A MCKENZIE RIDGE NOVEL

FEARLESS

USA TODAY BESTSELLING AUTHOR

STEPHANIE
ST. KLAIRE

FEARLESS

A MCKENZIE RIDGE NOVEL

STEPHANIE ST. KLAIRE

BOOKS BY STEPHANIE ST. KLAIRE

ALSO READ

Don't forget to check out Stephanie St. Klaire's alter ego,
USA Today Bestselling Romantic Comedy and
Contemporary Author of Clean & Wholesome Romance,
Stephie Klaire.
Get started FREE…
www.stephieklaire.com

ACKNOWLEDGMENTS

My dad likes to give me writing "advice". This advice usually earns a chuckle and a facebook post that gets more likes and comments than anything else I post – we're talking hundreds of likes and comments. But, because he's my dad, the "advice" usually ends up in my stories somewhere – like Ruthie, the duck in Hidden. Dad was right – she was needed! (snickers)

"Advice" now comes in the form of well-planned plots and vibrant characters. A phone call full of silent giggles on my part became a full blown sub-plot in Fearless. Thank my dad for the Stone Williams' story line and Ol'Twister. It's all his – just my words.

My dad is a quiet, humble guy who loves to go fishing, work on his cars, and do things around the house that will inevitably make my mom crazy – he also listens to SSK romance novels now. This one is his…

To all of my readers – *Thank you!* You have loved me, loved my books, and continue to ask for more! As long as you keep reading, I'll keep writing… and so will dad…

1

GLOOMY WHITE SKIES THREATENED OF SNOW AS THE TOWN'S people of McKenzie Ridge circled the graveside of one of their own – one of their beloved – creating the heavy somber mood resting on each of their shoulders. Everly took in the tear filled eyes and hiccuping sobs as Pastor Henry gave his final words while they lay to rest a dear woman, a town favorite. McKenzie Ridge would sorely miss such a well-liked member of their small community.

Evie scanned the crowd, taking in her friends, each at her side. Their emotions were raw but more visible than her own. Friends who were family in every way that mattered, they supported each other, and loved each other through every high and every low. This was most certainly the lowest of lows they had been through together.

It was odd. As painful as this loss was for the town, Everly's sorrow was trapped somewhere deep inside her. The flawless timing had its way with her this time. Unsure whether to feel sorry or relieved, for the number that was called to the beyond, Everly had no trouble recognizing her feelings of guilt as she thanked God it was *her* inside that coffin, *instead.* She struggled with that thought, it was deranged and ugly, but it was Everly's truth...at least for now.

Who thinks like that? A person who had struggled with loss her entire life, closing herself off to avoid moments like this very one. The tears were absent because she had trained herself years ago not to emotionally invest – to keep everyone at arm's length. The sting was less that way when life happened and the heavens came calling.

Pastor Henry opened the gathering to those who wanted to share kind thoughts, words, or memories. This was the part where bleeding hearts were laid out for all to see. Where the flood gates cracked wide open – a real bitch for those who didn't wear the right mascara. Another reason Everly didn't do the crying thing.

She faded away in thought, drifting back to where life played its little trick, shouting *plot twist*, as she remembered how she came to know about the death of the dear woman laying six feet deep in front of her.

* * *

TWO DAYS EARLIER IN PORTLAND...

WITH HIS LARGE STRONG HANDS TRAILING UP HER THIGHS, HE kissed a path that left his intentions undeniable. Everly Shaw was ready to lose her composure and give in to ecstasy before they had really begun. The sheer thought of what Doctor Mason Charles was about to do to her had her breathless as her body hummed. She was anxious for his mouth to find her heated hungry bundle of nerves that would scream orgasm with a single stroke if she wasn't careful.

Doc Charles was handsome, smart, kind – the kind of guy you take home to meet the family, and marry. That was all nice and sweet and entirely *not* for Evie. It was his intimate knowledge of her female anatomy that kept her coming back for more – making him a god in bed – which was where they had spent every spare moment over the last week.

Evie was an independent, no non-sense girl who took charge in everything she did, always willing to take a risk and live on the edge. Except in bed, with the man who rocked her world. Doc made her putty with a simple sultry look or the teasing hand that rested just on the small of her back, at the high side of her ass. He played her like one of his instruments, and played her well, making beautiful breathless music as he did.

With her legs wide, draping over his broad shoulders, her moans were getting deeper, breath pitchier when he added a finger, then two to his assault. In and out, he stroked her as his tongue lashed against her swollen bud over and over, circling and sucking as he did. She started to move against him, unable to control the blazing desire he was tormenting her with, making him smile.

For good measure, his free hand quickly yanked her bra down exposing her full breasts and hardened nipples. He twisted and pinched, pulling her rosy peaks as he went, driving her straight to the edge.

He suddenly pulled his mouth from her and said, "Don't get greedy baby. You know what happens when you finish before I'm done."

The deep threatening tone of his voice, playful as it was intended, was nearly her undoing. She wanted him to show her what would happen, again and again. As if he could read her wicked mind, Doc pulled his fingers from her, causing her to cry out, before grabbing her hips and pulling her to the edge of the bed where he flipped her over.

Standing at the edge of the bed, leaning over her backside, he said, "Nice try sweetheart. Is this what you want?"

His hands slowly slid down her back before gripping her hips and lifting her to her knees with her head still down. Yes…this was *exactly* what she wanted. Doc down and dirty, threatening with the kind of *punishment* a girl on the edge of bliss begged for.

Pressing against her from behind, he teased her opening with his hot hard length before he entered her with one quick lunge, causing her to cry out in pleasure. His generous length and weighty girth filled her to the point of just enough friction to offer the aching delight of a joyful ride. He was perfect, and she couldn't get enough.

The intensity built with every plunge, faster and harder with each pleasing movement. Evie was lost in him and everything he made her feel. Gripping the sheets with white knuckles, she moved against him, grinding, unable to control the desire he was manipulating. He reached around and stroked that one little spot that held all of the cards – he knew what she wanted – he heard it in her cries and moans for more.

Unable to control her urge, her back arched at his touch and her knee's spread wider to gain more of him. Doc grazed her back, with a subtle touch that left a trail of goosebumps. He reached the nape of her neck, digging his fingers into her hair and grabbing a handful of her golden locks.

Like a puppet with her master, she pushed up on her hands, gaining the leverage she needed to mirror his every move. Her hips were grinding, pounding against him with as much force as he delivered in return. Her breathy sighs became seductive *OHs,* bringing her closer to the edge before finally coming undone around him.

She fell back down to the bed, exhausted from the lust filled ride, with Doc falling right behind her. He rolled them to their sides and pulled her into him where he held her close peppering her with kisses. Never losing their connection, they rode the waves left by their passionate lovemaking.

"Wow…you're really good at that," Everly said, still a bit breathless, causing him to chuckle.

"We should high five over that one! I mean, I *was* great… I really need a cape. It's super hero worthy. Man of steel, right?" he joked.

Evie laughed, covering her face. "Aaand, he's back folks! Dirty Doc has left the building and we are now left with dorky Doc and all of his bad jokes. Hear that? The crowd is chanting…they want dirty Doc back."

"You're not too bad yourself, Shaw." He planted a long drawn out kiss on the back of her neck before finishing, "All this practice has been paying off."

"I could get used to this, ya know? Just coming and going as we please, no sneaking around…just…being us," she admitted.

"We don't have to sneak around back home either. You know that right? We can do whatever we want, wherever you want. Besides, McKenzie Ridge isn't exactly the place for secrets…I'm pretty sure we aren't as under the radar as you think, Ev."

"We *do* need to sneak around at home. We've talked about this, Doc."

He sighed. "You've talked about it. I'm game for holding hands, kissing in public, and letting everyone know when I'm sleeping over at your place."

"Which is why we sleep at your place. If Gran saw your

car in the driveway at my place, in the middle of the night, she'd have us married and making babies by morning."

"And what's so wrong with that. Maybe I should stop by for a...check up one night. I'll honk first, let you know I'm there...Gran too."

She turned to him, eyes wide and jaw dropped. "You wouldn't!"

"It'd serve you right. That's what you get for living next door to your Grandmother who happens to also be the town bugle." His voice softened as he dropped another kiss on her neck. "I wouldn't mind it at all...I'd love for everyone to know you're mine."

She hesitated for a moment, enjoying his heated kisses and sentiment before whispering back, "You know why we can't. This isn't forever, Doc."

He pulled away, breaking their connection, disappointment hanging in the room. "I know...I get it. I guess we'll just have to make the most of the last few days here and find more medical conferences to escape to for more of this!"

He smacked her ass and turned her to her back, pulling her to the edge of the bed where he leaned over her. Wrapping her long tone legs around his waist, she drew him closer to her and accepted the deep arousing kiss he was offering. Her body was humming again. She was noticing a distinct pattern.

Doc turned her on with a simple steamy kiss that made her want to do really bad things with him, to him, and receive them from him. He had turned her into a libidinous wanton sex fiend. She wasn't complaining, she really could get used to this. Damn her for being her own worst enemy when it came to relationships.

Doc interrupted her thoughts, suspicious of her change in demeanor. "Race you to the shower."

"I have a better idea." She wrapped her arms around his neck with her legs still around him, "Take me there, Doc."

He smiled and lifted her from the bed, walking them to the large marble bathroom in their suite. Just outside the oversized glass shower, lips locked, she was already grinding against him when there was a loud knock at the door.

Pausing for only a moment, Doc sat her on the vanity counter and went back to kissing her when another loud knock came.

"Maybe we should get it, Mason," Ev said with slight concern.

In between kisses around her collarbone, he said, "I hung the sign...do not disturb...they'll go away."

Everly's head rolled back and she let out a silent *oh* as she thoroughly enjoyed the attention Doc was giving her.

Pounding louder, a deep voice followed with, "EEEV... DOOOC. Open up!"

Doc straightened and turned toward the door, shielding Ev in a protective manner. "What the fuck? Who is that?"

"C'mon guys." the man yelled. "I'm coming in, you better have clothes on."

"O'Reilly! Oh, geez, it's Wylie!" Ev said full of surprise.

Doc squinted his eyes, confusion crossing his expression. "Carigan's brother?"

Carigan O'Reilly was a friend from home, in McKenzie Ridge. She was an EMT who partnered with Dawson Tayler, all part of the same family-like group of friends. Her brothers, all five of them, lived in Portland, where as she lived in McKenzie Ridge – a solid five hours away from their overly protective ways.

"Do you know anyone else named *Wylie O'Reilly*? C'mon...he means it. He'll open the door!" she said in a hushed voice as she jumped off the counter, covering her body as if he could see her.

"Shit! Hang on!" Doc shouted to Wylie through the door, before handing Everly the robe and panties he had peeled off of her earlier that afternoon. "Throw these on."

He pulled on a pair of sweats that hung low around his narrow hips, putting his well sculpted abs on display, and went to the door. Looking back to make sure she was covered – he wasn't sharing peeks of his girl – he caught her licking her lips as she scanned him head to toe. With a shake of his head and raise of his brow, he let out a low chuckle before he opened the door to a giant.

2

WYLIE O'REILLY WAS THE YOUNGEST OF THE FIVE O'REILLY brothers, Carigan being the only girl and youngest of six children in all. Wylie was by far the biggest of the brothers, topping even the oldest, Declan. Growing up the *baby* of the bunch, with a name like *Wylie Riley O'Reilly*, in a very Irish home full of rowdy Irish boys, did that to a guy. Despite his size and intimidating presence, one glimpse of his mega-watt smile and charming dimples put any stranger at ease.

Today he wasn't wearing that smile, and his dimples were absent. His handsome mug was drawn and serious with a furrowed brow. Sadness marked his mood, something that didn't represent the fun loving prankster on any given day. Wylie was named such because he was *wily* and mischievous even in the womb, according to his mother. Today though, he was anything but cracking jokes, lighthearted, or cracking smiles. Something was wrong.

Evie's heart dropped at his appearance. The O'Reilly boys had no idea she or Doc were in town and would only know where to find them if they were sent looking. Sent by someone from home. The unsettled feeling that rested in her gut was starting to stir, as old memories and emotions threatened to surface. She knew this was for her.

Everly lost her parents, as a small child, in a tragic hiking accident. They had been too close to a loose edge, snapping a family picture, when the ground beneath them gave way and they plummeted to their deaths, landing on a narrow ledge below. All but Evie, anyway. She survived the fall.

Nobody knew why, entirely, other than something divine must have intervened. If you asked her, though, she died on that cliff that day too. She waited with her deceased parents, on that narrow ledge for days, until they were finally found, and she was rescued. Having lost her grandfather just years before that, it left just Evie and Granny Lou...the only person that she gave her heart to, and even then, it was well guarded.

"You know, it's pointless to reserve two rooms if you're just going to use one," Wylie teased, trying to lighten the dark mood he knew he brought with him.

"Oh, uh, I just came up to see if Ev wanted to grab a bite later." Doc was determined to protect their secret – that's how Everly wanted it.

"Really, Doc? So why are your clothes here too, and suitcase...and I'm guessing toothbrush? I didn't see any of those things in your room," Wylie teased.

"Wait, you were in my room? How did you...ah, you're an O'Reilly. Never mind."

Wylie grinned and nodded, glad his reputation still held. "Exactly. You know everyone knows, right?" He waved a finger between the two. "The only two who believe you aren't here together or aren't together in general is you two."

Doc cringed. He knew deep down that in a small town like McKenzie, there was no such thing as keeping secrets. Add to that the many *medical conferences* they both happened to go on. Everly believed they had a good cover and no one was the wiser, and he had just let her believe her false truth.

"Wylie, what is it. Who..." she asked, her voice cracking in anxious emotion, trying to keep her panic at bay.

"Um, well...I got a call. Blake. I guess they've all been trying to reach you and couldn't so they sent us. Well...me." Wylie danced around the issue, trying to deliver the blow gently, especially since Everly was already seemingly worried.

She quickly turned, making her way to the nightstand, searching for her phone. When she didn't find it at the other end of her phone charger, she moved to the small table near the large floor to ceiling window and grabbed her purse. More frantic with every step, she dumped the contents of her bag on the table, most falling to the floor, before finally finding her cell phone in the mess.

She held it up, her face paling. "It's dead. Oh my God, I..."

Doc came to her side and pulled her close, walking them to the bed where he sat her down. Wylie never took his eyes off of her, sympathy lacing his gaze. Doc knew this was a call for her as much as Evie already knew, too. She reached for the charger and plugged in her phone, dropping it on the nightstand like it burned her hand.

"Ev...I'm sorry, but it's Lou...it's Gran. We need to get you home." He paused, letting her take it in. The sharp gasp she let out was hard to take, he needed a minute too. Gran was loved by everyone; even the rambunctious O'Reilly boys had a special bond with her.

"Is she...?" Everly's words trailed off, a near whisper, afraid to voice what she really needed to know.

"No. Sorry, I didn't mean to make it seem as if... Shit this is hard. Now I know why those assholes sent me. She had a massive heart attack…she collapsed in Baker's Bakery this morning. She was in surgery last I heard."

Doc abruptly stood and quickly made his way to the closet, tossing clothes and shoes in the first suitcase he came across. "I'll drive you. Hurry, let's go."

"No! I mean, we drove separately, we should…"

With a dramatic eye roll, Wylie interrupted, "Beck sent his plane, its already waiting for you. Grab what you need, and we'll get the rest and your cars over to you."

Everly shook her head, eyes filling with tears, and started to toss things in a bag. "No, no…that's too much to ask, I can't."

"It's a five hour drive, Ev, and there is snow on the pass. Beck's plane will have you there in less than an hour. We'll be heading over anyway so bringing the cars isn't a problem," Wylie reasoned.

Doc put his hand on her shoulders while looking her in the eye. "I'm still coming with you."

"No, it's too…weird. Let's just stick to…"

"Everly, I'm going with you. Not a request, got it? You aren't going alone. I don't fucking care what anyone thinks or what that damn town wants to talk about. Understand?" His stern tone had her attention, leaving her no other option but to agree.

"Okay…yeah, okay." The tears that had been welling, finally spilled over. Everly didn't do tears, she didn't cry. Until now.

Wylie dropped his head, feeling her pain. He gave them a minute together. "I'll be waiting downstairs, I'm parked right out front. Just come down when you're…ready."

As Wylie opened the door to leave, he paused at the sound of buzzing. Everly's phone had enough charge to come back on, and all of the missed calls and text messages were buzzing and pinging. Everly's gut wrenching sob was the last thing he heard before the door closed behind him. "Fuck. You can't do this, old woman. You can't do this to her."

* * *

BECK MCCAIN WAS A WEALTHY MAN – ORIGINALLY FROM Seattle where his corporation was, he now resided in McKenzie Ridge with his new bride, Morgan Jameson. He had an accident on her property and suffered memory loss, so he went by Guy until he regained his memory after his best friend turned on him and was set on murder. He and Morgan had the kind of whirlwind love affair that belonged in a swoon worthy romance novel.

Beck had a landing strip on his property in Arrow Springs, the next town over, but they had put one in at Pinecrest Ranch, where he and Morgan lived for convenience. He was the newest addition to their family-like group of friends, but fit in perfectly with his kind demeanor and generous heart.

To Everly's surprise, it wasn't Beck who met them at the airstrip, but Blake Cooper. He was the town hunky cop who looked over his close-knit group, albeit from a distance. He had his own secret past and demons to battle, but he put the gang first...kept them safe.

"Doc," he greeted with a nod and handshake.

"Hey man, you our ride?" Doc questioned.

Blake took one look at Evie, her dark shades not fooling anyone, and pulled her into his strong embrace where she wept. Blake wasn't one for emotion of any kind, certainly not the affectionate type, but Granny Lou was as important to him as anyone and they shared their grief for a moment.

"You hangin' in there kid?" He kissed the top of her head before letting her go.

"Yeah. I mean, I guess. I don't know."

"It's going to be okay. She's a tough broad. All that whiskey has her so well preserved, she ain't going nowhere!"

Both Doc and Ev chuckled at the somewhat endearing thought before Doc put his hand on Blake's shoulder, appreciating the effort he made for Everly. "I suppose we ought to get out of here?"

"Yep, I brought the work car…lights and shit. We'll get through traffic faster," he replied, pointing at the police SUV parked by the hangar.

"Traffic? It's McKenzie Ridge…" Doc joked, trying to make light of the situation.

"Yeah, well, if I'm going to drive that fast, I need the lights and sirens. I need to set an example. We'll call it traffic."

Doc put an arm around Everly and walked her to the waiting squad car. "Touché."

A lazy bark came from the front seat, grabbing their attention – Blake didn't have a dog. At closer inspection, a slight smile came to Everly's face when she realized who was responsible for the not so intimidating bark. It was a grey and black dapple dachshund, with mismatched eyes and a belly so big you couldn't see his legs.

Stepping around the rear passenger side door, she went to the front and picked up the obese dog, Gran's *wiener*, as she liked to call it, and said, "Moonshine."

"I grabbed him on my way here. He can stay with me until we get things sorted. It was…the least I could do," Blake offered with sympathetic words. He too had a close bond with Louise Shaw. Though she was the leader of the town gossip squad, Blake confided in her with secrets he didn't share with anyone. Those secrets, as juicy as they likely were, didn't go any further than Granny Lou.

Moonshine licked her face, enticed by her salty tears, and suddenly she felt a bit closer to Gran and a bit more hopeful. She was glad Blake was taking him, but she didn't want to inconvenience anyone. Moonshine was a high maintenance pet. He was lazy, but required extra care because he was so lazy.

"Blake, I appreciate that, and I know Gran would too, but Moonshine is a bit of a handful," she reasoned.

"I've had dogs before, Ev…big dogs. Moonshine is nothing but a lap dog…not much of a handful. Besides, you sit him down and he's usually right where you left him an hour later."

"Well, that's what I mean. He can't be left alone long and you have work, so…"

Blake interrupted her before she could finish. "He's going with me."

"To work? Won't you…you know, get in trouble?" she asked.

"First, I'm the boss. Second, no. And third, I'm putting him in the K-9 program." He deadpanned that last one. Moonshine in the K-9 program was like feeding a cop a carrot in a donut shop…it just didn't happen.

"The K-9 program?!"

"Yep. He's about to get in shape – add some years back to his life. Lou's going to need him healthy when she gets home," Blake assured, his expression blank, giving away nothing.

"Oh, well…okay then." She stroked the dog all the way to the hospital, while Moonshine howled from her lap in response to the blaring siren.

McKenzie General Hospital was a short fifteen minute

drive to the opposite side of McKenzie from Pinecrest Ranch where they started. Blake had them there in just over five. He opened the rear door, grabbed Moonshine from Everly's lap and placed him in the awkward baby carrier like sling draped across his body. He had Granny's dog packing sling. She carried that dog everywhere in that thing – because *he* needed to go for *walks*.

Without a word, Blake turned and walked into the hospital, as if there was nothing odd about his presence. Everly and Doc followed close behind, anxiety running high. As much as Everly wanted – needed – to know how Gran was, she feared that knowledge.

Seeing big, beefy, gun toting, super cop Blake Cooper walking in front of her, with a dog hanging from his hip, like he owned the place, gave her a little sense of normal. The man who hadn't let go of her hand since hearing the news, standing at her side, gave her comfort and calm.

"Uh, Blake…" a nurse said, confusion in her voice, "that's a dog."

Blake turned his attention to Captain Obvious, gave her a tight grin and nod, causing her to swoon.

"Yep, sure is." And he kept on walking like there was nothing unusual about it at all. That was Blake Cooper.

An elevator ride, and several floors later, brought them to the level that made Evie shudder, Cardiac Intensive Care. This was where the worst of the worst landed to battle the odds of life over death. Being a nurse, Everly had the advantage of field knowledge, which was also the disadvantage – she knew too much.

Sighs of relief, even a few light sobs greeted them in the waiting room of the unit. Warm embraces, and sympathetic greetings were shared among the group. They were all there, every one of them, except Sam Tayler. Sam and Everly grew up the best of friends, as close as sisters. When Sam's mother wanted to be anything but, Gran and Evie took her in and the girls grew up together.

Sam was a lot like Everly when it came to men and love until life intervened a few years back. She was now a stay at home mom, only volunteering and covering nursing shifts when absolutely needed. She and Dawson Tayler, an EMT, had their own steamy love affair that finally led to a happily ever after.

Scanning the room, she couldn't find Sam, who was probably the one person who understood how she felt the most. Not only because her love for Granny Lou ran just as deep, but because she was also a nurse. Before she could ask for her, the sterile metal double doors swung open and out walked Sam and Doctor Drake Sterling, a well-known Heart Surgeon – the best in the State. He serviced McKenzie General a few times a month, and consulted remotely, but he resided in Portland at the state's largest hospital.

It was unusual for him to be here at the end of a week, this time of the month. Beck. The man had money, power, and influence. Everly met his gaze, and the smile and nod he returned told her what she already knew. He brought Doctor Sterling here for Gran, for *her.*

As Sam and Doctor Sterling got closer, their low toned conversation came into range. With Sam's emotion drawn face telling part of the story, it was her words that set Everly Louise Shaw into a dark abyss.

"She didn't make it?" Sam choked. "Oh, God, I just can't believe she's gone."

"NO!" Everly cried out before losing her legs beneath her, while the room spun around her, taking her to the ground in a total state of darkness…Gran was gone.

3

DOC'S HAND GENTLY STROKED EVERLY'S BACK, BRINGING her back to present. He was watching her, his stare full of worry. She gave him a weak smile to assure him she was okay and received one from him in return. He hadn't left her side for more than a minute since they returned. Though she didn't voice it, she was damn glad. She needed him.

Back from her dream like state, the rest of the memory from the day of Gran's heart attack passed through her mind. She remembered waking on a hospital gurney, surrounded by the people she adored, each staring at her with fearful eyes. Then it hit her, the reason she was there, and why she apparently blacked out.

Everly began to sit up, tossing the light hospital blanket from her lap. "Gran!"

Strong arms embraced her from behind, and held her close, rocking her from side to side while shushing her and saying, "She's okay, she's alive," over and over.

"Honey, I am so sorry to have scared you," Sam said, choking on a sob. "Gran is alive. She is in ICU, but alive."

A sudden wave of relief washed over Everly. Gran was alive. Oddly, the part about being in the Cardiac Care Unit – ICU for heart patients – didn't even faze her after the scare she had just moments ago. The thought of losing all that she had left in the world had overwhelmed her, literally knocking her to her knees.

"But you said – and Doctor Sterling said…"

"I know, Ev. We were talking about Mrs. Burton. June Burton? She came in yesterday in full arrest. Heart failure finally claimed her, honey. She's passed," Sam calmly delivered, knowing June's passing would sting as well.

As quickly as the hint of joy came at knowing Gran was okay, it left again. They all knew June was on borrowed time, but hearing of her passing was no less of a blow. The loss sat in Evie's gut like a heavy brick while she contemplated life's crazy game. Two lives were gambled, one lost, one still in play.

June Burton was an elderly woman who lived off the grid in the woods. The town's people referred to them as *The Woods People*. They lived away from society, many without indoor facilities, electricity, or running water. They lived off the land and, typically, sold crops or wares in town to earn what little money they had to get by. It was a chosen lifestyle – the only one they grew up in and any of them ever knew.

The gang each held positions in fields that benefited these people. From fire, to police, with Doctors and EMT's in between, they all brought something to the table, especially with their extensive training as Search and Rescue. They volunteered their time and made their rounds, checking in on the people who would allow them near. They brought basic medicine, first aide, and food when available through town donations. A very primitive lifestyle, but a common one in areas such as these.

June Burton was a lovely lady who happily lived this lifestyle along with her son, Clyde. He was Everly and Sam's age, and went to school with them through middle school before dropping out. He was quiet, introverted, but sweet and kind. Everly always had a fondness toward him, defending him when the other kids would pick on him for having strange clothes or smelling like the woods.

When Everly's parents passed, she withdrew. She returned to school not long after the accident, but didn't interact with any of the other students, or staff...she was broken. At recess, while all of the other kids played ball, or chase, she sat alone on the swings. Clyde would find her every morning and sit on the swing next to her. He never said a word, would just toss her a friendly smile and sit there with her, a silent bond between them.

June was equally kind. She had made special visits to town to check on her and Gran, bringing her special beeswax candles, her special honey, or preserves for pies. They were simple people, but kind people. They got by, selling those very items in a few of the town's shops, and the seasonal Farmers Market.

When June fell ill and her heart was failing, they tried to get her the care she needed, at no cost to her, but her pride wouldn't allow it. She said she would go willingly when the Lord called her home, what was meant to be would be. They all spent as much time as they could with June, trying to make things easier for her, but the decline was rapid and she lost her battle quickly it seemed.

Today they were burying this kind and gentle soul, June Burton. Everly felt the loss deeply. She adored June. She also felt guilty. She knew better than to think that getting into heaven was a matter of standing in line and that June's passing meant Gran got to stay, but…what if? She wouldn't wish this outcome on anyone, but she would be lying if she said she wasn't grateful to be at someone else's funeral and not her grandmother's. The guilt was two-fold as she sat and watched Clyde Burton weep over the loss of his mother, when her loved one was still alive, albeit, in a fight to remain so.

Gran had been hospitalized for two days in a medically induced coma. Though she had surgery, she wasn't responding as they wished and this was the only way to control her vitals. She was a fighter, not one to sit still, so Ev had a hunch that she was her own worst enemy while trying to heal. Bed rest and low key were not words to describe Louise Shaw, hence the medically induced coma. Her body needed rest, needed to heal.

Everly hadn't left the hospital, but once to shower and change, since being back. It was to change for the funeral of June. She hated being away from Gran, and standing over a grave wasn't easing the anxiety of being away any easier. She had come so close. This could have been Gran if not for the immediate care she received from their dear friends who happened to be on duty when the call came in. Interesting how that worked out.

The service came to an end and everyone went their separate ways after paying final respects to Clyde. The gang gathered to the side and quickly discussed who was going to see Gran and who was grabbing food to keep everyone fed. Nobody wanted her left alone, and everyone felt the need to stay close.

"Clyde, I am so sorry for your loss." Everly embraced him in a sweet hug, her condolences sincere.

"Th-thank you, Evie. I appreciate that. I heard about Lou.

I am sorry she fell ill. I hope she pulls through okay. Please give her my best," he replied with a brief smile.

"She's not awake yet, Clyde, but I'll still tell her. They say, even in a coma state, patients can hear you. And I know she'll be glad to know you're thinking about her."

He looked at her for a moment, as if searching for words, not sure what to say next. All he could conjure up was, "Thank you."

"Of course," she smiled. "If you need anything, you know we are all here for you, right? Even if it's just to talk."

He nodded and looked at his feet, the conversation getting entirely too personal for him. "Yeah, I do. Thank you. I'll be okay."

With her hand still on his shoulder, she gave it a squeeze and offered a sweet smile as Doc came up behind her and wrapped his arm around her waist. "I know you will, Clyde. You're going to be just fine."

Doc reached out to Clyde to shake his hand. "I'm really sorry for your loss, man. Your mother was one of the finest people I knew. She will be missed."

Clyde's eyes remained at his feet with his head bobbing up and down. His hand rose to his face, pinching his eyes, and he wiped away the tears that were threatening to spill over. "She was, Doc, she sure was. Thank you. I already do miss her somethin' fierce. Guess no matter how much warnin' you get, it's still tough."

"I understand," Doc offered, "If there is anything we can do, if you need *anything*...well, just know you aren't alone out there, okay?"

With no words to follow up with, Clyde pinched his lips together in a straight line, and nodded, fighting the emotion before walking away with a quick wave.

Doc and Everly stood there and watched him climb into

his old pickup truck and drive off in the direction of the hills that lead to where they lived in the woods.

Evie laid her head on Doc's shoulder, and let out a deep sigh. "You're a good man, Mason Charles."

Tipping his head to plant a kiss on her forehead, he whispered, "A man is only as good as the woman at his side."

She wrapped herself in those words and all the comfort and ease they granted. Any other day, she would have brushed his arm from her waist, told him to stop talking like a pansy, and remind him she wasn't his woman. Today, though, she needed him, just like she had the previous handful of days. He made everything better. He spoke for her when she was all out of words, held her when she needed comfort, stayed awake when exhaustion claimed her in the wee hours of the night. That man practically breathed for her, and she was sure he would find a way if she really needed him to.

"Are you guys going back up to the hospital?" Sam asked, bringing Evie back to the conversation.

"I think we'll…"

Everly quickly interrupted Doc. "I need to. We've been gone too long. I don't want to miss rounds or…anything else."

"You don't want to go home and change? Get more comfortable?" Doc knew she wanted to be close to Lou but also knew she couldn't stay holed up in that hospital all day, every day, without compromising her sanity. Watching a person in a coma was like watching grass grow.

"No, I'm good. I'll be fine," she rambled with an anxious tone.

Truth be told, Everly was struggling with the guilt of being so far away when Gran needed her most. Of course there were no warning signs or indications that Granny Lou was on her way to a severe medical crisis. It just happened, that's how it went sometimes. But she couldn't help but feel the way she did, and regret not being there sooner.

"Look, we need to get home to check on the kids. How about I head up there in a bit, and I'll grab some things from your house on the way?" Sam offered as a compromise.

"That's a good idea," Blake chimed in. "I was going to bring Moonshine up to see her. I read that animals are good for that kind of thing, you know, with sick people. Good for healing. Therapy dogs or whatever."

Colton, the animal lover of the group, who had his own menagerie of misfit pets with varying disabilities, smiled. Blake was speaking his language. "You're right. Good call, man. It will be good for both of them. Meg and I can grab some food, meet you all there."

Having a toddler daughter who was the light of their lives, Meg and Colton had their hands full, adding to the equation the animals they'd rescued. Especially since he was a fire-fighter, working on the same engine as Jessie Clarke, and Meg owned the local floral shop, Blooming Grounds that doubled as a coffee shop. Meg had moved to McKenzie only a handful of years back, looking for a *do over* after a comfortable life as a New York socialite that felt tawdry compared to her new life the two enjoyed.

"Oh, I got food!" Jessie interrupted, her eyes on Blake. Their relationship was like water and vinegar on the outside, but everyone knew there was a deep affection there. Everyone but them.

Jessie being Jessie, rude, crude, and a basic asshole, couldn't let a moment pass with anyone thinking she was kind. "Besides, Fancy Pants there will probably bring some of that macrobiotic green sludge shit that no one likes. How about pizza?"

"You called it macrobiotic! You *have* been paying attention!" Meg clapped her hands, pleased with her normally filter lacking friend's slip of knowledge.

Jessie rolled her eyes, her intentional lack of filter back intact. "Whatever. It gives everyone the shits, we aren't eating it."

"Oh, that's just the detox par…"

"Nobody cares, Princess. Pizza. See you guys there." She walked toward the parking lot before looking over her shoulder, tossing them a final thought. "Someone sneak in beer."

Beck shouted, "Got you covered, Jess!"

Laughter erupted for the first time in days. It felt good to laugh a bit, but it also felt wrong without the family of friends' matriarch at the helm. At least they had each other, and they could include Gran in their own special way.

Everyone went their separate ways, each with their own mission to accomplish. It was family dinner night with Gran – pizza at the hospital.

4

DRIVING HOME FROM THE FUNERAL, CARIGAN O'REILLY decided to stop at Baker's Bakery and grab a dessert to take up to the hospital. Beer and Pizza was covered, but nobody mentioned dessert, and this was very much the time to indulge. Sugar from Baker's fixed everything.

Sugary goodness to drown their worries in wasn't the only thing Carigan was on a mission for. There was more. A six foot something brawny man in a bun, who happened to be a beast in bed…to be exact. It felt weird returning to Baker's. The last time she had been there it was to rescue Gran and save her life – a little heavy for a light and fluffy bakery.

Emotion coursed through her when she pushed through the front door. Looking around, she noticed the place was quiet, just a few families and a handful of teenagers scattered about with soft music playing in the background. She looked first to the back corner where the world had shifted, knocking them all off balance. She could still see Sam and Meg at a corner booth, comforting each other – Morgan and Blake over Gran…it was surreal. There was another memory etched in her peripheral, BJ Baker. The beast in bed.

Jed Baker owned the bakery, it had been in the family for generations. He had his own health challenges over the past year – a fall that required hip replacement. Age and hips that were never the same after surgery required him to slow down and let others run the business. She didn't know that *other's* included BJ coming back to McKenzie Ridge.

Once upon a time, Carigan and BJ were an inseparable couple of high school sweethearts with dreams of forever. That was until forever was put off while he finished his culinary studies at Le Cordon Bleu, then again after traveling abroad to finesse his craft in the kitchen. Bartholomew James Baker, of humble roots in McKenzie Ridge, was a world class chef with one of the highest sought out restaurants on the West Coast – Chez Sol in San Francisco. It was a five star dining experience that would knock your socks off and break your wallet in the process.

The relationship had been off and on long distance for a few years before eventually fizzling out. Seeing him again brought back a flood of emotions from anger to excitement. Even the rush of twisted butterflies had returned from their long hibernation. It was kismet seeing him again. By the expression he wore, she could confidently say the feeling was mutual.

After leaving Lou at the hospital the night of her heart attack, Carigan came home to find a strange car in her driveway. She shouldn't have been surprised to find it was BJ, concerned for her well-being. He was a McKenzie native and understood the blow Lou's condition had on the community, he just wanted to be there for her.

Oddly, they were completely in sync as if no time had passed at all, talking well into the night. Though there was one distinct difference, he wasn't a high school boy anymore – he was a hot virile man. BJ was the epitome of tall dark and handsome with a hint of long haired hippy all rolled in to one. His scruffy beard and dark shoulder length locks that had sun bleached ends caused her to wipe the drool from her chin often and cross her legs a bit tighter. A man bun wasn't her idea of sexy, but he wore it well, too well. He was damn hot with his rock hard physique and sultry gray blue eyes.

BJ and Carigan had been inseparable since that night, and as she found herself approaching her home with the brownie bottom cheesecake she'd picked up at the bakery, she noticed his car in the driveway and hoped she would find him in her bed right where she left him. She sat in her car for a moment, staring at her house, the lights on inside suggesting someone was home. It felt nice, it felt right to come home to someone. Shaking her head at the premature ideas of forever, she reminded herself that he left once, he could leave again. She would take whatever this was one day at a time, leaving all expectations at the door.

Damn, he wasn't in the bedroom like she'd hoped. She found him in the kitchen, cooking – she hoped they'd do some cooking of another kind in there too. Why not?

He greeted her with a long, heated kiss that was both spicy and sweet, matching the intense aroma that she couldn't quite identify. "It smells amazing in here! What are you making?"

He held her close and stole another kiss before putting a small piece of what appeared to be bacon in her mouth. "What do you think?"

"Oh, my God, is this bacon?" She let out a throaty moan and reached for another piece.

"It is. I take it you like it?"

"Um, I love it! What is it for?"

"It's bacon crack!"

"You can say that again, I'm already addicted!"

He tossed his head back and laughed. "No really, that's what it's called. It's bacon rubbed in a variety of chiles and brown sugar to give it a crispy, sweet and spicy edge."

"Well, I love it!" Proof of such was in the handful she was feasting on.

"I use it for a lot of things. I was testing recipes for the bakery."

Her eyes widened, surprised by his admission. The menu at Baker's hadn't changed in years, if ever. "You are going to serve entrée's at the Bakery now? Interesting! This stuff will sell out, I can tell you that much."

The smile he gave in response to her compliment would get him anything he wanted from her. She was starting to sweat and it wasn't from the spicy bacon.

"Well, dad says no, but I think McKenzie can use a little flavor like this. Why not? I use this bacon on a lot of things. I like to toss it with asparagus, wrap it around chicken, on top of a cupcake, even in ice cream for those with a daring palate for flavor..." She hung on every word, her mouth slightly open, eyes heavy with sensual intention, and she was shifting from side to side as she devoured him with a single look.

"God I love it when you talk food to me." She moved closer with a slight arch in her back putting her breasts on display. "I'm getting...hungry."

Leaning her small body against his oversized frame, he lifted her as if she didn't weigh a thing and placed her on the counter. Not wanting to lose the intimate contact they had, he stood between her parted legs, brushing a lock of coppery hair away from her face, resting it behind her shoulder with a two finger sweep. Those fingers were teasing her.

"Are you now? What are you hungry for, baby? Just tell me what you want and it's yours." He ducked down and took her mouth. Soft and sweet at first, then swept her lips with his tongue until she let him in and he went to work.

"I'm...supposed to... meet everyone at the..." Her words were lost in a mind full of sultry thoughts he was generating with every kiss down her neck and across her collarbone.

She felt him grin against her neck as he said, "At the what, honey?"

"The..uhhh..." She licked her lips as her head rolled back and her eyes closed, completely lost in him. "Hospital... pizza. We're having beer and pizza."

"Uh huh. I heard. I'm going with you." He continued, "But not until we are done with this."

His mouth drifted lower, peppering kisses on each exposed shoulder, following the trail of goosebumps his hands made pushing down the sleeves of her dress and straps of her bra. The top of her black dress continued to fall, BJ trailing close behind, meeting the tops of her breasts with his wicked tongue. He took one step back and drank her in while he pulled down her bra, leaving nothing to his imagination.

"You are so fucking beautiful." He pushed up her skirt, revealing the V at the top of her legs. "I'm glad you wore this dress today. I need the lace."

"The what?" She was rummy from his intoxicating touch.

"Lift your ass baby, I want your panties. I think I'm keeping those." Happy to oblige, she lifted while he pulled, sliding them slowly down her legs, then put them in his pocket for safe keeping. With a hand on each knee, he quickly parted her legs, exposing her completely, an act that would probably embarrass her with anyone else...just not BJ.

He looked her over, head to toe, taking in her creamy alabaster skin, emerald green eyes and the copper hair that made her his feisty little Irish vixen – he spent more time staring at her perfectly pink core that matched her hardened nipples, debating where he should begin. He knew one thing, it didn't matter where he began, he was having every last inch of her, right there on the kitchen counter.

"So fucking beautiful."

His hands were on each inner thigh, sliding up to heaven where he pushed her legs wider, opening her to him. He fell to his knees, his mouth at just the right height to take her in. A single stroke of his tongue down her center earned him an arched back and a moan that made him so hard he was sure he would have tracks from his zipper.

He pulled her ass to the edge of the counter and placed her feet there as well so her knees could fall open, giving him better access to what he was after. Her moans turned to cries when his fingers stroked her, pumping in and out of her faster and faster, his mouth matching the intense pace.

He watched her react to the intense pleasure that came over her when she tightened around his fingers and cried out his name. With her body limp, completely sated, he quickly undid his pants, pushing them to the floor. BJ pulled her from the counter and wrapped her around his waist, standing in the middle of the kitchen like she didn't weigh a thing.

Resting her on his steely length, he leaned her back, ever so slightly, gaining access to her hardened rosy buds. He plunged into her just as he clamped down on her breast, causing her to cry out in pleasure. He filled her completely, like a glove, their connection familiar from years ago.

His brisk steady movement continued completely in sync with the tongue lashing he gave her plump breasts. As her first wave of passion subsided, a new one was brewing, causing her to ride him back hard, taking what she wanted – all of him. The friction they created was hot, and uncontrolled.

He let go of her breast with his mouth, tossing his head

back on the brink of spilling over – his own moans matching hers. Her hands snaked through his hair, pulling herself closer so her now lonely breasts could rake over his chest with every rise and fall of her hips. Carigan O'Reilly was his sexy muse, taking her dirty fill before tightening around him for a second time, milking him to his own satisfied happy ending.

With her still cradled in his arms, and wrapped around him, he took them to the floor, leaning against the cabinets while they each caught their breaths.

"We're going to need to bleach that counter," Carigan joked, still a bit breathless.

"Probably the floor too," he chuckled and stroked her back while she leaned against him, head on his shoulder.

It didn't take long before she started to rock against him, slowly at first, picking up the pace as she felt him harden inside her. He pushed forward and laid her on the ground. Where it was fast and hard before, this time he made slow sweet love to her on the kitchen floor. Cooking in the kitchen had an entirely new meaning to them.

Their pizza was going to be cold by the time they made it to the hospital, but that was okay, they'd already had their dessert.

5

STIRRING FROM A LOUD BANGING SOUND SHE COULDN'T YET identify, Carigan reluctantly woke from a sound sleep. The banging continued to earn her attention as she finally got her wits about her. Disappointment filled her heart when she noticed the empty spot to her left that BJ had kept warm all night.

His intoxicating scent was still there when she hugged the pillow he had used, only to find a sweet note had been resting on it. It was from him.

Good morning, beautiful! I had to open the bakery for Pop, but I'll be back later to pick up where we left off. Why don't you take a nice, long, hot bath and relax...maybe I'll meet you there? See you soon, B.

As soon as she finished, she read it again, letting out a breathy sigh at his words. She thought about where they had *left off* the night before – or early morning, rather – driving her libidinous desires wild.

They had eventually made it to the hospital, spending time with their friends, waiting for Granny Lou to wake up. Evie was having a rough time with her grandmother's condition. She looked pale and tired, so it was nice to be there for her and the others. Even sleeping, Lou had a presence that gave them all comfort after such an emotional day, burying a dear friend.

When Carigan and BJ got back to her place, the mood transitioned from low and somber to hot and bothered. She and BJ tore up the sheets all night – and the shower, and the kitchen again of all places. Sweet and kind Carigan was becoming an insatiable sex monger who couldn't get enough of the delicious man who never left her fantasies and dreams. Something about him being back drew out a side of her that she didn't even recognize, and reading his note for a third time, she pictured all of the things she wanted to do with him in the bath and everywhere else.

Obnoxious knocking pulled her from her sexy wanderlust daydream. She pulled herself from beneath her warm blankets and tossed on a pair of yoga pants and a sweatshirt before making her way to the door. More impatient pounding had her half ticked when she realized the ungodly hour. Her pace quickened when it dawned on her that perhaps it had something to do with Lou. BJ had a key and nobody else would think to interrupt one's sleep at the ass crack of dawn…unless something was wrong.

With eyes wide, prepared for the worst, she swung the door open with a force and said, "What happened?!"

"Jesus, Squirt! Is that how you always answer the door, or just for your brother?" A tall guy with muscles for days, short spikey hair with shaved sides, and a too tight t-shirt greeted her, Luke O'Reilly.

"Luke O'Reilly, you nearly rose the dead in me boyo!" she replied with a hint of her Irish twang and hand to her heart. "What are you doing here – and so early?"

"First, it's polite to invite people in and *not* make them

freeze their balls off in this weather. Second, you didn't even look out the window to see who it was. What if I was a crazed loon? You could be dead right now! Last…brought the car back. Wanted to check on Lou." He tossed a thumb over his shoulder, aiming at the small red car in the driveway.

"Evie's car. Oh… It's not even seven in the morning', that means you left after midnight to get here? What are you up to, Luke?"

She knew better than to think that this was simply a quick courtesy delivery – that was just a convenient excuse. Carigan was the baby of the family, and the only girl, with five bossy, overly protective older brothers. If she didn't know better, she would think they could literally smell a man in her presence from hundreds of miles away. She needed to play it cool, see what he knew.

Luke, the third oldest by just three minutes – his twin brother Liam beat him to the second-in-charge title – was also third largest in size, just inches behind Wylie and Dec. That didn't mean much, however, because the O'Reilly brothers were all tall, built, and intimidating as hell, especially Luke. He was as alpha tough guy as they came, with a military background full of top secret macho elite forces crap that no one except their brother Declan and Blake Cooper really knew much about because they shared the same story.

Luke retired early, against his will, at the hands of an injury that nearly claimed him. A special mission gone bad, but not before he saved his crew and took the final blow that left him with a permanent injury, PTSD and a big ass chip on his shoulder. He hadn't been the same since his accident. He was now very introverted, a loner, battling his deep rooted demons.

One thing that hadn't changed was his big brother bully routine. It became obvious he knew about BJ when he started scanning the room, looking for clues. This was why Carigan lived in the family home in McKenzie Ridge, while her brothers lived miles and miles away in Portland. Apparently, that was no longer her safety net.

"Luke..." she said again, "What are you up to?"

"Me? Oh, nothing. Just bringing back the car and...you know...Lou," he said with a mischievous smile.

Eye's narrowing, she puffed out her chest after noticing the duffle bag in his hand. "So, you'll be leaving now?"

"Oh, nawwww. Thought I'd stay a few days, visit with the gang. Maybe get some training in with Blake and the boys." His wink told another story entirely.

"Boys? What do you mean *boys?* You mean Blake, Dawson...Colton, right? Those *boys?"* She held her breath and waited with a prayer on the tip of her tongue – *please don't let it be the O'Reilly boys.*

Reading her mind, and being an ass, he smiled and answered, "Sure!"

"*Sure*...that's encouraging." Rolling her eyes, she went to the kitchen to make a strong pot of coffee. It was going to be a long ass day.

Luke hollered behind her, "Hey, heard that Baker kid was back in town."

And there it was, Luke's sole purpose for showing up at zero dark thirty...to ruin her life. "So that's why you're here. Had a feeling. You might want to work on your clairvoyance skills, they're getting a little weak. That's a job hazard in your line of work." By job, she was referring to the elite high profile security company he and the other brothers owned.

"No, that's just for fun. Everly needed her car back, along with the things she left at the hotel, and I wanted to visit Lou. Plus McCain is one of our clients, we have business to discuss." He was referring to Beck McCain who became their client after a major security breach that nearly cost him his life just over a year ago.

"Uh huh. And where do you plan to stay, brother?"

"What do you mean? Here of course!"

"Oh, of *course*." Sarcasm and a bit of spite rolled off her words, coaxing a smile out of Luke. He knew he was pushing her buttons.

"What? This is the family home. I'll just take my old room!"

It was time to fight fire with a little fire. If she learned anything from her overbearing brothers, it was how to play dirty. "I had a feeling… BJ stays here, you know."

"Aw, well, looks like he'll be staying somewhere else." He winked.

With her arms crossed and a snarly scowl, she charged off to her room in a mock toddler fit. She grabbed her cellphone to send a text – two could play at this game.

Change of plans. Luke is in town. I'll come to your place tonight. See you then, have the bath ready. –C

CARIGAN SPENT THE DAY RUNNING ERRANDS AND LAZING around the house after making a stop in at the hospital to take Everly food, and checking on Granny Lou. Under the veil of darkness, however, later that night, Carigan made good on her promise. After excusing herself to her room, she readied herself for the night by putting on her sexiest lingerie under a simple dress and crept out of the house. Carigan one, Luke zero.

"Hey," Luke said into the phone. "Yeah, it's me. No, no… he's not here. She fucking snuck out though! Can you believe it? What is she, fucking 16? No, I'm not following her, I know where she's going. Okay…let the others know. See you then."

And he hung up the phone, sitting in silence, waiting for his little sister to sneak back in.

"Game on, Squirt…game on."

* * *

LIKE DÉJÀ VU, CARIGAN WAS STARTLED AWAKE BY MORE pounding. She was fricken tired after a late night of romping and rolling with her new addiction. It didn't help that she had to sit in her car up the street for over an hour, waiting for her brother's bedroom light to go off so she could sneak back in. She loved her brother, but hoped his stay would be short and sweet.

Pulling her pillow over her head, she ignored the pounding. If Luke wanted to stay in the *family home*, he could answer the *family door*. But the pounding didn't stop, Luke wasn't answering, and there were very few people who would stand there that long, waiting for someone to answer.

"Bloody hell!" She tossed off the covers, glad she had decided on pajamas for bed, and charged the front door.

She swung the door open with a fury and threatening tone, "WHAT?!"

"Whoa, Squirt! What the hell?!"

"What are you doing here, Wylie? And stop calling me Squirt! Christ, I'm closer to thirty than twenty now, I think that nickname died a decade ago."

She walked away, leaving the door open so he could let himself in. "Why are *you* here now?"

"Oh, Doc Charles's car…I brought it back for him."

"Doc doesn't live here, Wylie. Take it to his house."

"No way. It's way too early to just show up like that…

don't want to be rude," he finished, with the classic O'Reilly brothers wink that worked on most women, but not her, because that would be weird.

"Of course you didn't, so come here instead. Makes sense." On her way to the kitchen to start a pot of coffee so she could start what was about to be another really long day, she hollered, "LUKE! Your brother's here!"

"Oh, Luke's not here."

"What do you mean, Luke's not here? Did he leave?" There was a bit too much enthusiasm in that last question and it wasn't lost on Wylie.

"Yep! Saw him on the road on my way in."

"On the road? He's walking back to Portland?" She felt bad for a moment, recalling her less than enthusiastic welcome and rude nature the day before.

"To Portland? No...he's just out for a run."

As quickly as that regret came, it was gone. She was being played by the master of all pranks and shenanigans. He could have just said what he meant, but Wylie liked to mess with a person so she tossed him a *closer to thirty than twenty* stink eye.

"Wait. If Luke drove over in Ev's car, and you Doc's... how are you guys getting home?"

"Home? Oh, I thought I would stay a few days! Check on Lou and..."

"Hang with the boys? Yeah, heard that yesterday."

"Exactly. McCain is..."

"I know...your client...business to discuss."

"Yeah! How'd ya know?" he said, a little too impressed.

"Gee, lucky guess."

The front door opened and Luke walked in. "Hey, you're up early Squirt! What's up, Wy?! Good to see you."

She did that mock toddler thing again, storming off to her room, slamming the door behind her.

Much like the day before, Carigan waited until close to midnight before trying to escape her hovering brothers. She crept down the dark quiet hallway to the living room, aiming for the front door. Nearly there, she was startled by a deep throaty voice.

"Where ya going, Squirt?"

"Jesus! You scared the shit out of me, Luke! What are you doing up?"

"Couldn't sleep, grabbing a movie. You?" His cocked eyebrow made her nervous, he was like a human lie detector and she was out of practice.

"Oh, uh, ice cream. I wanted ice cream."

"Uh huh. Sounds good, I'll have some too."

"Of course you will...be...right...back." Slamming the door behind her was becoming a thing. She picked up her phone and sent a quick text to BJ.

Change of plans. I'll be a little late. Wylie's here now too. Ugh. – C

Carigan drove to the end of her street and sat there for a bit, while sexting back and forth with BJ. She couldn't wait to see him, and make good on all the promises he was sending her. When enough time had passed, she pulled back in the driveway, and went inside to face what she was now referring to as the cock blocking spawn of Satan.

"Hey! Where's the ice cream?" Luke asked, a stupid grin plastered on his face just to piss her off.

"Ate it."

"Then where's the trash?"

She paused, gave him an *if looks could kill* glare while tossing her hands in the air, and said, "Tossed it out the window!"

"Wow, Cari! Why would you do…"

She didn't hear the rest of his annoying BS because the door slamming behind her made it hard to hear.

An hour had passed and the house was silent. She heard Luke trail down the hallway just minutes after her followed by the sound of his door closing. The routine was already getting old, but she wanted to see her guy, so she made her way down the hallway. As she got closer to the living room, music came in ear shot and she found all of the lights on. Standing in the middle of the room was Wylie, shirtless, in a pair of basketball shorts. He was dancing around an ironing board using the iron as a microphone.

"What the bloody hell, Wylie?"

Not even startled by her sudden entry, he smiled and pointed to the ironing board. "Ironing!"

"I see that, but in the middle of the night? Wait…let me guess…you couldn't sleep?"

"Yeah...that obvious, huh?" His tone was as condescending as hers.

"Something like that. Um, why are you ironing t-shirts… and are those underwear?"

"Yep! I don't like wrinkles and want crisp lines. I like to look sharp!"

"But it's t-shirts, and…whatever." She turned back around, and back to her room she went.

"Goodnight, Squirt."

SLAM.

* * *

AT AN UNGODLY HOUR, BEFORE EVEN NATURE WAS AWAKE, Carigan woke to the sound of a motorcycle parking out front. Well aware of who it probably was, she beat him to the punch and headed for the front door.

She waited there, leaning in the doorway with her arms crossed, to greet her brother, Dace. Dace was the fourth brother – the tattooed, pierced, motorcycle riding bad boy of the bunch.

"Hey, Squirt! What are you doing up so early?"

"Seems to be a new habit, thought I would let you in so you wouldn't have to wake the squirrels, pounding on the door like Luke and Wylie did."

"Oh, they're here? Cool."

She turned halfway to the kitchen and shot him an unimpressed look and the middle finger. Something she didn't do often, and something he wasn't expecting based on his shocked expression. Carigan one, Dace zero.

"You should have stayed in bed and slept. I have a key, I could've let myself in."

And she flipped him the bird a second time for good measure. "Let me guess, you saw Luke and Wylie out running on your way in."

"No, they're running later."

"So you *did* know they were here!"

"No, I just know their schedules."

"Right."

"So what's with Bart Baker?" Dace asked, just as Luke and Wylie walked in.

"Yeah, what the hell kind of name is *Bart*? C'mon Squirt…you can do better than *Bart*!" Wylie added.

"He hasn't gone by *Bart* since grade school! It's Bartholomew…" Carigan defended.

"Oh, 'cause Bartholomew Baker sounds better. I hear he's

all Grizzly Adams nature boy with shit livin' in his beard and birds layin' eggs in that shit bun on his head…you're seriously into that?" Dace did tattoos, piercings, and was anything but the straight and narrow kind of guy…but he drew the line at au naturel and lack of manly grooming apparently.

Carigan put her coffee cup down a little harder than intended, splashing its contents about, "He goes by BJ…got it? *BJ*!"

Luke nearly dropped his mug. "For fucks sake! Are you serious? *BJ*? Really? BJ…you have got to be kidding me. C'mon Squirt…Bart is better than…*BJ*!"

"Blow Job Baker…you just can't make this shit up!" Wylie laughed.

She stood there in silence, trying to reign in her calm because these boys had her halfway to that new toddler thing she was doing. After a quiet moment and a few deep breaths, she excused herself. "I need to get ready for work. I won't be home until really late tonight…pulling a double shift."

She left the room, pleased with the way she'd pulled one over on her brothers. So what if her second shift was at *Blow Job* Baker's house. Carigan for the win…

6

CURLED UP IN THE CHAIR NEXT TO GRAN'S BED, EVERLY held her hand and talked to her like she did so many times when she needed advise or just to vent.

"They say you can hear me, so we'll just go with that. They say there's a silver lining in everything, maybe right here, right now, the silver lining is that you can't interrupt me." She laughed at her poorly played joke, making light of the serious situation.

"Moonshine has taken up with Blake nicely, he doesn't give me the time of day. Blake doesn't say so, but I think he is really fond of him. He needs someone, or something, to keep him company, I think. Maybe Colton should find him a dog too. I don't know. I guess I'm just rambling right now. Maybe I do want you to interrupt me with some of your inappropriate sayings and vulgar words. I really need you Gran, so come back to me. Okay? Soon."

A tear had spilled over, and made its way down her cheek. She wiped it away with her sleeve, and laughed...Gran would have had a heyday with that. Something about crusty sleeves grosses out the boys. She rubbed Gran's hand, working on her composure before she finished.

"Gosh...I think you would looove this one, Gran. Life is playing non-stop tricks on me these days. I keep thinking I am going to wake up and this will have all been a strange dream, but nope! My life is turning out to be anything but what I planned or expected. You told me that would happen. You said to *get it together and find me a man before fate steps in and I'm stuck with whatever it leaves me*." She laughed at her own attempt at sounding like her Gran. Her voice was just a sound that couldn't be mastered.

"Well, you were right...*again*! I know you don't get tired of hearing that. You were right, you were right, you were...right. So, things are going to be changing. I don't know exactly how, but I'll figure it out, I always do. It would just be easier with you. Here's a good one...everyone figured out Doc and I have been *canoodling*, or whatever you call it. Bet you called that one too." Oddly, it didn't feel like she was talking to herself, like she originally thought. Gran couldn't answer, but Everly felt like she was being heard and that brought her much needed comfort.

She looked around the room, taking in all of the flowers that had accumulated. They were starting to place them at all of the nurse's stations, and various areas of the hospital. It was like Gran's joy and presence was everywhere – Everly liked that.

"You seem pretty popular around here. I hope you wake in time to see all of these flowers, I know how much you love them. Mostly fall flowers, like those wild ones you love so much." She scanned the room again, taking in just how many bouquets were the same or similar flowers. Her brow furrowed, there were so many, and no cards that she could see with the matching bouquets. Interesting.

"Who keeps sending those wild flowers. They are too similar to be a coincidence. Do you have an admirer, Gran? I bet you *do*! Well, how about that! I'll have to ask Meg if they're from her shop. Hopefully, it's someone who paid with a card so we can see who it is. See, you've rubbed off on me, that's something you would do!" She laughed.

"Anyway. I'm just stalling. This is where you tell me to *spit it out, girl*! So I guess I'll just spit it out. Back to that curveball I guess. I don't really know what to think, or what to do next, but I know that after everything, Doc probably isn't going anywhere...even if I wanted him to." She giggled.

"I wish you were awake, I know you would be enjoying the shit out of this. I know I swore off relationships and marriage, but I don't think I'm going to get away with that. He's a good guy, Gran. Such a good guy – he hasn't left my side through this and I'm sure he'd walk through hot coals laced with shards of glass if I asked him too. As much as I think I don't need him, I want him. Especially now. I know you're fond of him, and if I didn't know any better, I would think you were behind all of this, you old broad. Gran...this scares the shit out of me. So much is happening, and about to happen, so fast...I...just come back to me. Okay? I'm about to..."

Out of the corner of her eye, something, or someone, caught her attention. Doc. He was leaning in the doorway with his hands in his pocket and ankles crossed. He wore a sweet smile while he watched her, not intending to interrupt her time with Lou. He knew she missed her terribly and worried despite her stable condition.

"Hey..." he said softly, "You okay?"

She smiled, her eyes filling again for reasons unknown, or maybe reasons that were overwhelming. "Yeah, I think so. Just miss her, ya know? It's weird without her. I guess that old saying is true...*you don't realize what you have until it's gone.*"

He came into the room, and sat in the chair next to her, scooting closer to her as he did, "I understand. But she's stable, babe. Just don't give up on her, because she's certainly not giving up on any of us."

Feeling comforted by his words, she leaned into him and rested her head on his shoulder. He calmed her, took care of her and made everything feel right when it was entirely wrong. As much as she hated needing him, she loved it too. He was all that she was lacking in her life. Doc gave her a kind of love she hadn't known she was missing, kept her safe...from herself. He was everything she spent her entire life despising and now she couldn't quit him even if she wanted to for reasons beyond her heart.

His arm draped around her and he held her for several long minutes, neither saying a word until she broke the silence, "You're a good one, Mason Charles."

A long lingering kiss to her forehead *said* almost everything she needed to hear without a sound between them. In a low near whisper, he confirmed, "I would walk through hot coals laced with shards of glass for you."

Emotions rolling through her, that unfamiliar sensation of tears streaming down her face hit her yet again. Normally one to detest tears, crying, or real emotion...she welcomed it. She couldn't control it if she wanted to anyway.

Not used to the butterflies and sweet nothings, she redirected the conversation to safe and easy. "So, what brings you by, Doc? Slow in the ER tonight?"

"Yeah, just a few ski injuries. New powder up above us drawing all the die hards. It won't be long before it drops to our elevation and we start getting the snow. Anyway, I came to take you to dinner."

"Oh, I'm not hungry. Thank you, though."

"Ev...you haven't left at all. I'm guessing you haven't slept or eaten either. Just a couple hours, anything you want. I mean *anything*."

She gave him a dramatic eye roll and silly giggle followed by an elbow to the ribs. "Nice, Doc. Look, I really want to stay here. Just in case."

"Compromise...dinner downstairs, in the hospital cafeteria. Not exactly fine dining, but we're already at the hospital if we choke on it." He tried to woo her with humor, but without much luck.

"Doc. Seriously, I'm not going anywhere."

"Evie, c'mon. This isn't healthy. You're pale, exhausted, and wearing the stress you're carrying. It's just a quick meal so you don't end up in a bed next to Lou." His tone was heavier than his typical happy go lucky. His concern was legitimate, but she didn't care.

"I just want to stay here, with..." she went to stand, but immediately lost her footing when the room began to spin and everything went dark around her.

Doc reached out for her and broke her fall. Holding her in his arms, he reached for the nurse's button on the side of Lou's bed and shouted toward the door for the nurse he recalled seeing as he came in, "Carly! Need some help in here!"

With his heart in his gut, Doc worked to bring her back. Her pulse was strong, she was breathing, all good signs. Had he jinxed her only moments ago when he mentioned falling ill? Time stood still while he held her in his arms, not as a doctor, but a man holding his love. Those moments he waited for her to respond to him felt like hours – he literally held his heart in his arms.

"What is it Doc Ma... Oh, God!" Carly, a newer nurse to

McKenzie Ridge and McKenzie General, rushed to his side to assist.

"I think she just fainted. Vitals are good, she's starting to stir a bit. Grab a gurney and a lab tech – let's also start a line and run fluids."

After rushing from the room, Carly was back in no time with everything but the lab tech. "I couldn't get through to the lab, so I just grabbed the kit. I'll draw whatever you need after I place the line. Help me get her to the bed?"

Doc nodded in appreciation, thankful for her attentiveness. Standing straight from the floor, he lifted her, cradled against his chest, and gently laid her in the bed Carly had rolled in.

"Or, you can just get her in the bed, Doc," Carly teased. "Step aside, I got this. Can you check Lou? I hear her monitor getting a little noisy."

He did as she requested, tending to Lou was a nice distraction. Normally he was the one calling out the orders, but he appreciated her taking charge of the situation. He figured it was in her nature to do so. She was a petite little brunette, sweet, bubbly, and…bossy. Doc had never been exposed to such fear in his life, nor responsible for a loved one as an instant patient. Lou was fine, likely just her body responding to the chaos around her.

"All done Doc. Drip's running, and drew for labs. Here are the vials, just need to know what you want ordered so I know if I pulled enough before that drip goes too long."

Carly took the vials of blood with Doc's lab order marked stat. He pulled the chair close to her bedside sitting between her and Lou, and buried his face in his hands. She had stirred, spoken, though it was mostly jibberish. Odd as it was, he took that as a good sign. She may have fainted from standing too quickly with a heated temper while likely dehydrated, but

now she had fallen to the mercy of sleep. Much needed sleep
– she was exhausted – and when you don't listen to your
body, it has a way of forcing the issue.

Never in his career had he felt as panicked over his most
critical of patients as he did over a stressed out, exhausted
Everly. As a doctor, he knew she wasn't critical – she was a
generally healthy, active woman who was always on the go,
seeking out new challenges from rock climbing to skydiving.
She wasn't afraid of anything. As the man who loved her, and
man did he love her, he worried.

She was the first thing he thought about in the morning,
and the last thing when he finally gave in to sleep at night.
She'd quickly become his every dream, desire, and future. He
needed her like the air he breathed, and she became his
constant hunger. She was his everything…and now she lay at
the mercy of her own demons, and he couldn't do a damn
thing to save her from herself.

Patience wasn't his strong suit when it came to Everly
Shaw. Fully aware that she had made a pact with herself,
never to become more serious than a romp in the sack – with
anyone, not just him – he knew, from the day he met her, he
would be the man to change that. Her life had been anything
but perfect, but given the circumstances, she had a full life,
full of love. She was just too blind to see it. His personal
mission had been to show her, wait for her, until she saw
what was right in front of her.

"C'mon Ev, why are you doing this?" he whispered, "Let
me give you everything. It can be amazing, you just have to
let it be. You don't have to worry or live in fear anymore
because your past is not your destiny. Let me carry your fear,
your hurt, and fill that emptiness. Jesus, I love you…so much
it hurts."

He kissed the back of her hand, holding it in his as he

watched her sleep. She was so peaceful, relaxed…and so damn beautiful with her golden hair, refined features, and full lips. That was only the tip of the iceberg because every bit of her was beautiful, inside and out.

Checking his watch, he noted enough time had passed for the initial labs to process. He leaned in to leave a kiss on her forehead as he stood to leave the room. Standing above her, he took her in.

He whispered, "What is going on with you Everly. Why do I feel like you aren't telling me everything?"

Before he made it to the door on his way to the nearest computer at the nurse's station, his attention was caught by the increasing tones of Lou's monitors. Stepping back to look them over and assess her, he couldn't find anything obvious to be concerned about. Was she reacting to him and Everly?

He noted the subtle change in Lou's expression, "Is that a scowl? What do you know old woman? What do you know?"

7

Up before dawn seemed to be Carigan's new habit and it was a real bitch. Work had kept her busy and away from her brothers, but between the two, she was also missing time with BJ. She vented the night before to her partner on the ambulance, Dawson, but he was no help. He had a good laugh and tried to convince her they just care. He may as well be one of her overprotective brothers too. If she was a gambling girl, she'd wager that all of the guys would say the same and side with her brothers. Assholes.

Standing in the kitchen, watching her coffee brew as fast as a slug could run, her attention was drawn to a sound she had actually been waiting for. The open kitchen and attached living room afforded a straight shot view through the large picture window on the front of the house. Just as she expected, number two was fourth to arrive.

Carigan briskly made her way to the door where two cooking pans were sitting on a side table. Her brothers underestimated her, she was prepared for this, they forgot she had the best teachers of all....them. With the door wide open she picked up the pans and banged them together as loudly as she could, yelling toward the hallway that led to all of the bedrooms.

She hollered, "Get up boys! Your brother is here, you lazy arses!"

Liam O'Reilly stood in front of her with a befuddled look of concern and maybe even fear. Mission accomplished.

Giving her watch a quick look, she was surprised. "You're late, Liam! It's nearly six thirty in the morning!"

"You...knew I was...coming? I didn't know I was on a schedule." Liam replied. Not sure what to think of Carigan's disposition, he kept looking over her shoulder, hoping the reinforcements would wander down the hallway.

"Ehh, the other boys got here much earlier than you." She looked around him, disappointed to see he was alone. "Where's the sprite? She didn't come with you?"

The *sprite* was Liam's ten year old daughter, Reagan. She was the spitting image of Carigan, interestingly enough, but with a fire about her that earned her the nickname, Ragin' Reagan. Liam was Luke's twin, and just as beautiful to look at as the other brothers, but he was the brain of the bunch.

Liam handled the IT side of their high end security firm and could hack anything and everything. The only reason he wasn't in a federal prison was because he worked for them often, and that afforded him some legal courtesies. While the other boys grew up in sports and going girl crazy, Liam was involved in every academic club there was and dated the same girl all through high school. He married that girl, she was his everything, but his world collapsed when she died, leaving Liam a young widower with a daughter to raise alone.

"She's not here, she's with...Cassidy's family for Thanksgiving this year," he said, pain crossing his face at the mention of his wife's name.

"Oh, I'm sorry...I didn't know." Carigan felt like an ass

now, giving the one brother a rough time who deserved it the least.

"It's…okay. Oh, and I was dropped off."

"Dropped off? By who?" She looked outside again, the car she knew she heard was nowhere to be seen.

"A friend." He made his way in the door, passing her with a wink and a cunning grin.

"How are you going to get home, and more important… how are you getting the boys home?"

"Huh…I hadn't really thought about that. Thought I'd stay a while. You don't mind, do you?"

A deep sigh later, she realized she was getting nowhere fast, and switched gears. "Where's Declan? Thought he may be with you?"

"Dec? He's on a project, he couldn't come. You're welcome." Liam gave her a wink, knowing Dec was the one she feared most. Everyone feared Declan most.

"Oh, well with *Beck McCain* as your client and the big *business* meeting you guys have, I thought maybe he would come too."

Liam gave her a cross look then noticed his disheveled brothers entering the room, still half asleep, nodding their heads. "Oh…uh…yeah. I'm here for that too."

"Sure you are."

His sullen mood was gone at the sight of his mischievous brothers, and it was time to get in the game. "So where's Bart."

Hands on her half-cocked hips, Carigan was ready to spit fire, "Holy hell, are we doing this again?"

"Again? Hey…" He raised his hands in an innocent plea, but the ornery grin gave him away. "I just got here! Catch me up!"

"He goes by *Blow Job* Baker now." Wylie deadpanned.

"BJ! His name...is BJ!" she ranted.

Wylie shrugged his smug shoulders and scanned the room for support. "That's what I just said!"

"You've gotta see this kid!" Dace added, "Boy got big... and probably stopped taking showers. Very *earthy*. He's like a giant hippy with granola and sticks stuck in his beard and everything."

"Yes! And he wears like this purse! A mountain man with a purse...and a twirly knot thing in his hair. What's it called?"

Wylie batted his eyelashes and sipped his coffee with pinkies out in a weak attempt to look and sound proper. "It's a *bun*, dear. Blow Job doesn't have a *purse,* it's probably a giant weed bag."

Awareness fell over her at the exaggerated, yet somewhat accurate descriptions of BJ. "Wait, you saw him? When?"

Muffled snickers and sly smiles filled the room and suddenly they were each thirsty, taking sips from their mugs. No one was going to talk, until one got brave... Wylie.

"Sure," he chortled, "many times."

"So you're following me! You're basically stalking your sister...and Blow Job! I mean BJ! And it's a *SATCHEL!*"

And there it was, a win for her brothers and pure fury for Carigan. It was time to play hardball. These guys may have been oozing alpha macho crap, unafraid of anything...but one person. Colleen O'Reilly.

"I'll call ma." Not a threat, or tease...just an *I dare you to do it again* promise.

Challenge accepted, Wylie fired back with his best bargaining chip, "Go ahead, we'll tell her you're sneaking out."

Smug grins and puffed out chests deflated the moment their little sister used a big girl word, in a calm promising tone, "Good. Tell her I'm having sex too. Lots and lots of wild sex!"

With that, she took her coffee and left the kitchen, headed to her room to get ready for the day. She was so pleased with herself and the wide eyed blank expressions she left her brothers with she would have high-fived herself, but she wasn't one to gloat.

She could hear their voices begin to echo down the hallway, "Wait, what do you mean? You're not... No way is she... Someone call Dec..." just as she closed her door.

WORKING THE LATE SHIFT AND HAVING HOUSE *GUESTS* HAD put a damper on Carigan's late night – and all day – shenanigans with BJ. Granted, they had only had a few days apart, after only days back together, but she missed him. She believed in insta-attraction, but insta-love? No way. But, the longer she went without him in her bed, or even just by her side, the more she realized maybe this was more there than just a good time.

Maybe the rules were different when you had a history with someone. Maybe having somewhere to start that was beyond the awkward early weeks, but just before the serious commitment that included cake and white dresses, meant something. Girls who fall head over heels and start naming their future children and puppies after the first few dates drove her crazy. Oddly, she was becoming one of those girls.

Her brothers had pegged him as a dirty hippie, but they would find something wrong with a guy with a fat bank account and fancy suits just the same, if he were dating her. Truth was, BJ's shoulder length, brown locks gave her something to run her hands through and his beard left a tantalizing sting that couldn't be matched.

He was health conscious, sure, but he was a chef and it was more about the chemistry of food than anything else. His satchel was their gym bag, tit for tat. He was a business man, a very successful one, and his work went everywhere with him while he was in between San Francisco and McKenzie Ridge. He needed that satchel.

Sitting alone in her room, defending him was just another reminder that she had it bad for the guy. They hadn't discussed long term plans, but she hoped they included her. She didn't think she could lose him again, not this time. She would be lost without him…and the hot sex. He ruined her.

A loud knocking distracted her from her deep thoughts on loving BJ Baker. Her brothers had left a while ago, she heard them leave, and she wasn't expecting anyone. BJ came to mind again, and her excitement grew. Maybe he knew they were gone…smart man.

Racing down the hall, she stopped to do a quick once over in a hallway mirror before answering the door with her best smile, which fell flat the minute she saw who was on the other side.

"Dec."

"Well, it's nice to see you too, Squirt. Where's the boys?" he asked, pushing his way past her.

"C'mon in." She waved her hand sarcastically, as if she had a say in him staying. "I don't know, they left a while ago. Wait, you know they're here? Great! You're their ride, right?"

Declan gave her a bewildered glance, "Ride? No. I'm here on business."

"Right, Beck…your client."

"You feeling okay, Squirt? I don't know what you're

talkin' about." He wasn't leading her on, he was being straight with her.

"So there is no business with McCain! They're all here because of BJ!"

"I know nothing. I'll just leave it at that." He smiled, something he didn't do often.

"You aren't here to get them? I swear, Declan O'Reilly, if you call Ronan and all the cousins in Deception Pass to show up next, I'm running away where you'll never find me."

"I haven't called Ronan. And Ma sent me. Thought you could use some backup."

"I love that woman." A sigh of relief escaped her, and her shoulders relaxed for the first time in days. She was no longer outnumbered because Declan O'Reilly alone was a hard match for the rest of their brothers combined.

Dec was the oldest of the clan, not quite biggest, but big enough to be scary. His work took him undercover a lot so he was the one who tended to be on the outside, keeping his distance to keep his family safe from whatever he was trying to bust. The brothers were each only a year apart – with twins Luke and Liam being the exception – but they all worshiped Declan like he was their ten plus year senior. If Dec told them to knock it off and jump off a cliff, they'd do both yesterday.

"So, where *is* Bart?"

"BJ. And I don't know. I think he's afraid to come around with you guys here."

"Pussy."

"No, smart. I don't blame him."

"Why? We're a fun bunch!"

"Sure you are, with all of that macho, alpha, special forces, gun for hire, we know how to get rid of a body charisma…beats me!"

"Wow, you make us sound pretty damn intimidating,

Squirt. Full disclosure, Da sent me too. He sent me to keep Bart in line."

"You are intimidating, not to mention giant pains in my ass! Make it stop, Dec. I like this guy...a lot."

"You always have, kid." His arm wrapped around her shoulders and he pulled her in for a hug right before he rubbed his hand through her coppery hair and messed it up, earning him a solid punch to the gut.

"Does Lydia know you're here?" she asked quietly, tip-toeing around the soft subject.

"No, why would she?"

Dec seemed to have his own bad luck in love. Lydia Prescott, Megan Sparks' sister, was one of his cases a few years back, before he left whatever secret government agency he worked for to work full time with their brothers at their security firm. She was his *last* case. They spent a year or so on the run, trying to stay alive so she could testify against her husband, who was a murdering cartel member. It all ended in McKenzie Ridge when they set a trap that almost went bad.

Her husband was dead now, thanks to Dec and Blake Cooper. Dec left McKenzie Ridge immediately afterward, and never looked back, though she knew it pained him to do so. He was still protecting Lydia, by staying away. Carigan found that to be one of the most heartbreaking romantic stories she ever heard.

"No reason, big brother." she hugged him, and he let her.

Her phone buzzed and she ignored it. Then it buzzed again, and again. She went to the kitchen counter where she had left it and found the same text from each of their friends. Everly had collapsed. She was not just a visitor at the hospital, she was a patient.

8

EVERLY WOKE UP IN A SEMI-DARK ROOM IN A BED TO THE right of Granny Lou. She looked around, not yet fully awake, trying to recall all that had happened. She noticed the wild flowers on the table between her and Gran. They were new and much like those that had been delivered before. Again, no card. The thought of someone walking in and her having no recollection sent a chill down her spine. She must have been exhausted, just like Doc said.

A large plastic hospital mug full of what looked like ice water sat on the table too. When she reached for it, the tug in her arm drew her attention to the I.V. in her arm. She traced the line up the pole to the bag it was all attached to – a saline bag – she was being treated for dehydration. She could have drunk and ate more, but between the stress and not feeling well, she hadn't.

Now she was stuck in a hospital bed, the patient, not the nurse, and the I.V. hurt like a bitch. Lesson learned. Thinking back to what happened, she closed her eyes and let out an annoyed sigh. She had made a complete ass of herself in front of Doc. First by refusing to grab a quick meal with him, something that likely could have prevented all of this. Then by blacking out for the second time in not more than a week's time. She couldn't keep up the charade.

"So when were you going to tell me?" Looking out of the window on the other side of the room, Doc didn't even turn while addressing her.

"Wha-what do you mean?"

He turned slowly, his hands in his pocket and wearing a long drawn face that told a story of sadness. He knew her secret and that scared the shit out of her. Would he go, or would he stay. She hoped it was stay.

"Ev, stop it. You know what I'm talking about. I ordered labs, but the one test I didn't *think* to run had already been run. I found it in your chart when I was looking for answers from the labs pulled today. Ev…a baby?"

A lone tear drifted down her cheek as she looked down at her fidgeting hands unsure how to answer. "I…I just found out. I needed time to process it. Decide what to do. Then Gran…"

"Decide what to do? Was I going to be a part of that? You aren't just a little pregnant, Ev – you are well into your second trimester. You're keeping it…right, Ev? We aren't talking about…"

"I am. I am keeping it and I was going to tell you. It's just…"

From sadness to anger, his tone took a sharp turn and it had her on edge. She knew this conversation was going to be hard, but not this hard. Fear had managed to interfere with even this for her, and rather than doing what she knew in her gut was right…she listened to that fear. Regret seemed to be her favorite company when it came to relationships.

"You just what? Say it!"

"I don't know! Alright? I just...you know what I've been through and I was scared!"

"Everly, if you don't know me by now, and know that I would do anything, *anything* for you, then I don't know why we're even doing this!"

Everly was speechless. She knew everything he was saying was true. Doc was the kindest most honest man she knew, he was upstanding and she could count on him. She also knew that no matter how much you love someone, or want to love someone, it's a gamble, and forevers aren't always real.

"This explains so much. Shit, even in Portland...you didn't eat much. You were tired. You even got sick! How did I not see this coming?" He raked his hand through his hair in frustration. "I thought you fainted the other day because you were in shock. You were getting sick! I'm not a very good doctor, shit, I missed all the signs. Fuck, this is why you've been pushing me away! I thought it was just how you were dealing with Lou being sick, but no...it was me."

He turned away, his focus back on whatever was outside that window, shaking his head slightly, frustration rolling off of him while he collected himself. This was a side of Doc Everly had yet to see, and it worried her.

"Look, I know losing your parents as a kid, the way you did, had to be awful. Those are wounds that never heal, but you are going to have to find a way to live with them. You're missing out, Ev...missing out on everything I'm sure they would have wanted for you."

His words stung. After all, that's how the truth worked, right? It was full of jagged edges and always hard to swallow, but it was what it was...truth. Somehow she needed to own hers.

"Those tragedies are once in a life time – it's okay to take a chance. You can love, Ev. You can love me, you can love the baby."

Doc turned to leave, but not before he finished what he *needed* to say, "Nothing bad will happen, I won't let it. I love our baby already. Nothing could make me happier except you – getting all of you. I love you Ev, I think I've loved you since that very first day."

Turning to the door so he could get some much needed air and a chance to get his head together, he saw that they had an audience in the doorway. Their friends were awkwardly standing there, straight faced and probably shocked. He stopped halfway to the door, turned and walked back to Everly and kissed her on the forehead before he walked out the door.

Of course there was one person willing to crack the awkward moment of deafening silence. Good, bad, or indifferent, you could always count on Jessie for honesty, hard truths, and bad timing.

"Holy shit! Someone's been playing doctor and got knocked up!"

Divide and conquer was the unspoken mission of the evening. The men, Blake, Colton, and Dawson, followed Doc at a safe distance so he could get it together privately. But, they were nearby if he needed an ear to bend. Filing in around Everly's bed, Jessie, Sam, and Meg huddled in to congratulate their friend and offer their support. This is what this group did for each other.

* * *

SITTING IN A WAITING ROOM ROW OF CHAIRS WHILE DOC paced the adjacent glass corridor, Blake questioned the men, "Did you smell that back there?"

A couple side-eye glances met his before he clarified the question, "The smell in the room, assholes. I've smelled it before, not just in there, but somewhere."

"It just smells like bleach and hospital to me," Dawson added, Colton nodding in agreement beside him.

"No, its…something. I can't put my finger on it."

Carly, the night nurse in the cardiac unit, walked through the corridor, her arms full of what looked like a lunch cooler, and a bin of baked goods.

Concern and with perhaps a little panic in her voice, she stopped and talked to Doc. "What are you guys doing out here, is Lou okay?"

"Oh, she's fine," Doc answered. "Well as fine as she was yesterday. We're just waiting on the ladies…they're planning something in there."

"Oh, good." she placed a relieved hand on her chest. "I was worried for a second there. Say, while I have you. That man, the one with the harmonica that comes most nights. Is that Evie's grandfather, or an uncle?"

"Her grandfather passed, and there aren't any uncles that I'm aware of." He thought the question was strange, but had bigger things on his mind. He wanted to get back to those, so he left well enough alone with Nurse Carly.

"Oh, well, I'll just have to ask next time. Probably just a friend then, still the new kid in town. I'll figure out who everyone is eventually. Well, have a good night if I don't see you on rounds later."

Doc went back to pacing, Carly walked by with a smile and hello for the guys, and Blake had a sudden inkling that something wasn't right. He had overheard the quick conversation between Doc and Carly and it didn't settle well at all. Between the odd smell that came and went, the excessive flowers that couldn't be traced when he looked into it, and now a mystery man…he had a heaviness in his gut that told him it was time to stay close, and keep eyes on all of his people. Something was happening and he didn't like it.

* * *

IT WASN'T LONG BEFORE THE SMALL CROWD THAT STUMBLED in on Everly's shocking baby reveal was reduced to one. The other ladies offered their support, congratulations, and hugs for Ev and Gran before gathering up their guys and giving her space. Sam knew better than to leave, though. Sister-like friends, Sam knew Everly better than anyone, and knew she was reeling.

"So, what do you *really* think?" Everly questioned, needing hard truths.

"I think you're going to be a *mom*! Ellie and Gavin will be excited, a new cousin!" Sam said, referring to her two children. She tried to find the silver linings while also trying to decide what Everly really needed to hear from her.

"Yeah, I'm sure El will have a list of her favorite names by tomorrow." Everly laughed.

"Seriously though," Sam started. "I know this isn't how you planned things or what you even wanted, but I have to think it's a sign of some sort."

"A sign? Really? Have you been sipping from Gran's flask?"

Sam laughed at the sarcasm, happy to see her sense of humor peeking through. "No, I haven't, but if you weren't knocked up, I'd sneak it in here for a few passes."

"I can't believe it, Sam. I still can't believe it. After days of mulling it over, and Doc's big moment…it still doesn't feel real."

"It will, honey. You'll get used to the idea and before you

know it, you'll be counting the days until you meet the little one. My guess is it will all get real around the first ultrasound. When you see him or her on the screen while they are kicking you inside, you can't help but feel how real it is."

"Yeah. I suppose." She looked at her hands, searching for the next words, when tears ran free and out of control. "I'm scared, Sam. I'm afraid to do this – to screw it up – or worse..."

"Honey, everyone feels that way at some point. You're going to be a *fantastic* mom – you're already everyone's favorite aunt. You can do this."

"And what if something happens?"

"Ev, that fear has nothing to do with what happened to you. Every parent has that worry, love does that, makes you worry. Why won't you let Doc in? You need him, you're literally carrying the other half of him."

"I know. I have been terrible to him. I think I just took him for granted and now...maybe I screwed things up for good. I am really good at that."

"You guys are good together. Really good. I think you underestimate him a bit. He's a good guy, it's obvious that he loves you, and he will make a terrific father."

Everly smiled, thinking of all that Sam said. Talking about Doc that way, thinking about him in that way, gave her those love drunk butterflies. "Yeah. He is a really good guy. I...I *really* like him."

Laughing at the admission, Sam replied, "I think you more than *like* him, but you'll figure that out. Just let him in. Let him love you, if not for you, then for the baby."

"I don't know if I can. When I love people, I lose them."

"You haven't lost any of us, and I know you love us. You can do this, Ev. You're the strongest woman I know, kid."

Placing her hand on her stomach, Everly said, "How did

he not notice before today? This is getting hard to miss. I look fat."

"Probably because you don't look fat, you look happy."

Sam leaned over the edge of the bed Everly was in to give her a hug before leaving. Sam was right, she really did love their little family of friends and they were all safe and fine despite her loving them. Maybe she *was* her own worst enemy and making things harder than they needed to be. Maybe, just maybe, this whole loving Doc and having his baby could work out for her and she could have a happily ever after like many of her friends had found.

"She's right, ya know." A gravelly voice startled her from the bed next to her.

"Oh my God! Gran!" Everly wrestled the blankets from across her lap and scrambled out of her bed.

She stood at Gran's bedside, hitting the nurse call button, and began to check vitals. "You're awake. I can't believe you're finally awake!"

Gran didn't seem herself, but that was to be expected given the tremendous trauma she had been through, so Everly didn't give it a second thought.

Granny Lou grabbed Everly's hand and locked stares with her. "I am so proud of you, Evie. So proud. You're mama and daddy would be too. You're going to be fine, girl. That Doc of yours will see to it. He's a keeper, don't toss that one back, you got it?"

Something odd settled over Everly, a sense of fear, like this was a goodbye, not a hello. "Gran I've needed you. I'm so glad you're back. I'm going to need you when this baby comes. I just…"

"No, honey. You have what you need – Doc and that baby. He's just waiting for you to realize what he already knows. That boy has forever in his eyes."

Gran dropped her hand and her head rolled back a bit as she let out a tired sigh.

"So you *have* been listening. I knew it."

"Oh, I've heard everything. It's all sort of mixed up in my head right now though, and I'm not sure why. You just let that boy take care of you though, you're going to need him, honey. You will need all of them…something…"

"Gran? Are you okay? Tell me what you're feeling." Everly began to panic, hitting the nurse's button over and over and she began to yell for help.

Doc ran into the room, pausing at the doorway, Carly right behind him.

"That sweet music, it never gets old. I remember it like it was yesterday. Willy always played beautiful music." A smile rested in her expression as her eyes closed like she was falling into a peaceful slumber.

Surrounded by Everly, Doc, and Carly, the machines attached to her began to scream something was wrong. Granny was no longer breathing, and her heart rate was barely traceable. All of the numbers on the monitors were a blur as Everly's world was crashing down around her…again.

The last thing she remembered as she sat on the edge of her bed was Doc shouting Code *Blue* and the code team rushing into the room, surrounding her grandmother. That's when she crawled back into that place inside herself where nothing, and no one, could reach her.

9

_____

DAYS HAD PASSED AND NOTHING HAD CHANGED. EVERLY SAT in Granny Lou's hospital room, leaving only to shower and change – never gone more than an hour. A stroke, they said. Something came loose, a clot, or plaque, they weren't sure. They also weren't sure if there was any permanent damage.

Early assessments indicated weakness on her left side, but they wouldn't know the full extent of her health until she was woke up. This time, they kept her in a medically induced coma, so they could keep her stable and rule out anything else that could possibly interfere with her recovery. She was weak, she was living with the help of a few machines, but she was alive. For now.

Gran's waking was likely some sort of fluke and precursor to the stroke. Beck McCain had pulled every string he had, and paid big bucks to bring in any specialist they thought could help with Gran's case and to help Everly.

Each one of those doctors, though, couldn't explain her brief waking and the odd circumstances surrounding her now stroke. McKenzie General and Doctor Sterling had provided the highest quality care available, nothing was left overlooked or undone. It was all just a fluke. Doctor Sterling was now at McKenzie General full-time through a Cardiology Grant sponsored by none other than, Beck McCain.

A neurologist who specialized in strange neuro anomalies was joining the team as well. Also on a grant, this time sponsored by the Tayler family. Everyone forgot Dawson came from money, and had a shit ton of it stowed away. He didn't like where it came from and didn't use it personally, but did use it for things like this – things that would benefit others. Dr. Skye Reynolds was the best of the best and her *only* patient at the moment was Louise Shaw.

Sitting in that room left Everly with a lot of time to do some soul searching. So many profound things had happened in such a short amount of time that she couldn't help but wonder if Sam was on to something with that whole *it's a sign* thing. Despite two major medical scares, Gran was still alive and there was hope.

She was pregnant, something she never planned. There was an amazing man just waiting for her to accept him. And her friends, they loved her and Gran so much that they were doing everything in their power to build a foundation for a happily ever after. All for *her.* If all of that wasn't cupid raining his shower of all things love on her...she didn't know what it was.

Every obstacle that landed in her path came with a resolution. Weighing the good and bad, she couldn't see a drastic influence from the bad. Sure, Gran falling ill was bad, but look at the good that came of it. In the end, when she was well, McKenzie would have not one, but two highly sought after doctors to tend to them. That was good.

She had a rowdy group of friends who were in her business at every turn. They interfered, annoyed, and overstayed welcomes…but they were her biggest cheerleaders and loved her unconditionally despite her own conditions.

Sure she had been *knocked up*, but now she was tied to the most incredible man she could have asked for. He was kind and loving, but more importantly, he was patient. There weren't many men who would put up with the boundaries and baggage she brought to the table. But he did, and he did it with grace.

Doc brought her every meal so she wouldn't have to leave the hospital, or Gran's side. If he couldn't, he arranged for someone else to do it. He didn't force the issue, just took care of her from a distance, giving her the space she needed to sort out her demons.

There were flowers, daily, also from Doc she thought. But he didn't say a word, about anything. She woke up some nights with a blanket over her and her head on his shoulder while he stroked her face with the back of his hand or caressed her arm. He comforted her.

There was no safer place than in his arms, and she was starting to see forever. Imagining a life without him was painful, whereas seeing a future with him felt like home. He doted on her like he needed her to breathe and if she was honest, she needed him just as much.

Life was funny that way. No matter how much you planned and stood strong in your personal convictions, it really wasn't up to you. Destiny, fate, kismet, they were all at work and we were at their mercy. The old adage of what was meant to be would be was the real plot twist in life. Doc was her plot twist, as was the baby, and everything that she cared so deeply about. Love – plot twist – and she was trying so desperately to let go of her fears.

She rested her hand on her belly, and looked down. "You, little one, changed my world. I think we're going to be okay.

Your daddy said we were and I've never known him to be a liar. You think we can love him back, forever?"

Startled, she placed both hands on her stomach and smiled. A very subtle hiccup of a flutter could be felt in her lower abdomen. She sat up straight, as quiet as can be, reminding herself to breathe. Another flutter. Her smile turned to a joyful giggle and she quickly grabbed her cell-phone that was on the table next to her and sent Doc a quick text.

Come to Gran's room – hurry. –E

Only a few minutes passed before Carly rushed in, Doc only seconds behind her in his scrubs, rubber gloves still on, and out of breath. He must've run the whole way. When Carly saw Everly's hands on her belly, and the tear stained smile, she grinned and backed out of the room.

"What is it?" he questioned, looking from Lou and her monitors to Everly. "What hurts? Are you okay? Jesus, Ev... talk to me!"

In a very calm and sweet tone she waved him closer. "Come here."

She placed his hand on her stomach next to hers and she giggled. "Do you feel it? Can you feel her?"

"Wait, what? He's moving?" The weight of the world fell from Doc's shoulders and an overwhelming sense of joy took over.

They sat in silence for a few moments while she giggled intermittently and he sat with a goofy smile.

"Can you feel her at all, Doc? All of those little... *blips*?"

"No, I can't. And why do you keep calling him a her?"

"I guess I just thought it was a her? I don't know...it just came out!" she joked.

"Well, it's probably still a little early for me to feel him.

That's the special part of this that's just between the two of you." He smiled.

"Him? So you think boy?"

He laughed. "I guess we both just unknowingly decided what we want him or her to be."

"I'd be happy with either one," she whispered.

"Well that's good because you're definitely getting one or the other," Doc teased.

"I was just talking to...uhhh...*the baby*."

"You were? What were you two talking about?" he asked, seeing the sentiment in her eyes.

"I was telling her...err...him...*the baby* about forever." Her eyes filled with emotion. "I'm so sorry Mason. I was so scared, am so scared, that I let it decide everything for me."

He pulled her close and held her, placing kisses on her forehead. "Shhh, it's okay, baby. I know this hasn't been easy for you, but you can trust me with everything. I won't let anything hurt you, or us."

A subtle sob escaped her as she felt every word he said, and believed it. "Promise me Doc. Promise me you'll never let anything happen like you said."

With his forehead to hers he whispered, "I promise, baby. You are my everything. I would've waited forever for you and now that I have you...nothing gets in our way. Okay?"

His emotion erupted in a long sultry kiss that he wouldn't let break free.

"Come home with me, Ev. You can get a good night's sleep and a decent meal for a change. You need this."

She was reluctant to go, turning to look at Gran. She hesitated to say anything.

"C'mon babe, it's just to sleep, eat, and shower. We're only minutes away and you know they will call immediately should something change. Carly is here, Gran is in good hands. Doctor Reynolds is weaning her meds anyway so she can wake up, you need to be rested for that. You can do this, Ev."

With a little hesitation, she nodded her head and stood to give Gran a kiss goodbye before walking out the door with Doc…to go *home.*

EVENING TURNED TO NIGHT AND BLAKE FOUND HIMSELF AT the hospital to put a nagging feeling to rest. The words Nurse Carly exchanged with Doc in the corridor were haunting him and he needed resolve. He exited the elevator on Lou's floor, and rounded the corner to the nurse's station that tended to Lou.

He played the conversation over and over in his mind, trying to identify the man Carly had mistaken as Everly's uncle or grandfather. The man with the harmonica who visited only at night and often. Granny had old roots in this town, and old friends too. People like Jed Baker from the bakery, and Chappy the ranch hand out at Morgan's ranch were old friends, but neither met the description and Carly knew both of them. They also came during the day, during regular visiting hours, and neither played harmonica.

A grey haired man in a cowboy hat, at the other end of the long hall, caught Blake's attention. He had a swagger that aged him and a certain limp that marked his pace. Blake didn't recognize the man from his back and assumed he was a patient's visitor.

When entering Lou's room, Blake was met by that odd smell again. It was something of a smoldering ash, with a hint of pine and something he couldn't quite put his finger on. It reminded him of campfire smoke and fresh cut Christmas trees, but he was lost on the rest of what lingered.

"Hey Blake!" Carly said from behind.

"Do you smell that?" he asked.

Carly tilted her head and stared for a moment with a puzzled look on her face, "Isss, that a joke?"

"Why does everyone keep asking that? I don't get it."

"Smell. Did you smell that…it's a joke to get people to smell the air after you…you know."

"No, I obviously don't know," he said, puzzled now himself.

"You know, when you…pass…gas. You ask if anyone can smell that and then they smell…it."

"That's disgusting," he deadpanned.

She laughed. "It is, but people think it's funny. So what do you smell?"

"That," Blake motioned to the room while sniffing. "I've smelled it several times now. Its woodsy."

"I suppose. I do smell that off and on. I just assumed it was the flowers or something."

"There's more flowers too. How often do those arrive?"

"Oh, Lou Shaw is a popular one – quite the fan club! Those flowers come in at all hours it seems. I can't keep up!"

With arms half crossed and a wide stance, Blake rubbed his chin trying to piece together what he had, but there wasn't a big picture forming at all. He was no closer to relieving the itch that told him something was off.

"I heard you talking to Doc about an old guy, you thought it was a relative? Plays a harmonica?"

"Oh, yes! We rather enjoy the late night serenades at the nurse's station – sometimes it's just too quiet at night. Don't know his name. Haven't met him yet, but he's friendly enough. He drops off goodies from Baker's for the nurse's every now and again."

"Hmmm, when is the last time you saw him?"

"Oh, he was just here a bit ago, you probably just missed him."

Blake was at attention, ready to dart, he asked, "Cowboy hat?"

"Yep! That's him!"

Blake burst from the room, running in the direction he had seen the man. The only way off the floor was through the elevator Blake came in on and the stairs next to it, or down the glass corridor to an elevator in another wing of the hospital – that's the direction the old man had gone. Blake looked all around, up and down the corridor and couldn't find the guy.

Doubling back, he realized that there was one more way to the elevator he had come from in the cardiac unit. The old man could have looped around the entire floor and taken the main elevator, but why. Why would he take a long route around when he could have caught it from only feet away, coming from Lou's room when he left?

Those hairs on the back of his neck were standing tall, indicating something was off in their little community and maybe in their family. He didn't take kindly to strangers in his town, especially when they were getting too close to his people. Who was the old man and how'd he know Blake was coming?

Catching up with Carly, he offered her his business card, "Hey, if you happen to see the old guy again, give me a holler. No one will know it was you."

"Sure. Uh, is everything okay? Shouldn't I just call security if he's not supposed to be here?"

"I need to find out who he is before we know if he isn't supposed to be here."

"Good point." She dropped her head a bit. "You all are lucky, ya know. To have each other – you all take care of each other. I admire that."

There was a sadness in her voice that struck him. He didn't know much about her other than she came from the city, lived alone, and worked a lot. He'd have to remember to pass that on to the ladies. It sounded like Carly could use some friends.

He smiled at her, "Yeah, they're all really good people."

Before leaving, Blake went back to Lou's room to check on her and say goodbye. After all, they said she could hear them. He wasn't expecting to find anyone in there, visiting with Lou at such a late hour though.

"Jessie? What are you doing here?" He would be lying if he said he wasn't happy to see her. As ornery as she was, and as big a pain in the ass she was, her face looking back at him gave him comfort.

"Same thing you are."

"Which is?"

"I know you can feel it. Something isn't quite right, is it? Can you smell that?"

Jessie Clarke was the thorn in his side that brought a smile to his face. *That's my girl,* he thought.

10

FALL IN MCKENZIE RIDGE BOASTED SUNNY CLEAR DAYS, albeit crisp – perfect for a nice drive which was exactly what Carigan and BJ were doing. It was far too cold to picnic along the creek, but the perfect spot along the banks and the scenery while eating a packed lunch from BJ's truck was actually pretty romantic – and warm. Alone time had been sparse, and both were missing each other. So a spontaneous almost picnic was perfect.

McKenzie Ridge was surrounded by beauty around every turn. Green pine trees, fall colors, snow-capped mountains all around, and nature in all of its glory – that was McKenzie. The stunning sunrises were only challenged by the breath-taking sunsets and the clear starry night skies. It was home for Carigan, and she hoped it would be for BJ too.

The couple sat along the creek, snacking on delicious yet practical finger foods BJ had put together.

"I've really missed this," Carigan said in between bites.

"My cooking?"

Carigan shrugged, and smiled. "Well, yeah, that…but I meant us."

"I know, just giving you a hard time. I've missed you too."

"I wish the boys would just go home, but sounds like they are planning on staying through Thanksgiving. Yay." Her cheer lacked enthusiasm and carried more annoyance than anything.

"Hey," he said, reaching a hand to her face and holding it, "it's okay, Cari. You know they don't bother me, right? We don't have to sneak around like teenagers."

She leaned into his hold, closing her eyes, accepting the affection and comfort. "I know. They just make me feel like…like a kid! And I don't want them giving you a hard time. They can be unbearable at times."

A chuckle escaped him. "That's very sweet, but we *aren't* kids anymore and the best they can do is give me shit. They can't dunk my head in the toilet for a swirly, or kick my ass behind the school. It's okay, babe. You know I'll respect whatever you want and go along with however you want to deal with this, but I'm really not intimidated by them at all. I actually kind of like them."

"Did they threaten you?" She sat up straight, squinting her emerald eyes, cheeks darkening with anger. "You don't have to listen to them you know!"

He erupted in laughter, finding her fiery side amusing. "You really are adorable when you get mad. I promise. They haven't said a word…really."

"Well…what do we do then. Sneaking off on a picnic feels ridiculous."

BJ leaned in, resting his hand behind Carigan's neck, pulling her in for a long sweet kiss. "We don't have to sneak off, Cari. We can do whatever we want. Right now, I want you."

Eyes wide, with surprise and a warm thrill rushing

through her, she pulled him closer. Happy to oblige, he slid across the bench seat of his truck. Maybe it wasn't such a bad idea to act like a couple of teenagers again for a steamy afternoon in the backseat – or front seat – neither were picky.

He leaned her back, reclining the seat as far as it would go to make room for what he wanted to do to her, and what she was more than hungry for. Unbuttoning her green flannel top and pushing it off along with the black down vest she was wearing, he kissed a trail from her collarbone to the top of her breasts. Pulling her bra down, freeing her full breasts, he feasted on each, pulling and biting as he went.

"So damn beautiful. Lift your ass, baby." She did as he asked so he could push down the black leggings she was wearing, giving him access to where she ached for him most.

His hand trailed up her thigh, slowly causing her ache to become a deep needy throb that had her so sensitive, just his light touch at her center had her breathy and crying out. Her legs fell open to him showing him what she needed from him. He stroked her with his fingers, swirling her core before slipping inside of her while still having his way with her breasts.

She reached for his belt, undoing each barrier until she reached what she wanted. Freeing him from his pants, she held him in her hand and began to stroke him, completely in sync with his own movements. The intensity hot, the pleasure sweet, they worked each other over fast and hard.

Without warning, he sat back down at her side, sliding one arm behind her when he lifted her so he could slide underneath her. He plunged into her as she fell to his lap facing away from him and she began to ride. The space was small, but they made due – her gripping the dash, him with one hand tugging and pinching at her hardened buds while the other hand stroked the sensitive knot between her legs.

He worked her over and ground her hips back into him,

picking up the pace until both of them spilled over into a passion driven bliss. They sat that way for several minutes before he slowly slid her bra back into place, kissing her shoulders as he did. Then her shirt was next, but left open. He laid her carefully to the side and helped her bring her leggings back up, then hovering over her, kissed her slow and sweet.

"I love you, Carigan O'Reilly. I've always loved you," he whispered into her ear.

Her breath caught, and she pulled away placing her hands on either side of his face, searching his eyes. She found sincerity and warmth, and maybe something that said forever. She was ready to speak her heart when the sound of an approaching vehicle startled them both.

"Oh, my God! There is a car coming!" she panicked, "Put your...thing away!"

He chuckled at her reference, but did as she said, while trying to see who was coming. "I can't tell who it is yet, they haven't rounded that corner...might be a truck? What are the odd's someone just happened to wander down this old road to this spot?"

"I don't know, but..." She stilled for a moment, closed her eyes and let out a deep annoyed breath. "I'd bet you money I don't have that I know who is about to round that corner! Are you all buttoned up...oh, my God!"

BJ had a feeling he knew who it was too, and her reaction to that had him laughing. "If it's the boys, maybe we should stay half dressed. It would make a point."

"What?! Out here? No witnesses? They know how to get rid of a body! No thanks! It *is* them!!!"

Carigan charged out of BJ's truck and rushed to her brother's vehicle as it pulled up behind them. She stood in a wide stance, hands on her hips, with a look that could kill. BJ got out behind her and leaned against the truck, ready for the show. Carigan's brothers got out of the vehicle, one by one, and walked to the back of it.

"What the hell are *you* guys doing here?" she demanded.

"Hey, nature boy, how's it going?" Wylie asked BJ with a friendly nod. "Hey, sis…fancy meeting you here!"

"Yeah…right…what a *coincidence.* So, what are you doing here?"

Luke was the first to walk from the back of their truck with a fishing pole and tackle box in hand. He held it up and said, "Fishing!"

"Yeah! Fish for dinner, Squirt!" Dace followed.

"In the middle of fall, when it's ready to snow? Fishing? It's not even fishing season…it's illegal if you catch anything," she replied, proud of her come back. They were caught. Or were they?

"Oh, we're just fishin' for fun! We were sitting around and thought, *wow it's been forever since we'd all been fishin' together,* so here we are! We'll just throw what we catch back…you know, for sport!" Wylie offered up, sarcasm lining his story.

"But I thought you were catching dinner? How does that work if you are just going to throw them back?" she asked, finding all of the holes in their story.

"You want fish for dinner, Squirt?" Liam asked, like it was her idea to eat fish in the first place. "We can grab some at the store back in town."

"Great idea," Dace chimed, "Family dinner night…fish fry!"

"Dec, do something!" she begged of her eldest brother who just smiled, leaning against his truck.

"I think you got this one, kid," he said.

"Hey Bart, you got any good fish recipes?"

"BJ!" Carigan yelled, correcting her brother. "How did

you find us out here? This isn't your old fishing spot and I've never known you guys to come this far out!"

"Oh…" Wylie laughed. "Heard it was a good spot so we followed…the trail out here."

"Followed? Are you serious?! Are you tracking my phone again? You have got to be kidding me! I'm getting a new number, and none of you get it."

Liam the hacker laughed at her confession. "Like I need the number to find you! Good one, kid. But that's not how we found…this spot."

"What do you mean?" she asked.

Wylie looked at BJ with an ornery smile, shaking his head before tossing a thumb Carigan's way. "It's like she forgets who she's talking to! *How did we find her*? Ha!"

The brothers were making their way past Carigan and BJ, following each other down to the creek's edge. Carigan stood there, watching each walk by, keeping a suspicious eye on each of them. Declan was the last to pass and dropped a subtle glance at the bumper of BJ's truck. Not one to miss a single detail, having grown up with this bunch, Carigan caught the clue.

She quickly turned, squatting behind BJ's truck, looking under the vehicle. She reached underneath, sliding her hands back and forth searching for something.

BJ squatted down next to her, with a half amused expression. "What are you doing Cari?"

"Finding it. They followed *you* – they probably have been. They are trying to catch us."

"Catch us, what?"

"Catch us…AHA! Found it!" Biting her bottom lip, Carigan placed both hands in the same spot under the bumper and tugged so hard she fell backward in the dirt. Quick to her feet, she stomped down to the creeks edge where her brothers stood, not one with a line in the water, and showed them her prize.

"You want to fish? Fish for this!" She threw the tracking device she found on BJ's truck as far as she could into the center of the widest part of the frigid creek.

"Hey! Those aren't cheap!" Liam reasoned.

"Good! Now leave us alone!" She hiked back up the slight embankment to where BJ was standing, a proud smile on his face.

"Hey, Granola?" Luke said, referring to BJ. "We're doing some special Search and Rescue training while we're here. Snow's coming so time for a refresher. You should come, we'll make a man out of ya."

"Yeah, we can all sit around and braid each other's hair when we are done. Or you can teach us how to do that bun thing." Wylie chuckled, swirling a finger over his head indicating the bun that BJ was currently wearing.

BJ added his own sense of humor to the hippy punch line, earning him several impressed grins and brows raising. "Sure! When and where? I'll pack organic, whole food, sustainable lunches! *Lots* of phytonutrients."

Turning a finger to BJ, Carigan scolded, "Don't you start too. Get in the truck, we're out of here."

"C'mon kid, this is all for your own good. We need to be sure this guy can take care of you," Liam reasoned.

"You're going to kill him! First football, then a ten mile run...*up* the ridge, you gave him a shotgun at the shooting range and *forgot* to mention the kickback one of those packs when fired. Now you want him climbing up the side of a mountain, or rappelling down the side of one...at *your* hands? You'll probably push him off the cliff!"

"Good idea, Squirt! Teach him to take a good fall! And

it's not our fault he fizzles out at around seven miles."
Wylie's taunting ways were riding Carigan's last nerve.

BJ put his hands on each of her shoulders and had her
undivided attention immediately. "It's okay, babe. I want to
go – might be fun."

He dropped his voice to a near whisper, "And if they
know I'm not scared of them, they might go away."

She smiled, this was definitely her man. She winked, and
said, "Fine! Give me your keys, I have to pick up the girls.
You ride with them and I'll meet you there."

BJ handed her his keys, tossed her a proud smile in lieu of
a high five, they were playing the game right back. To add
insult to injury, she pulled him in hard and laid a long, hard,
sultry kiss full of roaming hands and even a smack to BJ's
ass. Her brothers were mortified. Mission accomplished.

Rounding BJ's truck to leave, she stopped and looked at
her brothers. "I'm calling Ma and telling her what you're up
to. Be careful, no funny business before I get there! If you
boys aren't careful, I'm going to run off and marry this guy in
the middle of the night."

She slammed the door, started the truck and spun her
tires, hauling ass out of there. Carigan O'Reilly had spoken.

"Let's go, boys!" BJ said, helping himself to the front seat
of the remaining vehicle.

11

_____

EVERLY WAS SITTING IN GRANNY LOU'S HOSPITAL ROOM, fuming, frustrated, and maybe even a little hurt. Confessing her affections to Doc was a big step for her and now she almost regretted it. His constant affection, and doting was sweet to an extent, but his overbearing ways were starting to weigh on her.

He promised to take care of her, protect her, and he was making good on said promise to the point of overprotective. Doc continued to bring her every meal so she could stay at Gran's side, but he brought what he _thought_ she should eat. She wanted something sweet, like a brownie from Baker's, or fresh baked cookies, and Doc brought her a bowl of fruit.

Everly asked for a hot chocolate, or heaven forbid a cup of tea, and Doc brought her a glass of milk. Warm milk. When the girls stopped in to visit with a pizza, Doc showed up like pepperoni was on his radar...with a salad in hand, loaded with every vegetable in season. She found out that Doc had recruited BJ to make her _healthy_ meals and deliver them daily to the hospital.

It was all sweet in the beginning and she not only invited,

but indulged his attention. It was nice to be taken care of for a change. When her boyfriend started feeling more like a babysitter, or worse, a parent...she had trouble seeing straight.

Her trips away from the hospital were only to shower, sleep, and change. That was a big step for Everly, leaving Gran alone overnight. Even that, however, came with Doc's monitoring since he had officially moved into her house. She was sure there was a chart somewhere with her footsteps taken per day to make sure she wasn't over doing it and a pie chart that reflected how much time was spent sitting and not stretching her legs because that required balance too, during pregnancy.

Doing rounds with the gang in the woods was no longer an option. Doc had plenty of support from their friends on that one. Carly volunteered to take her place there.

If hiking into the woods was a no, then winter Search and Rescue training with the O'Reilly brothers was definitely off the table. She couldn't even go watch because apparently there weren't any seats available at the edge of the cliff they were training on. Daredevil and risk taker were no longer her middle name – she was now Everly Knocked-Up Shaw.

Doc brought her endless books with marked paragraphs and chapters full of information on *how to be pregnant*. If it wasn't a book, it was a story from someone in the ER, offering advice. He expressed that he was torn between one breast pump from another and types of storage versus best practices in reheating of breast milk. He was obsessed.

At night though, or the wee hours of the morning, when he would pull up a chair next to her at the hospital, or crawl into bed at night next to her, he was a different man. He just held her. Pulled her into him, cradled her against his body, and kept her safe. With pregnancy hormones raging, it was all she could do not to pin the man down and have her wicked way with him. Even if she did, though, he wasn't interested.

As annoying as he could be with all of his advice and hovering ways, he was sweet, and his actions endearing...and entirely too hot. Attraction wasn't something they struggled with, it was instant with them. But pregnant, even his dark framed glasses that he wore on occasion made her body hum. More and more, Doc Charles was becoming *her* muse, and his every step was another orgasm waiting to happen.

When he played video games, all she could think about was what game she wanted to play with him – naked – she'd play the bad guy and let him tie her up any day. When he got ready in the morning, in nothing but his superhero undershirt or ridiculous superhero boxer briefs, all she could think of was his *man of steel.* When he was up late, strumming the guitar because working random ER shifts screwed with his sleep schedule, all she could think about was being strummed by the talented fingers of a dirty rock star. Doc was her rock star. .

What's worse is despite her shameless flirting and endless attempts to seduce him at all hours, she was shot down at every turn. Everly had become a hormone induced, sex crazed insatiable vixen. She was like a free classy prostitute, offering endless goods, and he wanted nothing to do with it. He wouldn't touch her. He didn't even look at her like he used to.

On a good day, her advances would earn her a kiss on the forehead, otherwise, she was at arms-length. Sure he smiled at her, watched her from afar, and went out of his way to either be with her or nearby when he wasn't working, but there was still a distance between them. One that left her hot, bothered, and insecure.

She reduced herself to traipsing around the house in next

to nothing. Then decided undressing and dressing was something for show. She noticed him watching, but nothing beyond that. Getting handsy and groping him in the middle of the night when she couldn't take it any longer just caused him to turn them both to one side where he held her all night, rather than having his way with her. Even when she was in bed – naked.

Doc said nothing was wrong, he wasn't upset with her at all, but it still didn't add up. She didn't understand the change between them. With a growing belly and changing figure, had she become unattractive? Was he no longer interested in her and only in it for the baby? She practically violated the man, doing things that could actually get her arrested, and to no avail. Despite the endless efforts on her part, he just wouldn't touch her.

This was all her fault. She had pushed him away far too long and her little secret was the final straw. How could she blame him? Months and months of *being together* without actually being together. Telling them they could never be more than a romp in the sack finally clicked and he believed it. She couldn't give him her heart, but she gave him a baby? What message did that send? She got exactly what she wanted, only now, she didn't want it. She wanted him, and he wanted the baby.

If he wasn't charmed by any of her usual tactics, she would just have to concoct a plan that would remind him why *he* wanted *her* so bad in the first place. Quite certain she was dying a slow death from toxic levels of horny pregnancy hormones, she acted quickly. All of the aching and throbbing of her most intimate parts couldn't be good for the baby, she thought.

Standing at the nurse's station in the ER where she was supposed to meet Doc for a quick bite to eat, she found Owen

Trent, one of her associates on the life flight team – something else she couldn't do for a while. Owen had all of the check marks most women looked for. He was a successful helicopter pilot with a war hero's past, easy on the eyes, a gentleman through and through, and the man was single.

Owen was the perfect prop. Never really having an interest in him other than professionally and perhaps friends, he was perfect bait. If Doc didn't want her, there were plenty of men that did. Owen would help her prove that.

Everly engaged in a flirtatious conversation that had Owen biting instantly. It also had Doc's attention from the other side of a desk where he was charting patient notes. Of course Everly saw his complexion redden, eyes squint, and arms cross from across the way, but that didn't stop her, she just kept going.

"Nice, Shaw," Owen replied to some random comment she had made about absolutely nothing of real interest. "Want to grab a drink one of these nights real soon? When's your next shift on the helo?"

"Oh...uhhh," Everly began to shift from one foot to the other, losing her confidence the minute he offered her a night of drinks. "So, uh, about that. I'm grounded for a while, won't be going out on the chopper. Uh, can't drink either. So, just until the baby is born, though, then its whatever goes!"

An uncomfortable chuckle escaped her as her own face reddened, she hadn't thought this far ahead. "Supriiiise, I'm...pregnant."

Owens straightened, losing his seductive stare when that *surprise* fully registered. "Oh. Um, well, I gotta go."

Backing away slowly, he put his hands together and pointed them at her belly. "So, good luck with that. Hope you and...the father...are happy."

Owen was out of there like his ass was on fire. Everly's

ego was crushed. Doc had a pleased grin. That was until Evie's next mark landed right in front of her.

"Hey, Jimmy! What've you been up to, hon?" she asked of the unsuspecting male nurse who made female patients hearts race.

"Hey, Ev…"

His words trailed off, lost on Everly as she watched Doc force his chair behind him and stomp off to places unknown.

"Ev?" he questioned. "Everly…you with me?"

"Oh! Sorry, Jimmy. What was that?" She slapped on a quick smile and popped out her hip for good measure, just in case Doc was still listening from somewhere out of her line of sight.

"I said, I'm gay," He deadpanned.

"Oh. Yeah…" She waved a hand like she already knew. "That's so great…for you. How's that…going."

Jimmy laughed at her, laying his hand on her shoulder. "He's gone, I think it worked."

Everly closed her eyes, a little embarrassed she not only hit on a gay man but that she was caught. "I'm sorry…I…you knew?"

"It's okay. I get it. He's hot, I don't blame you. Congrats on the baby!" Before she could say another word, Jimmy was gone.

Everly stood there for a long moment, thinking to herself, *I hope Jimmy is right, and how did I not know he was gay?*

* * *

WITH HER HEAD HELD LOW, AND SELF-ESTEEM EVEN LOWER, Everly stepped off the elevator onto Granny Lou's floor of the hospital. From the hallway, she heard a voice coming from inside Gran's room, so she paused to listen. It was Doc.

He must've left the ER and went right upstairs to vent to the one person who everyone went to when their world was off kilter.

It seemed the apple didn't fall far from the tree because Everly found herself eavesdropping, unable to pull herself from what she knew was wrong. She couldn't help it if the traits she inherited from her grandmother included such. With her hand resting on her growing belly and a surly scowl, she listened to him unload without an ounce of guilt for her intrusive snooping.

Doc ran his hands through his hair before resting his elbows on his knee's to cradle his head. "Lou, I just don't get it! I don't know what else to do for her! She just frustrates the hell out of me! What am I doing wrong?"

His words felt like a sharp hot dagger to the back. The audacity to express such strong opinions, when clearly he was the non-interested party in this little thing between them, was mind boggling.

"*You're* frustrated with *me*? Are you serious?" Her words were like fire to his icy stare.

"Um, yeah! What the hell were you doing down there, Ev? Trying to land a date? Newsflash, I don't share!" He kicked the chair behind him as he stood, taking his place at the window.

This felt all too familiar to Everly and she was starting to get that inkling in her gut that maybe she was wrong...again.

"Why do you even care, Mason? You don't want me, so why not put myself out there?"

"I don't want you? Ev...why would you even say that, especially now?" His face softened and his hand extended, gesturing to her belly.

Oddly, the change in his tone and demeanor ignited her anger. "Are you serious? Are you really going to make me say it?! This is ridiculous! I get it, don't worry. You're off the hook, okay? I won't keep the baby from you, but we don't have to be a package deal."

Shocked by her words, Doc took a step back tilting his head while the hurt in her words washed through him, leaving him more confused than before. A near whisper, and perhaps a bit hurt, his reply was desperate. "What do you mean, Ev? I don't want to be off the hook. You're all I have wanted since...since I don't know when. Why would you even say that? Do you mean it? You don't...want this? Don't want... us?"

"If you want me so bad, why do you avoid me? You barely look at me, much less touch me. Sure you bring me food and check in...on the baby...but that's why you're still around, right? I have paraded around the house *NAKED*, and you barely notice. Not feeling very *wanted.*" her rant faded in a near whisper as she watched her words assault him to the point of sadness and what appeared to be pain.

"Ev...you have it wrong. Sooo...wrong. I want you more than anything. Everything I'm doing is for us. I made you a *promise*, to protect you, and the baby... That's what I'm doing. Or at least I thought I was."

"It all sounds good, but you know what they say about actions and how they're louder than words and all...Doc, you don't touch me...at all. I can't get a hug, much less anything else. I know I am starting to look different, but..."

"You're beautiful...stunning. I can't see any other woman but you...the rest just don't exist. You have ruined me for anyone else, Ev. You know that? You consume my every thought, and I can't see anything but you when I think of days ahead. I don't know how I made you feel any less than my everything, but I'm sorry."

Perfect words from a perfect man, Everly couldn't hold

back the lone tear that trailed her cheek. If that was how he felt, then why *did* she feel so neglected and abandoned? He had been attentive, just not in the way she was used to with him, or in a way she desired. She didn't have all of him and she needed to communicate that with him, but couldn't find but one word that she would blame entirely on hormones.

"Sex. Okay. You won't touch me! Why won't you have sex with me? It's us, it's what we do...and we are *really* good at it! So good we made a baby doing it! Remember that? The sex? How can you say all of those things about me and then not want me in that way?" She covered her mouth with both hands, shocked by her own outburst.

"Is that what this is all about? We haven't...*you know*? Is that all this has been for you, because it's much more than that to me. And of course we are...*good at it*. There's a reason for that...it's called love, Ev."

Still saying all of the right things, she was beginning to feel like an ass until she realized he was deflecting. He was completely avoiding the *why*. At this point, she had nothing to lose, it was all out there, and she wanted a real answer, even if her being upset over no sex was starting to feel cheap.

"Then why, Mason... You still haven't said why. If you love me so much, and find me so irresistible...then why?"

Pacing now, he looked to the floor as if the answers laid there. Rubbing his chin, he became very uncomfortable and his cheeks began to redden. "The baby, okay? You have no idea how many cold showers and long runs I have taken just to shake the need – especially when you walk around... naked! I'm afraid...to hurt you...and the baby. I don't want to hurt the baby."

Stunned by his confession, Everly's jaw dropped in surprise. Playing his words over and over in her mind, she tried to wrap her mind around what *Doctor* Mason Charles just said. Disbelief and flat out hilarity overcame her and she burst out in laughter. She tried to cover her mouth and muffle her amusement, but Doc dropped a bomb she was not at all prepared for…a ridiculous one.

Too overwhelmed by humiliation to withstand the spotlight he had drawn to himself, Doc threw his hands in the air and rushed out of the room, leaving Everly alone in a hysterical fit.

Funny how the truth can set you free from so many things. Everly suddenly didn't feel rejected any longer, quite the opposite in fact. Doc loved her so much he would take endless cold showers…for her.

12

FALL WAS IN FULL SWING, THANKSGIVING ONLY TWO DAYS away. With Gran still hospitalized and her condition unknown, things would certainly be different. Upholding tradition, despite her absence, the gang got together for holiday prep, and a break from the stress that came with holding vigil at the hospital. With their family of friends growing more and more, Sam and Dawson volunteered to host since they had the space.

Gathered in the kitchen, the women divided out the recipes, Gran's recipes, and went to work. Pies, and other baked goods were just the beginning; there were even seasoned bread crumbs in the making for stuffing just as Granny Lou would do.

"So what's up with you and Doc? Feels a little tense," Morgan asked of Everly.

"Oh, nothing. Just a little misunderstanding…and bruised ego," she chuckled.

Sam stopped chopping the apples she was working on, intrigued by topic at hand. "Uh oh…do tell."

"I...can't. It wouldn't be right," Everly defended, but the laughter kicked in yet again.

The ladies had all stopped doing whatever task they were charged with and came together, time to tag team Everly and get some answers. Though Everly was amused by whatever was going on, the tension that stilled the air between her and Doc was a contradiction that had them swarming like bees to honey.

"No really...I can't," Everly insisted with a stupid grin and snort.

"Jesus, Ev, just say it. We're going to figure it out anyway, you suck at secrets," Jessie chimed, her lack of filter fully intact.

"What is that supposed to mean?"

"It means you suck at secrets. What part of that is confusing?" Jessie deadpanned. "We all knew you were screwin' Doc. Parking in front of each other's house in the middle of night? C'mon... Even knocked up, you tried to hide it. Then you act like he's just a booty call baby daddy when it's obvious you love the shit out of him."

Nothing could quiet a crowd to the point of hearing dust fall like hard truths. Everly sat in her chair, leaning from side to side, unsure of what to say next. Tension among the ladies was high until Everly finally relaxed and a grin turned to a giggle, the ladies joining in the laughter.

"I guess that was pretty stupid."

"Yep. Now what's going on. Doc's not bailing is he?" Jessie asked, sounding concerned. She may come across as a real hard ass, but she had a heart of gold and loved her people hard. "We can bust his balls if he is."

"Oh, my God. No. Nothing like that. Quite the opposite actually." Everly looked around taking in the curiosity amongst the hens.

"I uh...had a hard time understanding Doc's...behavior."

"His behavior?" Jessie chimed, again. "You mean his obsession? That guy has it bad for you, I'm surprised he lets you pee unattended."

"Well...yeah. He has been a little overwhelming, but with good intentions. I got upset though because...well..." her silly grin broke into a chuckle again and she couldn't help herself.

"He won't have sex with me." Everly was in a full blown fit of ab busting laughter. "He won't...touch...me."

Unsure what to think of Everly's admission, the ladies and their laughter stalled. It wasn't funny, it was sad really, and they were worried for their dear friend.

"Everly, honey," Sam interrupted. "This isn't healthy. What do you mean he won't have sex with you. Are you... breaking up?"

A room full of nearly silent awes and ohs of sympathy made Everly laugh even more. Their concern was endearing, but completely unnecessary so she thought she would let them off the hook.

"No, no...he's afraid to. He's afraid to hurt...the baby!" And there it was, Everly's confession and Doc's humiliation. "I thought he didn't want me, that I was getting too fat...he just doesn't want to hurt us! I've tried everything!"

The giggles were matched with adoring sentiments as Doc's silliness was actually quite sweet. His love for Everly had been obvious, but now it was more so.

* * *

WHILE THE WOMEN WERE BUSY AT WORK, PREPARING FOR A big day of cooking, the men worked on tradition of their own. Sam and Dawson lived in a semi-secluded area, on several acres that were mostly forest. Directly behind the house was a fair sized yard, with all that comes with outdoor living, like seating, a swing set for the kids, hammocks, and then some.

Just beyond the soft grass, but before the tree line that bordered the property, was a small slope that dropped into a prairie like field that was mowed and painted every year for the annual Thanksgiving Day football game. Any other day of the year, you might see a herd of deer, or even elk, but on this day, it was white lines and make shift goal posts made from fence posts.

It is said that women hunt and circle gossip like a flock of hungry vultures, but truth be told, men have them beat ten-fold. Working alongside the guys, Doc was quiet and in an obvious pout that had the other men giving each other questioning looks. Doc was the guy who always had a smile on his face and couldn't be brought down by anything – even the shit he saw at work. Today, though, he was in the midst of a silent tantrum that was lacking only a single foot stomp and folded arms.

"Hey, Doc? You okay over there?" Dawson was the one to bite first.

"Just fine," was all he had in return – short and sweet – also not like Doc. He was far too outgoing, loved to talk, hear himself talk, and had no issue with being the center of attention – hence being the lead singer in the band he was in.

"You seem a little...*off*," Blake offered, looking to the others, shrugging his shoulders, throwing his hands out, unsure what to say. Just like it wasn't like Doc to be quiet, it wasn't like Blake to pry or generally give a shit about *feelings*.

Laughter came drifting from the house above them grabbing their attention with its ebbs and flows of intensity.

"Wonder what's so funny up there?" Colton asked, resting

his hands and chin on the end of a shovel he had been using to dig holes for goal posts.

Doc's stare was locked on the house. "Probably me. I bet she's telling *everyone*. Real fricken funny!"

More confused looks were exchanged between the men as they watched Doc watch the house. Curiosity was getting the better of them, they wanted to know what was so funny because it obviously was the source of Doc's pissed off demeanor. There was a silent debate, all with eye contact and eyebrow gestures as the guys tried to decide who was going in. When all eyes looked away from him as if he drew the short straw, Beck rolled his eyes, tired of the *let the new guy handle it* mentality. He was hardly new, but he was the newest and took a lot of crap for it.

"So, uh, what is it you're, uh…worried about over there, Doc?" Beck was about as good at this as the other men.

He turned and looked at them with a surly look. "Why… you want to laugh at me too?"

Hands going up around the group, they all shrugged it off with each saying, *not me* or *not at all*. There was even a *just here to listen, bud* in there. Doc sighed again, looking at his feet, a pattern he was getting really good at.

"So, I upset Evie. Like really upset her and didn't mean to. I was just trying to…protect her, and the baby. Well, it didn't go as planned."

Protective instincts were kicking in from all the alphas in one place and chests began to puff a bit, each wondering if there was honor to defend on Everly's behalf. The change in the air, and smell of testosterone wasn't lost on Doc when he looked up. "Calm down. Nothing like any of you are think-ing. Christ…I could never hurt her. Not like that."

"Oh, uh…go on then," came from one of the O'Reilly boys.

"Look. I promised her. I promised nothing would ever happen to her or the baby. She's fragile that way, you know? Or at least *she* thinks she is. I think she's kind of a fearless bad ass, but…"

He looked back up at the house, noticing Everly standing at the sliding glass door looking back at him. She smiled at him before walking away from the door, returning to whatever she was doing.

"I uh, upset her because I was taking care of her *too* much."

Dawson gave him a cross look, "How does that work? What's too much? I mean, I know you have been helping her out so she can stay with Lou. Sam actually complained that I don't do nice things *like Doc* anymore. How does that get you in trouble, it only got *me* in trouble."

"Me too…" Colton added.

Beck nodded, "Yep…and me."

"She thought I didn't want her anymore. That I wasn't… I swear to God I will kick any one of your asses if this turns into a…*thing*, got it?! I don't care if most of you are bigger than me, I'm faster."

Grins were brewing as they all nodded in compliance, damn, this was going to be good.

"I won't sleep with her. There. Ya happy? I won't have sex with her, I hurt her feelings because of it. I didn't want to hurt the baby."

Oh, Doc stepped right into that one as far as Wylie was concerned. "I thought you were a doctor? You know how it got in there, right?"

Then came the laughs. He should have known better. He realized how ridiculous he had been, especially now that he said it not once, but twice.

"Oh, fuck off, O'Reilly."

"Whoa, Doc. Easy. Give us a minute. We are mere mortals and know that shit can't hurt the baby. So give us a second because it's...well, it's *funny.*" Dawson tried, but lost his composure too. Doc's fear wasn't unheard of, it was just something you didn't typically hear from a Doctor.

"I know. God, I know it's so stupid. I know it's safe, have even told patients to go for it. There's just all that medical jargon in my head that says, hey...but there is that rare oddity that is medically possible. Then it's all about the science, and odds...and that promise. It's like I can't turn it off. God knows, I want to turn it off because she's..." he stopped himself before saying more and disrespecting her, they weren't blind after all.

"You aren't going to hurt her, or the baby," Blake said, matter of fact, drawing attention from the others. Blake was the least likely to understand that concept, and even more unlikely to give a shit so it took them all by surprise.

"I know! Gah! I finally, after all this time, get the girl and then..."

"You *do* love her – you got it bad, Doc." Colton snickered.

"I do. I bought a ring. Months ago, long before the baby. I wanted to have it in case she finally came around and, well... now maybe she will?"

"Wow...man, that's great. Really fucking girly, but great. We grew up with her, she's a great catch, Doc. Hang on to her," Wylie added. As much as he was playful and full of mischief, he was the sentimental and sweet one of the bunch.

Awkward was about the only word to sum up this conversation for Blake. He cared deeply for his people, but bedroom talk like a bunch of pansies was really making his skin itch. "Yeah...you might want to...*you know*...before you blow it.

If you want to give her that ring but no...*stuff*, she might say no."

Doc nodded, he knew Blake was right, they all were. He went into the conversation feeling like an idiot, telling his buddies he was afraid to have sex. Now he felt like an idiot because they were not only still talking about it, but they were giving him advice...good advice. Even if his man card was likely to be revoked.

"Now that we are all done *feeling* and *supporting* each other's *needs* with an estrogen loaded pep talk, can we finish this thing up? I'm about to grow tits and an ovary over here." Declan earned a round of laughs, and raised eyebrows. There was a woman inside that house, who'd haunted him since the day he left her behind, and had him twisted in knots. Another one who thought he kept his secrets on lock down, but wore them on his sleeve...Lydia Prescott was inside and it was either burning a hole in his heart or his dick – maybe both.

"Thank you! Jesus, it's like you guys left your balls at home or in your women's purses. Football field and emotions...I only signed up for part of that. Let's finish, I'm hungry." Luke was haunted by a lot more than a woman. Feelings – he just didn't do those.

Jessie stuck her head out the sliding glass door and yelled for the men, "Food's here! If you stink, we'll bring your plate outside!"

Food meant BJ was there. He had to run the bakery for the first half of the day but promised to bring lunch and help finish up whatever they had left to do. It was Thanksgiving Day that they really wanted him for. They could make the pies, bread crumbs, and even make a football field, but BJ Baker, five star world renowned chef, was charged with the one thing he did better than anyone...make Thanksgiving dinner on Thursday.

Quick to clean up their tools and supplies, the men made their way up to the house, ready for whatever BJ whipped up. Even the O'Reilly brothers were looking forward to BJ's lunch feast, though they wouldn't admit it and added plenty of organic hippy food jokes. Coming through the backdoor, laughter from the ladies could be heard from the adjacent kitchen. Doc froze when he was within ear shot and realized the conversation was still about him.

"Don't worry, Ev. We'll get you a bedside boyfriend for your nightstand drawer. Just need to give him new batteries once in a while," Jessie teased.

Meg was the last one in the group to have been pregnant, and added, "Pregnancy hormones...she'll need lots and lots of batteries."

Colton was in the door and heard the gist of the conversation, and added his two cents before wrapping his arms around her waist and kissing her hard. "That was my favorite part of you being pregnant!"

Laughter and *get a room* floated through the room, but Doc stood right where he was, just outside the door, too embarrassed to go in. He considered heading right back down the steps and running around to the front of the house, where his truck was parked, and leaving.

"Ignore it, Doc. They're just messing around. Jessie makes fun of the Pope so of course she'll make fun of your situation," Blake said from behind Doc.

"I can't believe she told all of them. Crap."

"Well, in all fairness, you told all of us so what's the difference?"

Doc just shrugged his shoulders, Blake was right, but it still stung. If he was being entirely honest with himself, he wasn't really mad or embarrassed by Everly's actions...it was his own. He waited so long to *get the girl* and when he got her, he didn't know what to do with her. He felt like an ass by his own doing.

"Look, Doc. You love her. It's obvious she loves you too, even if she's being all *Evie* about it. You guys are having a kid… Don't let this get away from you over a few jokes and your *weird* paranoia. Family is everything, man, and you have one of your own now."

Blake patted Doc on the shoulder as he walked past him, headed to the kitchen where everyone else was. Shocked at the sincerity and that odd sense that Blake was speaking from experience, Doc couldn't help but feel the words that he spoke. He *was* lucky, and the only real problem he had was with himself. It was high time he got his shit together.

* * *

LAST ONE TO ENTER THE KITCHEN, DOC WENT STRAIGHT TO Everly, wrapped his arms around her, and locked her under a long hot smoldering kiss that made her sweat. Without a word, just a confident swagger, he continued on, as if she were just a quick pit stop, and washed his hands like nothing just happened. Snickers and snorts quickly began the clapping of hands with a few high pitched whistles mixed in.

Speechless and in shock, Everly stood there and watched her man come back to her. It wasn't clear what came over him, or her for that matter, but she had wicked romping butterflies. That was her libido, not the baby.

With two plates in his hand, Doc tipped his head in Everly's direction and motioned for her to join him while he plated up food for both of them. The sentiment was sweet, his doting was back in play, and the other ladies were side eyeing their men, wondering where their plates were. Doc may have been getting out of trouble with Everly, but he was quickly becoming well hated amongst the other men with the example he was setting.

Everly sat at the large table, looking around the space at each and every one who was there. Their small family of friends was much larger than she really gave it credit. They no longer managed to fit at a single table when all together like this. If she had any doubt left about her lack of family or ability to love anyone completely, it was gone now.

Confident and loved were the two things she felt the most in that moment. This was going to work out for her, she could feel it and it wasn't just the kicking baby, it was hope and forever with Doc. She rubbed her belly and had a secret agreement with the little person growing in there about its daddy. Everly had room in her heart for one more and what he provoked in her far outweighed the fear she had lived with most of her life…it was love.

Doc watched Everly look down with a smile on her face as she rested her hands on her small baby bump. Something had changed and for once, it didn't worry him where she was concerned. Joy, pure joy, was rolling off her and he couldn't help but feel it as he looked at her bump and had a silent promise of his own with their baby.

A lifelong promise is what he vowed – to love them, cherish them, and be everything they wanted and needed him to be. He couldn't wait to live that truth. A weight had been lifted, and a hint at forever replaced it.

But first, he had some advice to take and a plan to put into action. Blake was right, it was all in his hands and he needed to claim his woman. And he would…forever was waiting.

They were living a season of change, a welcome one full of firsts and fresh new starts. As if on cue, the universe threw him a sign as the season outside had changed a bit too with its own first and fresh new start…it began to snow.

13

Lighting the last candle, Doc looked around the room, proud of the romantic scene he pulled together. Various candles sat on almost every available surface, providing most of the lighting in the living and adjacent dining room that Everly would soon walk into. Meg had helped him decorate a perfectly set table, full of romantic gestures, including a silver ice bucket that had not champagne, but a nice sparkling apple cider in its place.

A perfectly romantic evening was staged with the lingering aroma from the meal BJ helped him make, warming in the oven, and light jazz music playing softly in the background. Everly had no idea what she was about to walk in on, but Doc knew she would love it. He had wasted too much time, acting like a fool, tonight everything changed. He was claiming his woman and the life they were destined to have.

"Right on time," he mumbled to himself when he heard her car pull into the driveway.

Like a giddy teenager, he ran to the door full of enthusiasm only to open it and lean in the doorway full of cool and calm. He was anything but. The excitement coursing through him was nearly more than he could handle and a challenge to contain. Especially when he saw beautiful Everly smile at him as she walked up the path to the door, home to shower and change before heading back to the hospital.

"Hey," she said, with slight suspicion and a look to match.

Shit, be cool, be cool...you're giving it all away he thought to himself.

"Hey yourself," he said with a cheesy wink and brow lift that immediately made him want to palm his face in embarrassment.

She turned a side eyed glance his way and let out a quiet chuckle. "You okay, Doc?"

"Oh, yeeeaaah. I'm good. Totally good, I mean fine. Nothing big...going on...in there." He tossed a thumb over his shoulder toward the interior of the house before awkwardly crossing his arms over his chest and crossing one ankle over the other.

Everly stood in front of him, just outside the door on the steps, with a sideways grin and suspicious tone. "Oh. Well that's good. So do you think you can...let me in, maybe?"

Straightening quickly, he fumbled a bit before moving to the side and stretching an arm inside, indicating she should enter. "Yes, of course! Come in...I mean, it's your house so... Anyway, just come in."

Her giggle was endearing as she walked through the front door, only to gasp at the sight before her. He watched her scan the room from one side to the other, pausing only to close her eyes and smell the aroma coming from the kitchen. She was speechless, standing there with her jaw slack and eyes wide.

Nerves took over and he started to worry to the point of nearly shuddering. "Crap, I'm sorry. I'm really bad at this. I was trying to...trying to...I don't know, put together a romantic evening and..."

"It's perfect, Mace. Perfect..." She turned to him with glassy eyes ready to spill over. "But I have to get back up to the hospital, and..."

"No. I mean, I took care of that too. Jessie will be there the rest of the evening and overnight with Lou. It's...your night off." An adorable shrug full of sweet boyish charm trailed his words while he hoped he had thought of everything and she would stay with him.

"It's *our* night off then." A single tear finally trailed her cheek, tempting more to follow. "I can't believe you did all of this. It's so...romantic. The flowers, candles...did you cook?"

"I did. Well, I had help, with all of it. But it's all for you, Ev." He pulled her into him for a sweet embrace, but she caught him off guard with a passionate kiss instead that went on and on.

Finally breaking the kiss, he grabbed her hands and pulled her the rest of the way into the house, kicking the door closed with his foot. "I suppose we don't need to put on a show for the neighbors, well...the wildlife anyway."

"I can't believe you did all of this, why? What's the occasion?" she asked, taking in the room again while she wandered to the table and pulled out the sparkling cider. She held it up and laughed. "You really did think of everything."

Doc pulled out the dining room chair she was standing next to and turned it away from the table, gesturing for her to sit. Taking the *not quite champagne* bottle from her hand, he opened it, filling both glasses halfway. Holding up a single finger to wait, he excused himself from where he stood and grabbed a small tiffany blue gift bag that had been sitting on the credenza by the front door. Somehow she had missed that when she walked in.

Doc nervously handed her the bag and began to speak. "I picked this up months ago in Portland. I've been hanging onto it, waiting for the right time to give it to you. Everly, I've known since that first day. You had my heart, my soul, my every breath from go."

He reached across the table and pulled a single rose from the arrangement and held it as he finished professing his love for her. "Meg helped me pick the flowers."

"They're gorgeous. Actually my favorite rose."

"Well, good! They serve a dual purpose then." he chuckled, trying to stay light while his emotions felt flooding. "They're fire and ice. We went through every flower in her shop and I picked this one because it's us, Ev. I guess the red at the tips represent a passionate and an unmatched intensity of eternal love. The white body means purity and unconditional love. This is us, Ev. This is how we live and love...like fire and ice. When I saw them in the shop, before I even knew what they meant, they had my attention. I couldn't see anything but these – they are stunning, just like you."

Everly choked on a small sob, tears flooding her face. Holding her face in his hands, he wiped at her cheeks with the pads of his thumbs as he knelt before her, taking a knee. He leaned forward for a small, sweet kiss then took the bag from her hands and set it on the ground next to him.

He whispered sweetly, "Don't cry, baby."

"It's...it's the hormones."

"I love you Everly Shaw. I love you so much it hurts and makes me do stupid things. I don't remember anything before you because I didn't start living until I met you. You challenge me, you make me laugh, you keep me wanting more. There isn't anything I wouldn't do for you – to keep you safe, to keep you happy, to give you everything you want. I will love you forever, Ev, and spend every single day of the rest of my life showing you that."

He reached into the bag and pulled out a small box that matched the bag with a white ribbon on top. Every woman knew what that box was and where it was from. Her body began to quake and he lifted the lid and revealed what he had been saving for her...for months.

"Everly Louise Shaw, I can't live another day without calling you mine. You've already made me a proud father, but I'd give anything if you would let me love you and let me be your husband. I want forever, Ev...with you."

He slipped the white gold and diamond dazzler on the fourth finger of her shaking left hand. She looked at it in awe before giving him a look he had yet to see before today. It was peaceful, content, and something he didn't recognize yet. Maybe it was the love she had for him and kept hidden until now.

Placing her hands on his shoulders, slowly snaking them around his neck, she leaned her forehead against his and whispered in a tear filled voice, "You've changed my life, Mason Charles. You conquered my demons and filled me with things I didn't know I would ever feel. I love you so much I'm almost scared to say it. You do make me feel safe, cherished, and so loved. I don't know how you did it, but I need you so damn bad. Don't ever leave me because I think this is the kind of love that only belongs to one person and that's you...forever. I will marry you, Doc. I'd marry you a hundred times over."

He pulled her into a sultry kiss that didn't last long before Everly slid from her seat and into his lap, causing him to fall to his ass, propped against the back of the nearby sofa. His hands drifted under her shirt, stroking the sides of her full breasts as she straddled him. Intensity building, he pulled her shirt over her head and unhooked her bra, freeing her breasts for his pleasure.

She arched her back, displaying her ample breasts as a tease to get what she wanted. She was hungry for his taste, his feel, his arousal. Rocking against him, she felt his hunger too, rubbing against her, long and hard. Her skin was on fire from the feel of his lips across her breasts as his tongue lashed at her sensitive nipples and his free hand gripped and massaged as he did.

She had missed this, missed him and couldn't get enough of him. She leaned back, bracing herself with one hand on the floor behind her, head tossed back, her breath quickening. With the other arm wrapped around his neck, he gently leaned her back to the floor and hovered over her. His eyes locked on hers, he smiled down at her before he trailed kisses and soft bites from her neck to her breasts, continuing down her abdomen.

He stopped for a moment and laid his head on her small baby bump before placing a kiss dead center and continuing his descent. He gripped the waistband of her yoga pants, and slowly pulled them down, devouring her as he went. She unwrapped her legs from his waist, setting her legs down wide as she lifted her ass so he could finish what he was doing.

Laying completely bare to him, he stalled, and looked down at her nude body and said, "You are so beautiful. So fucking beautiful."

In a bold move so seductive and intimate, her heavily hooded eyes closed as she let out a deep breathy sigh and let her legs fall completely open for his viewing pleasure. He pulled his own shirt over his head, tossing it to the side, and quickly undid his jeans, freeing himself so he was ready for her, but not until he worshipped her, devoured her, and loved her first. Sitting between her legs, he leaned forward, placing the back of his hand on her face and slowly dragged it the length of her body until it finally rested exactly where she wanted him.

The catch in her breath and arch of her back when his fingers stroked her center was nearly his undoing. Provocative, highly sensual, and oh so hot, he had missed her as much as she him. It had been weeks of watching her, seeing her body, and not touching it and here he was with her at his mercy, crying for more. It was all he could do to contain his own desires and early finish. He was going to pleasure her until she couldn't take anymore and then he would do it until he couldn't.

Stroking her slick heat, his finger slipped inside of her, the act as pleasing to him as it was her. He stroked her in and out, over and over, finally slipping a second finger inside of her. Pure ecstasy washing over her as he did. He took her mouth in a primal move of ravishment, his tongue slipping in through her throaty moan.

His pace increasing, he moved down her body once more, paying attention to her collarbone, then her tight, hard rosy buds, down her abdomen. His thumb had been swirling her swollen bundle of nerves driving her to the edge. His mouth took over, finally covering her center adding more pressure to her most sensitive spot as his fingers continued to plunge in and out.

With her tightening around him, he felt her reach the peak of euphoria. Removing his fingers, and moving up her body, he took her breast in his mouth biting down on her while his hard length plunged into her. She rode him back, grinding her hips against him in search of relief, she finally found it when his free hand slipped between them and pressed on her swollen and needy middle, flicking it once then twice before she crashed down around him.

She rode him through the waves of pleasure, her tight grip around him bringing him to his own finish. They laid on the living room floor, never losing their connection, while they caught their breaths and regained their wits.

"Finally." Finally was right, both had been desperate for such intimacy – especially Everly.

"I've missed this. I've missed *you*," Doc said, interrupting the silliness.

Everly chuckled. "So have I. Let's never go that long again."

Kissing him again, her hand stroked his side, up and down before grabbing his ass.

"Doc…" she said in between kisses to his neck. "Can we…I want…"

"Insatiable, I see…"

"It's the hormones…and you naked on top of me."

Finally, Doc scooped her off the floor and carried her toward the bedroom.

"Wait! The candles! The oven! We can't leave them unattended."

Doc paused and scanned the room before moving toward the dining table where his cellphone was sitting. He picked it up, tapped the screen a few times and the candles went out in unison.

"How did you do that?" Amusement danced on her face, impressed with what he had just done.

"Candles aren't real. They all have a Bluetooth smart sensor and I can control them with my phone from anywhere…cool, huh?"

Her head fell back in laughter, this was typical Doc. Handsome, virile, and rugged as he could be, he was a tech nerd at heart, in love with his video games and gadgets. Even romance was wireless with Bluetooth with him.

"I'm guessing the oven is on your phone too?" she teased.

"No…the warmer is on a timer."

They finally made it to their soft bed where he made love to her again, slow, and sweet, and he loved every inch of her

14

"I DIDN'T KNOW IT COULD BE LIKE THAT...LIKE *THIS.*" Everly ran her finger up and down Doc's chest, swirling her finger in the peppering of dark hair there. The sparkle from the ring he put on her finger catching her eye, making her smile.

"What? Pregnant sex? All the hormones? I'll keep you knocked up if this is what's going to happen every time." An ornery edge wound through his teasing words.

"No, pervert, I mean this. Us. I just didn't think...I would have this. I fought it so hard and now I can't imagine a life any different than what we are building."

He kissed the top of her head, feeling every single word she spoke, "I'm glad you fought it. If you hadn't, I might have missed my chance."

"I don't know about that." Everly laughed, trying to lighten the heaviness of his words. She was on board with the relationship and opening her heart, but old habits die hard and she was still getting used to the feeling it brought.

"You're a total babe, trust me...you wouldn't have been on the market long. Especially with that ass." It wasn't lost on him that she was still a bit uncomfortable with not only having, but discussing *feelings*. He would do anything to protect her from that unease and set back anything they had gained, even crack bad jokes loaded with truths.

"I don't know Doc, many men have tried, only one survived and conquered…planting his *seed*."

"Now the jokes are getting really bad," he teased. "I'd plant my seed over and over again too. I want lots of babies with you, Ev. A big family."

"I think I can handle that, Doc. You, me, and our own little band."

"Now you're talking."

They laid in each other's embrace, hanging on those words, each imagining the life they were planning. Doc gently stroked her arm while she continued to run a finger through the light hair on his chiseled chest. Happy. Loved. Content. They were finally there, wholly and completely.

The intimate silence surrounding them was interrupted by a loud hollow growl from Everly's stomach leading them both to laughter.

"I guess Junior is trying to tell us something! I'll be right back." Doc jumped out of bed, tossing on a pair of loose, low hanging sweats that showed off his perfect V and boasted defined abs, giving Everly something else to hunger for.

Clanging of dishes and a few expletives could be heard from the kitchen as Doc rushed around, causing Everly to laugh while she pulled one of Doc's t-shirts over her head. She stared at the ring she wore, his ring, and her heart swelled. Recalling the romantic proposal, she was hung up on the idea that he had purchased the ring months ago. He really had loved her all along – a true testament to his devotion – he believed in them even then and was willing to wait for her.

She could kick herself for nearly missing out on what

was becoming the best part of her life, but she was glad she finally saw what was right in front of her. An incredible man who would *walk through hot coals laced with shards of glass* for her – she didn't doubt that for a second now. Her faith in them had finally outweighed her fear of the past and she couldn't wait to see where that faith took them.

A heavy tray in hand, overflowing with glasses and plates of food, the accompanying aroma that entered the room with him had her mouthwatering. Doc's upper arms were pinned to his body, holding the bottle of apple cider under one arm, two of his electric candles under the other and bulging pockets full of what appeared to be utensils and napkins on one side, and salad dressing in the other. A sight to be seen, Everly couldn't help but let out an appreciative giggle, laced with an endearing *awww*.

This is why she loved this man – he didn't do anything small and nothing was impossible. He provided for her every need, fulfilled her every desire, and nurtured a love that was beyond measure. And in this very moment…he had food.

"Oh, my God, that smells amazing. Let me help you." Before she could leave her spot in their bed, she was quickly stopped with a side eye look.

"Sit, woman. I got this." There was a cocky demeanor about him that was as much serious as he was kidding.

Playing it smug, she was actually amused by the lengths he went to for her. Even the smallest of things were big for him. With her arms crossed, she watched him pull it off and crawl into bed beside her.

"Wow," she said, looking over the large wood tray between them. "This is quite the spread! I don't know where to start."

"How about we skip the salad and roasted chicken and

dig right into that chocolate cake thing with raspberry something or other all over it?"

"Now you're talking! Thank you, Doc." Her tone had changed from enthusiasm over dessert before dinner to a quiet sincere plea. "I don't think I've ever said thank you. Tonight was beautiful, so thoughtful and sweet. I put you off for so long, took you for granted, while all along you were planning this…or, some form of this. I don't know what I did to deserve you."

Tears were welling again, and not entirely due to hormones, but also because her heart was swelling to the point of almost hurting.

"You needed time, and that's something I had. I wasn't going to give up. I knew we would get here someday, baby, and I wanted to be ready when you were ready."

All the right words at the right time, Doc had a way with them. With one hand wrapped around his neck, she pulled him in for a long kiss full of promises, and forever. She wasn't good at verbalizing how she felt yet, but she could sure show him.

"Looks like I'm making dinner every night," he teased. "I could get used to your thank yous…in fact, I think I already am."

Under the dim light from his remote control candles, they fed each other a divine chocolate dessert. There was something seductive and slightly erotic about the intimacy involved that made their unsated libidinous state burn, leaving them full of desire and need. They had always been good together in bed, it was their initial attraction to each other. A new commitment between them, however, changed that connection to something indescribable. What had always been *good sex*, was now a beautiful entanglement where words weren't needed because *making love* said it all.

It was well into the night when the tray of food had long been picked over, and they laid in each other's arms catching their breaths once again.

"I loved the flowers." Everly didn't want to forget a single detail of their magical night. She let it play over and over as she recalled the flowers sitting on the coffee table when she had walked in.

"When Meg showed me the roses, I knew they were you." He rolled her to her back and hovered above her with a sly grin. "I am going to cover this bed in fire and ice petals and make love to you over and over in them. Or maybe fill the tub…"

Laughter shook them as he teased her with all of the ways and places he was going to claim her over and over. Placing a single finger over his mouth, she silenced him. "Though I love how you think, and I *am* taking notes…I meant the other flowers. The bouquet, like Gran's. I knew that was you taking them to her every day. When I saw them…ugh…these hormones. I think you found the last piece of my heart with those…it's so sweet."

Doc's expression dimmed, his lighthearted smile had become a furrowed brow with questioning eyes. "What other flowers? Grans? You mean the wild flowers?"

Slow to respond, an unease curdled in her stomach, letting a little bit of the fear she'd been fighting so desperately back in. "Yes…just like the ones from Gran's hospital room. Those are from…"

Finishing her thought wasn't necessary, his reaction said it all when he rolled off of her and sat near the edge of the bed; that unease she was feeling was ever present in his grimace and stiff posture. "Everly, I didn't bring those home. I haven't been bringing them to Lou either. I thought with so many flowers that we ran out of room at the hospital and you had brought those home. Baby, tell me you brought those home."

"I...I didn't. I was here last night and they weren't here. Doc..." Emotions were taking over at the idea that someone had not only been in her house but had left a gift, an unwelcome gift.

Rummaging through the miscellaneous glasses and plates that had accumulated on the nightstand from their evening, Doc found his cellphone and placed a call.

Running one hand through his hair as he paced the room, he finally got an answer on the other end. "Blake, I think we have a problem. How quick can you get here."

* * *

WITH JUST ENOUGH TIME TO PUT ON DECENT CLOTHES AND clean up the traces of their evening to a presentable state, a loud urgent knock sounded at the door. Before they could get to the door, Blake let himself in, leaving the door open while giving directions to someone over his shoulder. Candles stilled placed throughout the room and evidence of a romantic setting, Blake gave the couple a set of raised eyebrows and a sideways smirk.

"So, you think someone broke in and made you dinner?" he teased, bringing a smile to Everly's otherwise distraught expression.

"Funny. We know who did that...it's these that we are unsure of." Doc walked to the coffee table where the large arrangement of wild flowers sat, hovering over it with a protective wide stance and crossed arms like the flowers were somehow going to react.

Blake met him at the other side of the flowers, matching his stare. It was odd that something so simple as flowers felt like a threat and had so much of their attention in that moment. Small town living didn't tend to bring large crime, but flowers?

Scanning the room and sniffing the air, Blake earned bewildered glances from both Everly and Doc. "I smell it. It's just like the hospital."

He roamed the room, and asked permission to look in the bedrooms and other areas of the house, checking closets and the like. Back in the living room, Blake was met by a quick knock and a young gentleman wearing a matching uniform standing in the doorway.

"Nothing, Coop. Outside door to the garage is unlocked, but that's it. I secured it, all locked up now." The handsome young man nodded at Doc and Everly then turned his attention back to Blake waiting for his next order of business.

"Ev, Doc…this is Logan Traynor. Rookie in training," Blake said.

Everly smiled and nodded back, as did Doc.

The tall dark haired man couldn't be but in his early twenties, but was built like a tank with dark hair and eyes, and biceps bigger than Doc's thigh. His hair was military short and he had a matching edge to his presence that screamed military obedience; the only thing giving away his age was the glint in his eye and obvious eagerness to please Blake.

"Pleasure to meet you folks, wish it was under different circumstances." *Folks* might have given away his younger age too.

Doc was polite but not interested in exchanging pleasantries and phone numbers, he wanted answers and to ensure Everly was safe. "What do you think, Blake? I locked Ev in the room and checked the house before you got here and didn't see anything out of place or order. It just doesn't make sense."

"You said smell…" Everly interrupted, "what smell?"

"It must be the flowers. I smell it at the hospital too, every so often. Must be when a new arrangement is left. I've noticed it all along, Jessie has too."

Logan chimed in, "I smell it…something earthy, musty, maybe woodsy like pine? It doesn't smell like flowers."

"Ev is there anyone you know, older man, who may be stopping in to see Lou at the hospital or even you? Family? Old friend?" Blake asked.

"No, not at all. It's just Gran and me. You know anyone else who would be coming by. It would be someone from McKenzie."

Blake nodded, placing his hands on his hips, looking around the room again as if there was an answer somewhere, contemplating his next move when Doc perked up and said, "The old man."

Blake quickly jerked his head toward Doc. "You've seen him?"

"No, nothing like that. Carly, the nurse. She asked if Ev had a grandfather or uncle who had been coming by. I didn't think much of it. I wasn't really…engaged at the moment. I had just found out about the baby." Recalling that day and all of the emotions that went with it, Doc briefly looked at Everly with a timid smile before finishing. "I thought maybe it was Jed Baker from the bakery or someone maybe Carly hadn't met yet, being new to town."

Blake rubbed his chin mulling over what Doc had said, sure they were missing something in the greater picture. "I heard her ask you. I actually talked to her about it. I may have seen him a few nights back, but he was gone before I realized who he was. Carly has my card and is supposed to call me if she sees him again."

"He was with Gran? Alone? What did he look like,

Blake?" Concern was building for Everly as the story continued to unfold and the idea that there was a stranger in the background of their little town who had access to her ill grandmother.

"I didn't see his face, he was walking away from me, already down the hall. Had on a black cowboy hat, pulled down low from what I could tell so probably wouldn't have got a good look at his face anyway. Silver and black hair… mostly silver, a cowboy swagger with a limp. Dressed like an old cowboy really."

"A cowboy? I just don't know who that could be…"

"Carly said he was sweet, but standoffish. Brought the nurses some donuts or something a few times. Played the harmonica. That's all."

Everly rushed to the long table by the entry and grabbed her purse in a panicked furry, "I need to get up there. She can't be alone, not with this…guy around. And the flowers…"

Doc pulled her into him and kissed the top of her head. "It's okay, baby. She's not alone and I'm more worried about you right now. Take a deep breath, this isn't good for you, or the baby."

"Jessie is with her and I've been up there every night you haven't, Ev," Blake assured her. "He hasn't been back and we don't even know who he is, or if he's even a threat."

"Someone broke into my damn house and left me the same flowers they have been leaving for Gran…it isn't one of us so forgive me if I'm a little panicked at the moment." Holding back tears was no longer an option as they streamed down her face, both from worry and fear, causing her bottom lip to quiver. "Not a dead bunny or something threatening… flowers. I'm sorry, but there is something a little more sinister about this. Flowers?"

"Doc's right, this isn't good for the baby, or you. I want you to stay here tonight with Doc. The house checks out, just make sure you're locking your doors. For all we know, this was a friendly gesture and someone dropped them by thinking it was Lou's house...an old friend who had the two houses mixed up since you live next door to each other. I'm going to stay up at the hospital tonight with Jess."

Logan stepped forward with a sympathetic look and calm but concerned tone. "Yeah, I don't live but a mile or so away out on the old service road by the creek. I can be here in minutes if you need me. I'll do some drive-by's in my own truck too, less conspicuous that way and less likely to scare anyone off like a squad car would."

"Thank you, Logan. We appreciate that." Doc didn't know Logan's story but he already liked him. His aim may have been more to please his boss, Blake, but either way, the effort was helpful and his sincere demeanor would be a perfect fit in McKenzie Ridge.

Blake pulled Everly in to a rare hug offering her comfort. "It'll be okay, kid. Don't worry unless we have a reason to, okay? I'll let everyone else know – if there is someone up to something, it won't take long to figure it out around here."

A quick handshake with Doc later, and Logan and Blake were headed for the door, each tasked with duties that would hopefully lead to answers. Before closing the door behind him, Blake stopped and turned to the couple.

"Congrats, by the way."

Everly and Doc looked at each other in confusion before returning their bewildered gaze to Blake.

"The engagement..." He nodded to Everly's hand. "Nice ring. Congrats."

On his way to the hospital, Blake dropped Logan off at the House where Police, Fire, and Emergency Medical all cohabitated, so he could pick up his own vehicle and Blake could get to the hospital. He had left Everly and Doc smiling, reminding them of their exciting news that he assumed was only hours old, rather than leave them lingering in worry. He replayed the scene over and over, trying to find the missing link.

Though flowers felt innocent and lacking danger or a threat of any kind, there was something heavy in the air that made his skin prick with an intuitive sense of menace. With only an old man of mystery as their clue, even he didn't feel like the missing piece. Something about his bumpy swagger and slow stroll suggested he was as ominous and scowling as the harmonica he was said to play the entire time, each visit.

There was something wrong, however, he felt it as he always did and would continue to keep an eye on his people until he could rule out imminent danger altogether. In the meantime, he would spend his time with the one person who shared his wary skepticism, watching over Lou...Jessie.

15

SNOW HAD BEEN TEASING THE MOUNTAINS FOR DAYS AND THIS day was no different. The gang had gathered for their last big series of rounds through the woods community before heavier weather prevented their ventures into the deeper parts of the forest. Woods people chose to live off the grid without modern conveniences, it was all they really knew, but they did depend on some of the simple amenities they were afforded on these rounds – the things typical people took for granted. Medical attention and treatment, limited as it was in such an environment, was especially welcome.

Blake and Morgan stayed behind to keep an eye on hospital visitors, sending Logan and another officer as the official *legal authority* in the event the group ran into squatters with something to hide. The regular population was fairly mild mannered, they just wanted to be left alone and didn't draw attention to themselves and the group avoided those who were ill-tempered and didn't want to be bothered.

The seclusion the thick expansive forests offered, however, tended to draw those above the law, or maybe it was below the law, types who *did* have something to hide. Occasionally they came across illegal marijuana crops, drug manufacturing, or stolen goods. Even more rare were dog and cock fighting rings off the old forest service roads. Those were the people who didn't belong in the woods any more than they belonged in the city and made the good work, the group did, a little tougher at times, requiring a few armed individuals to accompany them.

Everly was passionate about this community service, but being pregnant with unpredictable weather looming, she had to stay behind. Much of their day would be spent on horseback so it might be not only uncomfortable, but it could be unsafe, travelling the terrain leading into those woods, especially with the snow making everything slick and hiding loose rocks. Strong will made it quite the task for the gang to convince her to stay, but when Nurse Carly volunteered to fill in and give her a detailed run down, Everly folded.

Carly had become quite friendly with the group of friends and well liked, fitting right in as a new member of the community. She promised to pay extra attention to the one Everly was most concerned about, Clyde Burton. She hadn't seen or heard from him since his mother, June's, funeral and wanted to be sure he was doing okay all by himself.

Doc was the only attending doctor on this trip, and greatly needed since it was their final visit for several months. He was reluctant to leave Everly behind, however, since everyone else from their small group, including the O'Reilly brothers who were still visiting, were all going.

Before leaving with the team, Doc checked in with Blake one more time, knowing he'd be heading to the hospital for the day and hoping there would be an update overnight, but understanding there was little to no chance of that.

"Nothing from the old guy last night, huh?" Doc asked.

"No. I don't expect him either. I think he saw me or knew I was coming, somehow, the night I saw him leaving."

Hands in his pocket, Doc kicked around a random pinecone on the ground. "You're not worried about this guy, are you?"

"I'm not. I want to know *who* he is and *why* he's here, the late night shit is weird, but I don't think he's the one dropping by flowers at the house *and* the hospital. Something is definitely off, but I don't know if it's the flowers, the old man, or someone else needs to be watched. I think we are still waiting for the other shoe to drop, Doc."

Nodding his head with a deep sigh, Doc replied, "That's what I was afraid you were going to say. I spent the morning looking for a note that may have fallen off the flowers and slipped under furniture or something before I even got here. You know, like from a friend who *would* just let themselves in and leave them. Nothing."

"Well, just keep your eyes open and let me know if you notice anything out of order. Logan has been assigned to Ev and Lou indefinitely and with discretion…today being the exception. I want to stay behind, see if anyone out of the norm stops by. Don't want her to know she's being watched over."

"Good idea, she won't go for that. Thanks man…for everything. You really have everyone's back…we're lucky to have you." Doc tried to maintain his man card while offering sincerities the best he could.

"Well if you assholes would stay out of trouble, you wouldn't need looking after, and if you hug me right now, I'll deck ya." A rare grin and slap to the shoulder as a thank you had the two laughing as they joined the rest of the group and headed out for their last full round in the woods before winter.

The two went their separate ways – Doc joined the team and they headed out. Their route took all day and consisted of traveling old Forest Service roads then hiking into parts of the forest, some required horses to get to because of the terrain and how far in they were tucked away. This trip was especially lengthy with the added winter supplies like blankets and socks as well as canned goods they were delivering for winter. It was good community service as well as an opportunity to hone their outdoors skills, which came in handy for Search and Rescue.

On the hike up, Doc was remembering back to when donations from the town's people were the sole funding for these supplies. He shook his head with a smile, remembering when Dawson Tayler asked if he could help fund the project, giving the group access to more materials and medications than they would have had otherwise.

Dawson had a ridiculously large bank account that he didn't want. It was dirty, old, family money that came with bad memories and a life he chose not to acknowledge. For him, the money was better used helping others...mostly because that would appall the family he inherited it from. Beck McCain was a major backer as well, with more money than God, he was able to add mobile medical equipment and supplies that made life easier for Doc and the nurses.

Their last stop was the Burton place at the top of a ridge that was anything but easy to get to and only had one way up, which was an old service road that started on the opposite side of the ridge from their destination. Carly hadn't been as prepared for the living conditions she encountered as she thought she would be. In her mind, it was going to be like large scale camping. Some of the conditions they came across, though, made camping look glamorous. The Burton place was one of those places.

Clyde was on the roof, nailing old boards together and securing a large tarp, apparently weather proofing the best he could, given the conditions. Several windows had cracked or broken panes, which explained why some had been boarded over, clearly another attempt to keep the elements out. The cabin itself was nothing more than a large shack that looked as though it wouldn't stand up to a brisk breeze, much less a heavy winter snow. While they waited for him to climb down the ramshackle of a ladder, Carly took a minute to take in the grounds without his watchful eye.

There were rows and rows of firewood stacked around the house that must've taken months to collect and chop. It was stacked like a barrier around the perimeter of the cabin, perhaps as a barrier and extra protection from the elements. Clever and resourceful, Carly thought.

Not far from the wood pile barrier was a three sided structure with a rickety roof and dead deer hanging from the center that made her cringe. Food for the winter, she presumed. The dilapidated structure had a small enclosed space no bigger than a coat closet attached, making up one of its three sides, with only a door and metal chimney on top with a slow smoldering of smoke swirling out. It had to be something of a smoke house to preserve the meats for the winter. Then there was the outhouse in the distance that made her shudder – she couldn't ever imagine using it, especially in the dead of winter or middle of the night.

"Hey there, miss," Clyde said, offering a friendly handshake and smile.

Carly looked around, realizing she was the only one standing there as the others already had a routine and were unloading supplies while she was snooping from where she stood.

"H-Hi." She forced a weak nervous smile, intimidated by

his height and overwhelming presence. "I'm Carly. I'm, uh, new."

Clyde tossed a wave to Doc and the others, looking for one in particular, "Where's Everly?"

No *nice to meet you,* or *how are you doing*...just where's Everly. His demeanor wasn't necessarily unkind, but it wasn't pleasant either, he was genuinely disappointed that she wasn't there.

"Oh. Uh, Everly couldn't make it out being pregnant and all. She did ask me to tell you hello and see how you're doing? She's been worried about you since your mama died. Oh! Please accept my condolences, I'm very sorry for your loss, Clyde."

"You knew my mama?"

"Well, no, but...I've heard great things about her and know she is missed by a lot of people."

"Oh, yeah, thanks." He nodded as he spoke and never lost eye contact with her.

Carly began to feel a bit uncomfortable in their awkward stand-off, trying to decide if there was any real menace behind the intimidating vibe or if he was just socially awkward. She guessed the latter of the two since Everly and the others were fond of him and continued to check in on him every month or so. She noted he could even be handsome under his shaggy hair, unkempt facial hair – a little hygiene could go a long way for this guy, she thought.

"She's pregnant?" he asked, pulling her from her thoughts.

"Oh...yes, she is. Very exciting."

"Huh. She will be a good mom." His gaze wandered to wear Doc stood and he squinted to a near glare before returning his attention to Carly. "Tell her I said congratulations."

Shifting from one foot to the other, ready to move on to where the others were, she said, "I will, I'm sure she'll be happy to hear that from you."

"Sure. Um, Everly is pregnant – is Doc Charles..." he tossed a thumb over his shoulder in the direction Doc had been standing, letting his words trail off and her to fill in the awkward blanks. He wanted to know if Doc was the baby's father – odd.

Carly offered a simple nod and kind smile before walking off to join the others, crossing Doc's path as she did.

"Hey, Clyde. How are things going. You doing okay?"

"Uh, sure Doc. It's a little quieter, but I'm doing alright. Winter is comin', we had a few flurries so I'm getting ready."

"Yeah, none of it stuck around long so that's good. You need any help getting the place together while we're out here? We have the O'Reilly brothers with us today...we can knock some stuff out pretty quick."

"No. I just have to finish boarding windows up."

"Wow, that makes it awfully dark and closed in. Make sure you get outside, even in the cold a little, alright? I left a well package for you. Just some vitamins and basic things like Tylenol and throat lozenges to get you through. I don't see your truck, you still able to get into town if you need to?"

"Oh, when the snow starts, I leave it down the ridge so it doesn't get stuck. We get a lot more up here than you guys do below. I'll be fine, Doc."

"Okay, good. Looks like you got a big one." Doc gestured to the deer hanging that was likely being readied for butchering.

"Yeah. Everly's pregnant." The curiosity in Clyde's voice had a hint of anxiety that had Doc feeling a bit wary. He reminded himself that Clyde wasn't necessarily tactful and struggled in social situations, chalking his odd behavior up to that. Clyde had always been partial to Everly, it made sense he would be concerned for her.

"Yes. She is. We're very excited."

Clyde watched his feet with his hands deep in his pockets, his posture rigid and stiff, "Are you marrying her? Because the baby and stuff...ya know? You should marry her, Doc."

Doc chuckled, laying a hand on Clyde's shoulder giving it a pat. "I am. Not just because of the baby, but because I love her. Look, I know Ev would like you there so when the time comes, we'll let you know, okay? As soon as Lou gets better, we're tying the knot."

"Oh. Yes, of course. Everly and Lou have always been good to me and mama. Well, to me. I will be there. After the winter passes I'm thinking of moving closer to town, maybe getting a regular job out there. Mama loved it here so I stayed to take care of her, but with just me now...well, it might get a little too lonely and I think I'd rather be...closer to people."

"That's great, Clyde. You know if there is any way we can help...we will. All of us."

Clyde nodded his head and walked off.

* * *

EARLY THAT MORNING, WHILE THE GANG WAS HEADED OUT for rounds in the woods, Everly was headed to the hospital. She hadn't slept well the night before, knowing something was less than right in their world and Granny Lou had a mysterious visitor stopping in every now and again. The flowers, of all things, really had her senses spooked. Knowing Blake and Jessie had both been with her overnight helped ease her nerves, but not entirely.

Jessie was heading out early with the team, so early to the hospital it was. The doctors were slowly weaning Gran from her meds, hoping she would wake soon. Given her fragile state and all she had endured thus far, slow and easy was the plan. Everly wanted to be there when she woke, wanted to see and hear first-hand what the heart attack and stroke had left her with.

She was disappointed that she had to miss rounds with the gang. She rather enjoyed it, felt like she was doing something profoundly important and helpful along with those closest to her. Her *family*. She stared at the ring Doc had sealed their future with as she sat by the window waiting for the sunrise that marked a new day. A new day and a new life – she was about to become Mrs. Mason Charles and was growing their family by not one, but two. Doc was already well loved by their family-like friends, but this made it official, as did the baby, and she couldn't be happier.

Thinking of the baby seemed to provoke the less desirable states of her current condition when her stomach began to roll and that donut from Baker's wasn't willing to settle. Morning sickness – it hadn't passed despite being as far as she was in the pregnancy. As much as she enjoyed being pregnant, this was one detail she wouldn't miss at all.

Cool water on her face only instigated another round of illness before she could leave the space. Finally feeling settled and able to regain her seat next to Gran, she left the bathroom and walked right into the very fear she had been trying to tamp down all night and morning. Despite the early morning hour, still dark outside in fact, there was a visitor sitting in the chair she had quickly abandoned when she rushed to the restroom.

A man sat in her chair, holding Gran's limp hand, with his back to her. He was large, filling the seat beyond its means with his long legs and generous height, dressed in old worn denim from head to toe and a tattered black cowboy hat. She noted his silver hair peeking out the bottom of his hat, peppered with some black yet to turn and surrender to age. He was talking in a low deep voice, though she couldn't make out the words, she felt a warmth in his lightly twangy tone…kindness and something sweet perhaps.

Her gasp erupted from being startled by his unexpected, larger than life presence causing the man to turn, slowly. She was met by a lightly pruned, sunbaked face that told a story of a life lived hard, but a pleasantry about him that suggested it was a good life. His smile friendly, his nod welcoming, it was his all too familiar eyes looking back at her that caught her breath.

With a tip of his hat, and charming wink he said, "Hello, Everly Louise…"

16

LOCKED IN EACH OTHER'S STARES, NEITHER EVERLY NOR THE gentlemen budged. As much as she wanted to holler for help, or scream even, she couldn't. This had to be the mystery man who had been showing up at odd hours, perhaps bringing the flowers, even letting himself in her home with a bouquet. Given he knew exactly who she was, using her full name, it made sense. As spooked as she had been by the idea of this man, standing before him, looking him square in the eye... she wasn't spooked at all.

Even when the man slowly stood and turned to face her, she wasn't frightened. Something still nudged her to call for help, but she was paralyzed where she stood and speechless, consumed by the familiarity that she saw in him, but couldn't quite identify. A warm smile that seemed to be his permanent expression reached his golden eyes that reflected kindness and what looked like longing. His chiseled masculine features, which spoke of refinement under the weathered appearance that age and something else had cemented, told the tale of something grand. She knew him, or felt that she did or had.

Rustling of a bag, and voices couldn't even break the entranced gaze between the two. With a bag of donuts from the bakery in Morgan's hand, and tray of paper mugs in Blake's, the two stopped in the doorway, stunned by the stand-off they had walked in on. The odd inkling of something awry that had haunted Blake all these days was subtly present, raising the hairs on the back of his neck. Through pure instinct, the tray of paper mugs, full of whatever drinks Blake was sharing, were tossed in the trash to his right, just inside the door, and his hand then rested on the gun attached to his belt as he moved briskly through the room, putting himself between Everly and the stranger.

Without a single look over his shoulder, Blake addressed Everly, not once taking his eyes off the older man. "You okay, Ev?"

Finally stirred from her unexplainable state, her eyes widened and she shook her head while taking a deep breath, "Uhhh…yeah. Yeah, I'm fine. I just…got sick and came out of the bathroom and…"

"And I was sittin' in her chair here, I presume?" The older man's deep throaty voice had a subtle drawl that was hard to identify as anything but a cowboy twang.

"Who the hell are you and what are you doing here?" With an icy glare and no bullshit resonance to his voice, Blake was not impressed with the hint at light hearted banter the man was offering. Blake didn't like strangers, especially strangers with secrets, and he could tell this old coot had a big one.

The man opened his mouth to answer, but was beat to the punch by Morgan's impressed introduction – clearly not seeing a stranger but an old familiar face before them.

"Stone Williams…" Her star struck eyes danced between the man and Blake who was still shielding Everly.

"You're Stone Williams. You're the mystery? I don't understand."

That kind smile brightened as his head dipped in a slow nod at Morgan while he closed his eyes out of what almost looked of defeat. "I am, Morgie. Surprised ya recognize me all these years later. How's your mama and daddy?"

Irritation consumed Blake and took over, using a hostile tone and ornerier glare when the man used Morgan's nickname – they knew each other which should have delighted him, but it did just the opposite. "Can someone tell me what the fuck is going on here? Who the hell is Stone Williams and what are you doing in my town."

Morgan relaxed her defensive state and moved into the room, sitting on the corner at the end of Lou's hospital bed, gesturing for all of them to take a seat. When Blake didn't move, she rolled her eyes and pulled an extra chair around for him so he could stay planted somewhat between Everly and the man he didn't yet trust. He didn't sit.

"Stone Williams. You've never heard of him?"

"I…I think that name is familiar, but…why?" Everly replied, finally taking her seat. She hadn't really felt uncomfortable with the man in question, but knowing that Morgan knew who he was and wasn't threatened, but more impressed, made her feel better.

"No," Blake deep-toned, not ready to let his guard down and holding onto that *don't fuck with me* glare.

"Rodeo Pro? The best rodeo bull rider in history?" When neither caught on, Morgan sighed and continued the hero worship introduction, "He's a rodeo legend that has the longest held world records in rodeo history…"

"What are you doing here?" Blake interrupted, arms crossed, still not impressed.

"Well, son, I…"

"Not your son…don't know you…can we cut the crap and get to it old man? Why are you here, why have you been in this room…hiding out."

"Oh, I haven't been hiding out. I just didn't want to interfere. I'm here for Lou – heard what happened and drove straight through from the panhandle."

"The panhandle?"

"Texas, boy, my home base…where my ranch is."

"That still doesn't explain what your business is with Lou and why you're hiding out."

"My business with Lou is personal. And I ain't hidin' out. If you'd been to that there equestrian center…Sugar Pines? You would know I've been there, bunkin' in my travel rig until the deal goes through."

Blake's glare narrowed and his tone stiffened, "What *deal*?"

"For Sugar Pines…I'm movin' home. With this busted up knee Ol'Twister gave me, it's time for me to head to pasture…I'm retirin' from the rodeo. "

"Home?" As much as Blake wanted to dislike the guy, and pin the eerie vibe in town on him, he was having a hard time doing so. The menace in the air didn't match the man – at all. But he was intrigued and wanted to know what his connection was to Lou…and Everly.

"Uh, Stone is from here," Morgan offered. "He actually worked with my dad on our ranch before he became a rodeo superstar."

"Ahhh, I don't know about superstar, but I did grow up here, on the land Sugar Pines is on."

Everly leaned forward, still trying to put together the missing pieces, watching his every move, hanging on his every word. "Sugar Pines has been there longer than….well, longer than I've been alive. How long ago did you leave?"

"Oh, I left long before you were even a glint in your daddy's eye...before he was born actually."

"You knew my dad?"

"I suppose you could say I knew *of* him."

"Then I'm lost. There is something oddly familiar about you. I feel like we've met, but I can't place it...I don't follow the rodeo circuit at all, so..."

"Yeah...I suppose I do. I see it too..."

"The eyes," Blake chimed, "high cheekbones...even the same heart shaped freckle on your left hand. I think we know where your height came from Ev. What's going on, Stone?"

Falling back in her chair, the air forced from Everly's lungs as reality settled in around her. It started to make sense, the familiarity. She didn't know Stone, never met him in fact, but she saw him every time she looked in the mirror. There was an undeniable resemblance between Stone and her deceased father, that is why it didn't come to her sooner... that's why there was a resemblance to *her.*

Turning to his left, Stone reached for Lou's hand, holding it in one hand while he pat the top of it with his free hand. There was something sentimental between them – the distant look that ended in a soft sweet grin gave it away. Gran only had a sister, that Everly knew about, and she had passed at an early age. Who was Stone to Gran that he could pass on inarguable characteristics?

A chain of emotions crossed Stone's face while he looked at Lou like he was running through memories, each one leaving a distinct imprint in his expression that told a story of something as grand as it was painful. A low chuckle escaped him as if a conversation was going on that only the two of them could hear before a pained sigh erupted. As if he had just remembered they weren't alone, his attention returned from wherever he was with Lou to the three sets of eyes that were pinned on him.

"I, uh, have known Lou my whole life – grew up together. There was a group of us, ya see…Lou and me along with ol'Chappy, Jed Baker, and Morgie's daddy…and your grand-daddy, Everly. We were always a group, did everything together. Back then, McKenzie was even smaller than it is now with just a single stop sign in a four corner town." He chuckled at the memory, lost in his own world.

Intrigued, Everly asked, "You knew my grandad?"

"Oh, yes…I sure did. He was the sensible one, good head on his shoulders and probably what kept us all out of trouble. Lou was as pretty as a Sunday morning sunrise, but as tough as a mean ol'rattle snake – she had no trouble keepin' up with us boys – in fact, we had trouble keepin' up with her."

The group laughed at the image of a younger Lou that didn't sound all that different than the Lou they knew now.

"Sounds like Lou." Blake snickered, relaxing in his seat with crossed arms and ankles.

"Oh, yeah, she was a feisty one. Probably what I loved most about her."

Dropping his affections for Lou like it was no secret spiked their curiosity, boosting their interest. Especially since they wanted answers, needed them now really because Lou didn't talk much about the past.

"The boys and I worked out at the ranch, Morgie's ranch now, and Lou met us there every afternoon when she was done working at the soda shop. It was summer, we'd been out of high school a year or so, maybe two. None of us were going anywhere – ya see, college was where you went if you wanted to be a doctor, or somethin' fancy. We were all about horses, ridin', and ranchin'. Lou and I had always had a bond of sorts, but that summer we were more…so much more. I was bull ridin' more, and more, had a few rodeos under my belt by then, and rodeo season was just around the corner. The boys and I practiced during the day, and Lou and I... Well, we had our nights." He drifted off for a moment, scratching his chin, lost in thought, before he finished his story.

"Long story short, we were in love, planned to marry, have our own ranch someday. What we hadn't counted on in all our plannin' was the rodeo. It came to town as it always did and the boys and I were there, competin'. Turned out, I was the best kid there on a bull...earned myself a spot on the circuit. I was in a tough spot, ya see – my girl, or an opportunity that could afford us our own ranch and that there future we'd talked so much about?"

Completely entranced by the story of her grandmother's first love, Everly finished his thought, beginning to see where the story was going, "You left...and didn't come back."

"No, I came back, but it was too late. Leavin' wasn't the biggest mistake I had made, it was not telling her the whole story. I was afraid of failin' and not makin' it that first season and didn't want to disappoint her if I came home with nothin' to show for the gamble. I was gone eight months. Longest eight months of my life. When I came back wearin' fancy new boots, and had a fuller wallet than I left with, I was too late. She wasn't stayin' at her place anymore. I went lookin' for her, stopped at your granddaddy, Hal's, and there she was. She was sittin' the yard holdin' a baby with Hal right next to her."

A lone tear trailed Stone's cheek, his pain evident by the crack in his voice as he remembered the moment his world had crumbled.

Being pregnant and starting a life with her true love, Everly's emotions mirrored Stone's as she thought about her grandmother so long ago. "What...what did you say? What did you do?"

"Left," he said with a defeated chuckle. "I went back to Texas to continue training, eventually bought my land and built my ranch there. I checked in on Lou from time to time, especially when the rodeo came through McKenzie, *she* just didn't know it. When Hal passed, then your mama and daddy, I stayed nearby but didn't interfere."

"Wait...why..." The tears started to flow as Everly pieced things together and realized why she saw herself in Stone Williams, her voice dimmed to a near whisper, "Why would you watch over us unless...you had reason. Gran always said her and grandad had a whirlwind love affair, marrying after only two months together – that's not enough time to get pregnant and have a baby only eight months later, Stone."

"I wouldn't be an expert on such things, but I imagine... you would be right."

"She was...she was pregnant when you left. Your eyes, your face...you look like me because you're my... grandfather?"

"I reckon so, kiddo...but Hal, he was your..."

"No...no need to explain, I understand. Did he know? Did my father know?"

"I can't say for your father, but I can tell ya that Hal knew...back then it was different. If you were pregnant and not married... Well, he did the right thing, did what I *should* have done and I don't begrudge him for that. He looked me up once when I was in town, ya see. Everyone ended up where they should."

Everly was speechless, completely stunned and unable to reconcile the stream of emotions flowing through her. As much as she should be disappointed by the secrets – lies really – surrounding her family, she wasn't. Losing her grandfather and parents had left a proverbial hole in her heart that would ultimately control how she lived for two decades because their love ran so deep and left her so hollow.

A sense of guilt tingled her senses when a bit of joy found its way in at the idea, however, that someone could fill those voids. Just as she had previously realized, little by little as the days went on, her circle wasn't shrinking simply by loving… it was growing. Perhaps it had just grown by one more. A premature thought, perhaps, but one that lingered none the less.

"So you have been bringing the flowers then?"

"Flowers? No. I tend to come by late at night when no one is around. When Jed called me and told me about Lou, I had to be here, but not to disrupt the life she had built. I figured that was her story to tell, until ya caught me." He chuckled, turning to Blake, "I saw this kid here one night and knew he was on to me, so I started coming mornings real early…guess that didn't work out too well either."

"Or, maybe it did…" Everly said with a glassy eyed soft smile, overwhelmed by the immediate connection she felt to Stone and clinging to the hope it left in her heart.

The afternoon wore on without notice while Everly and Stone became acquainted and Morgan brought him up to speed on her family. Blake sat back, listening to the stories, still not convinced that their threat was merely an old love hiding in the background. There was still something wrong, he knew it, he felt it.

"What's going on?" Interrupting the conversations, and thoughts swirling through the room, Doc and the rest of the gang had returned from a long day in the woods – first stop, the hospital.

"Hello, Doctor Charles…the name's Stone Williams." Shock and confusion over the gathering in Lou's room ended with a trip to Ponderosa Pizza, just across from the hospital where the group took over a large backroom and they were apprised of all that had happened in a single day. They welcomed a new friend back to town over pizza and beer, a fitting end to a busy day…that was McKenzie for you.

* * *

BLAKE RETURNED TO LOU'S HOSPITAL ROOM BEFORE THE others, feeling a bit of unease. He already knew what he needed to know about Stone, and he wasn't even on his radar. He actually liked the old man. Sitting in the chair next to Lou's bed, he watched the sour scowl on Lou's face, wondering what he had missed the short time they were all gone.

He sat trying to piece together the few clues he had, trying to solve a mystery that had yet to reveal itself entirely. Traces of dirt marked the floor when he returned, and a small dusting on the table where a new bunch of wild flowers sat in a vase. In the time that the room had been free of any onlookers, someone had been there…but who?

Something notably odd was the condition of the flowers. Bouquets past had been neatly cut and carefully arranged before placed in the vase. This bunch was hastily picked, evident by the crushed leaves, broken or bent stems, missing petals, and dirt clad roots that were undoubtedly ripped from the ground in a hurry or haste. No matter the reason, that alone suggested escalation in whatever was happening around them and swirled in his gut like a painful twist of a knife.

Attention turning to the door, he saw Stone walk in, but Doc was stopped at the door by Carly who was only there to check on Lou after her long day in the woods with the team. As Carly's fondness for this group of friends increased, their worries and concerns slowly became hers – including Lou. The conversation that unfolded twisted that knife a little tighter and if Blake was a betting man, he suspected Stone felt the same painful stab.

"So our mystery harmonica player is no longer a mystery?" she asked.

"It seems so, pretty incredible really. This stuff only happens in movies," Doc teased offering a nod to the men in Lou's room.

"I really didn't mean to eavesdrop, but I thought what you said to Lou was so sweet, Evie is a lucky lady. It set Lou's monitors off, it had her heart racing…she must've been pleased."

Baffled, Doc raised his brow in question, looking from the room then back to Carly. "I'm sorry? Where's her chart? She's okay, isn't she?"

"Oh, I'm sorry to worry you – she is absolutely fine. I just meant what you said about Everly, the baby and taking care of her…it was quite sweet. Don't worry…I made myself scarce pretty quick and your secret talks are safe with me!"

"Huh…I haven't been here. I was across the way at Ponderosa, just getting back now."

"Oh, really? Well, that's odd." She looked down, and scratched her head. "I'm sorry, I guess I misheard something else…huh."

Carly walked off, leaving for the night before her shift the next day, and Doc stopped to review Lou's chart at the nurse's station just across from her room. One look at Stone and Blake knew he picked up the same concern from the conversation – who had been here while they were gone.

Pulling up a chair next to Blake, Stone leaned forward, resting his elbows on his knees, eyes pinned on Lou. "What do you suppose that was about, son?"

Not quick to correct the use of *son* like he had before, Blake matched Stone's pose and posture and shook his head. "I don't know but it's been going on a while now."

Nodding in agreement, Stone let out a nervy groan, "I s'pose you noticed the smell?"

"Yep…how 'bout you? See the dirt?"

"Sure did, and those flowers don't look too carefully picked either."

Blake stood, patting Stone on the shoulder. "Why don't you head out, get some rest and you can take the early shift… I'll hang out here tonight."

"That sounds like a right nice plan, kid. I'm not far if…"

"I know," Blake replied before he could finish. He found the idea of needing the old man's help in an emergency a bit humorous but respected the sentiment just the same. "Give me a minute, I'm going to go grab a coffee, if you don't mind?"

"No need…" Jessie walked in the door holding two large paper mugs of what was assumed to be coffee. It appeared Blake had company for the night.

17

CARIGAN LOVED HER BROTHERS, BUT SHE DIDN'T EXACTLY like them. Sure they meant well, but they weren't kids anymore. She was an adult, perfectly capable of sorting through her love life without their help, or interference rather. She had tried to send them home, many times, but since their parents were on an extended trip to Ireland, all five insisted on staying through Thanksgiving...at the very least.

Though BJ wasn't intimidated by their many attempts to do so, she was. She knew them, what they were capable of, and just how ornery they could be. Of course they weren't so full of malice that they would hurt him intentionally, but they certainly weren't afraid to taunt, tease, and lightly bruise the guy. It had been Carigan's experience that most men eventually fled, not so much breaking up with her, but breaking up with the brothers.

Not this time, she refused to let them get the better of yet another relationship, especially this one because BJ really felt like the one – her true soul mate – and she wasn't about to lose true love twice. But alas, they didn't listen to her despite her own bodily threats and wish for wrathful harm to rain on them. They thought it was cute…of course.

She had even reduced herself to asking Blake to arrest them for everything from harassment to trespassing, but the law wasn't on her side, nor was karma or any other universal force that tended to right wrongs. She was desperate, not just to get rid of them, but to be with BJ; she missed him and was beginning to crave him. If only she knew how to dispose of a few bodies…she was sure Blake knew how, but asking would make her an immediate suspect should one…or five…go missing.

Exhausted by their shenanigans, she was done with them and had been tempted to call their mother, as childish as that seemed. Colleen O'Reilly was every bit as sweet as she looked with her petite frame, and soft voice – unless you pissed her off – or one of her boys was causing trouble. Then all Irish hell broke loose and she was a larger than life force to be reckoned with. Carigan was saving that as her last hand to play because it would likely end in an *in person* scolding for which she would bring their father too. Dad was on the boys' side.

Every time she and BJ made plans, or worse, were in the middle of hot and steamy bonding, the guys would show up or find a way to interrupt them. Other times, they just swept him away for some macho man challenge in an attempt to scare him off or humiliate him. BJ could hold his own, though, and rather enjoyed those moments. In more desperate attempts, it was Carigan they whisked away in the name of family dinner or game nights, sometimes both if they wanted to keep her busy late.

Conveniently, the only time her brothers gave her to herself, were the times in which BJ was working at his family bakery. She was wise to them and their ways and assumed they had found a way into his schedule and planned accordingly. They probably hacked BJ's cell phone, an easy amateurish task for these boys.

Sitting in her room reading a book, or really just pouting and licking her wounds, her last thought inspired an idea that couldn't go wrong. If they had hacked his cellphone, which she was certain they had, she decided to give them something to read while they were in there. Worst case scenario, they hadn't hacked it, and it was just a little fun flirting with her guy – a win/win.

A heated slew of steamy words full of suggestive innuendo were quickly wrangled and sent to her favorite guy in the form of a text. His reply was nearly immediate, picking up where she left off adding his own ideas and memories of some of their favorite *acts* together. Their exchange ended with a plan full of promised acts that were sure to elicit sensual pleasure…more than once.

Odd that a few weeks back in each other's company could go such a long way. She supposed it was because neither ever truly got over the other and their love was kismet. Regardless, she loved him like they were never apart and hoped it would stay that way, despite the interference.

Shaken from her thoughts, the rowdy entrance of her loud brothers had her back to boiling. Timing about right, they had read the texts because they were originally planning to be out all day working with Beck McCain on a new venture he was establishing. Even in her bedroom, with door closed, down the long hall from where they were, she heard them plain as day which meant their intentions were to interrupt whatever they put together from reading the text exchange between Carigan and BJ.

Something she had neglected to think through was what would she do should she confirm her suspicion and catch them spying like the juveniles they were behaving as – or what *could* she do. She could scare them off. Let them think they were too late and stepping right into the middle of what they were trying to prevent from starting in the first place.

Laughing to herself, she looked around the room, plotting as quickly as she could. Tossing a few pairs of shoes and books ahead of her, she climbed up on her bed, standing near the headboard. Her bed sat on the wall that separated her space from the space which the guys were occupying so this couldn't be more perfect. With her back to the door, and steadying herself on the bed, she began to jump. It was time to let them think she didn't care if they were around – for anything.

Her squeaky metal bedframe noised, and her headboard hit the wall if she jumped just hard enough. This was perfect. Her intensity increased and she tossed a shoe to the carpeted floor for a muffled thud that she followed with a provocative moan. Quickly covering her mouth to muffle the laughter building, she continued to jump wishing she could see the looks on their faces when another brilliant idea struck.

Cellphone in hand, she scrolled to find the right *mood music* to really get things going. She tossed the phone behind her and let it play, volume all the way up, and slapped both hands against the wall for good naughty sounding measure. Oh, this was good, so…so…good. Another shoe to the floor and headboard against the wall, she decided to increase the *heat* with more breathy moans and a few random high pitched squeals.

Completely jaw dropped and red faced, all five of the O'Reilly brothers stood cemented to the floor where they stood in the living room. Fists were clenching while knuckles went white as heads began to shake in disbelief. First unsure of what the banging was, it quickly became apparent when the banging lead to moaning.

"Are you fucking kidding me?" Dace spat.

Wylie covered his ears and shook his head rapidly, "No, no, no…I can't hear this. How the hell did this… When did she start… Oh, my God!"

"I must have found a lag in the system, those messages must have been from earlier. We're too late," Liam surmised, confused by his assumed error.

"Look, this was all just for fun, but he's… That guy is in there…you know, and she's our baby sister, just a kid!" Luke lunged toward the hall only to be stopped by Declan who tried to offer reason.

"Guys, she's an adult. What are you going to do, charge in there and kick his ass? He's naked…she's naked…you want to see *that?* I'll tell you this right now, I won't hold him down for you unless he has clothes on."

Timing couldn't be better, or perhaps worse, when BJ himself walked through the front door behind them. "Oh, hey…guys. Is something….wrong?"

Another bang against the wall and drawn out moan coursed through the air. BJ's brows furrowed and his chest puffed out, taking on the same clenched fists and white knuckles the brothers had.

"What the hell?" he questioned.

"Yeah…what the hell, *Bart?!*" Wylie's sharp tone was as threatening as it was sarcastic, "We were wondering the same thing! What the hell?"

"What…what's going on in there? Is that Cari?" Hot and bothered for all the wrong reasons, BJ was ready to come undone.

"What's going on in there? Seriously? We read the texts…you know exactly what's going on in there." Anger was clearly interfering with logic at this point, given the direction Luke had taken the conversation.

"Wait, you read my texts? How did you…" BJ looked at Liam who had a smarmy grin that screamed *fuck you and I'll drain your bank account next if you touch my sister.*

"Asshole…she's just a kid."

"First…she's not a kid. Let's just be clear about that. Second…how can I be in there with her, if I'm standing out here with you guys?"

"Oh…well, that was our next question too. Who *is* in there - *asshole.*" *Asshole* was added as a distraction, and for good measure, by Wylie who was feeling about as lowly as his brothers at the realization that they looked like a bunch of Neanderthal idiots.

"That's what I would like to know, I'll kick his ass." The moaning quickened as did the squeaking from the bed, fueling the fury consuming BJ. "Cari wouldn't…"

Declan grinned with a surprised, or maybe impressed, expression as awareness washed over him, "You're right, *Squirt* wouldn't. I think I know what's going on. Follow me…quietly."

Six oversized men tip toed down the hallway with faces of disgust and covering their ears. A few *I'm going to be sick* and *my ears are burning* were shared in whispers as they approached. The same sounds could be heard from outside Carigans door, as they heard in the living room…just louder, and clearer, making their stomachs roll.

Declan chuckled, certain he knew what was going on in Carigan's room. He raised his finger to his pursed lips, indicating he wanted them all to be quiet then slowly and quietly turned the door knob, opening the door. Just as he thought, Carigan was in there, alone, covering her mouth to muffle her laughter.

What Dec hadn't expected was the lengths she had gone to, but knew exactly why. Had BJ not walked in when he had, she would have succeeded. She jumped hard enough for the headboard to hit the wall and tossed her head back to moan, quickly covering it to shield the fit of laughter.

Unable to stay quiet, the guys in the hallway began to snicker as they watched their sister jump on her own bed and have fake sex. The sound of their laughs stopped her mid-jump. She stood there for a long moment before slowly turning to face them. First mortified, her expression transitioned to a red fiery anger and she had the tight fists and gritted teeth to match.

"Yooou…" she said with a sharp steely glare.

Declan shrugged his shoulders, and tilted his head toward the rest of the guys as if declaring innocence and indicating blame where blame was due. "What's going on here, Squirt? Not quite a pillow fight you got going on there."

"Or a pillow biter." Wylie laughed.

"How dare you. I knew you were reading those messages. You five are leaving, understand? If you don't, I will." She paused to step off the bed and move closer to them and continued her scolding. "This is ridiculous! If you have a problem with me and BJ, well that's *your* problem. I love him, probably have forever, and you won't change that by acting like a bunch of fucking buffoons so go beat your chests somewhere else and maybe work on your own love lives so mine won't be so appealing. Now get out, go pack – something – because I'm sick of the sight of ya!"

She stared them down with her hands on her hips silently challenging them to say something, anything, so she could inflict another round of her tempered wrath on each of them.

"Squirt, look…"

"Carigan, Cari, Sis…*that* is what you can call me. I may

be your little sister, but I'm a grown woman and you need to start treating me like one. Now get out."

BJ smiled with pride. Declaring her love for him so boldly made his heart swell, being a total badass while doing it turned him on. He pushed through the guys, into the room and pulled Carigan into his arms, kissing her hard. When grunts from the hallway festered, he kicked the door shut with his foot and reached for the door knob, locking it, without breaking their kiss.

BJ and Carigan didn't leave the room once, the whole night...

18

THANKSGIVING WAS A TIME FOR REFLECTION AND OF COURSE, thanks, especially for this group. They had a rough fall, thus far, but all in all, things could have always been worse, as they say. Lou wasn't with them, but she was improving each day. Each prayed for a full recovery so their world could return to normal, or what was their normal anyway.

In Lou's absence, however, the group of family-like friends was happy to have additional guests to celebrate with them exactly as Lou would have wanted. Carigan's brothers were there, of course, as well as BJ who was also cooking the meal. Carly was new to the area and without family but quickly fit in with this crowd and was excited to be there.

It seemed there may have been something romantic brewing with Carly and another of McKenzie's newest citizens, Logan Traynor. Match making tended to be Lou's job in town, but it seemed Stone had a knack for it too and was greatly invested in seeing that connection turn into something. Having Stone there was comforting to Everly. After extensive thought, she surmised that it had something to do with seeing her father in him. Both in looks and demeanor, for two people who didn't spend any time together, or even know each other, they were a lot alike. Stone was something special, Everly counted on it.

Taking a break from football, while BJ ran inside to check the turkey, the men gathered around the sidelines, joining in the conversation the women were having. Stone had played sideline ref from a chair with one of the handful of kiddos on each knee at any given time, marking him as family already.

"So when is this wedding, Ev? I swear if you make me wear some fluffy shit like fancy pants did when she married Colton, I'll teach your kid to spit before it can walk." Jessie didn't tell half-truths or bullshit, she just made promises and kept them so Everly took notes. Fancy Pants was her nickname for Meg, when she wasn't calling her Princess. It was actually an endearing term – if Jessie called you something other than your name, it meant she liked you.

"Hey," Meg chided, "those dresses were gorgeous and couture. You looked *amazing*, you're welcome."

"Yeah, well, I cut off the sleeves and over half the length…it's better now." Jessie would say anything to get a rise, but again…if she said it, she meant it.

Doc sat in a chair and pulled Everly to his lap, kissing her shoulder. " I've been waiting long enough. If I had it my way, I would have married Ev forever ago. I'd do it today, if someone could make that happen."

Placing her arm around his neck, Everly leaned down for a sweet kiss. "I agree…soon. I really want to do it before the baby is born, but I also want Gran there. I'm thinking simple, but elegant. It may be a last minute gig and that would make it hard to plan anything extravagant anyway."

Meg clapped her hands in delight, as the self-appointed party planner, and town florist who still had elite socialite tendencies running through her. "Oh, my God…I can make magic happen on any timeline honey. Anything you want, big, small…"

"Are we still talking about the wedding here, or what happens *after* the wedding?" Wylie laughed at Jessie's quick wit, something he had and few could match.

"Little ears, cool it." A warning from the moms in the group seemed to happen more often than not…when Jessie was around.

"I agree…Lou should be there. I can wait for her. She's off the meds now and can wake up. She's been stirring and showing signs according to the team so…"

"So we could be getting married any day now? That feels so weird. How do we even plan for that though? We need a license and someone to marry us…"

Stone chimed in, happy to have something to offer, "Well kid, you get that license, it's good for a time. When you're ready, if you would like, I can marry ya. I'm ordained and performed more cowboy weddings on the road than I can count. But my feelin's won't be hurt if you'd rather not since we are all still gettin' acquainted."

"No, I would love that, Stone. It would be perfect."

"Then it's a done deal, little one. You just let me know when and where. I'm stayin' on here while my ranch in Texas sells, I won't be goin' back. I can be ready at a moment's notice, ya hear?"

"You know we've had two weddings at the ranch now, why not a third? It can be our family tradition. Meg could turn the big barn into something amazing I'm sure," Morgan offered.

Meg gasped in excitement when Morgan started speaking her language. "I can already see it. Winter country chic, it could be beautiful."

"One wedding was up North, Deception Pass," Beck

reminded the group then turned to Stone to clarify. "Colton and Meg got married at my place in the San Juan Islands."

"Oh, that sounds real nice too. Sounds like you have some good options, kid."

"Same offer stands as before. You want to go to the islands, we can use the jet, get everyone there, make Lou real comfortable while we're at it. I just need a day's notice for my pilot," Beck added.

"Fancy Pants will pull a wedding out of her aaa...purse and have it ready in fifteen minutes. Sounds like you're all set Ev. We just need Gran." Remembering the reminder of little ears, Jessie quickly cleaned up her language, even if *ass* made a better point.

Overwhelming emotions consumed Everly, evidence streaming down her face. Her life had transformed so much in such little time, it was hard to process. Just a short time ago she was locked in a hotel room having a steamy weekend with someone who was nothing more than a long term fling. Now she sat with that same man, the man who she would spend her life with, while surrounded by the people who loved her...and who she loved.

A lonely life was what she had subscribed to in an effort to preserve what was left of her heart. Love with boundaries and from afar was all she allowed herself. Now she stood among the people who meant the most to her, without boundaries, planning a happily ever after with the man of her dreams...her *new* dream. That was the beauty of dreams, they could change, without limits or timelines and the sacrifice was worth it.

BJ had called out from the rear door, letting everyone know dinner was served, changing the sentimental moment to one of mouthwatering excitement. It didn't require any nudging, they were all headed up to the house, ready to celebrate all that they had to be thankful for which was a lot, despite the missing piece to their puzzle.

"You okay, baby?" Doc asked of Everly, wiping her tears.

"As much as I hate using the excuse so much…hormones. I don't cry, yet I've done more in these past weeks than my entire life combined."

A beautiful table was set, a golden turkey as the centerpiece, they all filled their seats quickly. Ready for their traditional rounding of the table saying what each was thankful for, followed by a prayer, another life changing moment brought it all to a grinding halt. A phone call was about to concrete the day as one they would never forget.

Dawson took to his feet, "All of the usual suspects are already here. Must be important if whoever that is, is calling on a holiday."

Quiet conversations stalled at Dawson's reaction to what was on the other end of the line. They took to silence, sitting at the edges of their seats and listened in.

"Oh my God…finally. Really? Yes, she's here… He's here too… Okay… I will…" he looked up, eye's full of emotion scanning the group with a satisfied grin on his face. "Yes …we're all coming."

Everly stood to her feet holding a hand over her mouth, waiting for him to hang up the phone. "Dawson…is she?"

"Your phone…they tried to call you. Looks like you're getting married – she's awake!"

* * *

IT WAS JUST LIKE LOUISE SHAW TO WAIT FOR SOMETHING substantial, like a holiday, to come back to her family. Rushing around to pack up the meal they had yet to eat, everyone agreed that dinner would be served at McKenzie General with the one they were missing.

"I can only imagine what she's doing to the poor nurses right now. I bet she's trying to get out of her bed and pissing and moaning about green jello." Breaking the thick silence full of anticipation and anxieties, Jessie did what she did well and made the group laugh as they finished packing up.

"Exactly! We better pack the extra pie for the nurses!" Everly teased.

Jessie grabbed one of the canvas totes used to carry the various dishes full of turkey dinner and unloaded it, earning her several sideways stares. She rushed to the refrigerator, going for the freezer, and began loading her bag, earning her an outburst of laughter. "And the vodka!"

She didn't find the humor in it, tossing them a threatening look before Everly chimed in, "The nurses are on duty! They can't have *that*! They're likely to stick one of us with a needle full of someone else's meds!"

"This isn't for the *nurses*, it's for Gran! What do you think she's trying to get out of that bed for anyway? Booze and her dog... Blake, grab Moonshine, she's going to want him." And out the door she went with a pie in one hand, bag full of booze in the other.

"Let's go..." Blake said, "we need to get there before Jess gets Lou drunk."

Something that had been missing was flooding back in, bringing them all a sense of relief with matched joy and laughter.

* * *

LOUISE SHAW WAS AS CANTANKEROUS AS EVER, NOT TO BE stopped by a heart attack or stroke, much less the meds that were supposed to keep her drowsy and calm. Her fitful behavior over being *stuck in a damn bed* was a welcome sight. Preliminary results showed that she was suffering weakness on her left side, causing a slight slur both of which would require therapy, but the prognosis was good. Unbelievable really.

"You all need'ta stop worryin' so much about me and just let me outta this here bed. Whoever thought it was a good idea to keep me sleepin' in this wreck," her hands spanned out, indicating the wreck was the bed, "owes me one of them massages and the *man* doin' it better be a looker."

"And she's back, folks!" Jessie joked.

Doc gave her a rundown of her condition and expressed why it was important they didn't rush things and just let healing happen organically, but that went over as easy as a snake in a boot.

"Oh, Doc...I feel fine. Just a little tired and my words are funny, but I can just blame that on whiskey if it don't go away."

Tears were brewing again, frustrating Everly. "Gran, you had us all scared half to death. Not once, but twice. We need you around so no more talk of whiskey, and you better listen to the doctors. You can't do this to us again unless you really plan on leavin' us, old woman!"

Lou reached for Everly's hand and held it in hers. "Oh, Evie, honey. I ain't goin' nowhere for a while yet. Still too much ta'do. Besides, heaven ain't ready for me yet and hell's afraid of me, so lack of options leaves me to all of you."

"Well, Moonshine missed you. He'll be happy to have you home soon," Blake said, pulling the dog from the sling he wore across his body and resting on his hip.

"What the hell did ya do to my dog?! Oh, my heavens,

Moonshine, you alright?" Lou gasped, doing her best to lift the dog and look him over.

Blake looked around the room, taking in the shrugging shoulders. He was suddenly concerned that she didn't recognize her beloved pet. "Uh…he's right there, Lou. That's Moonshine."

"Well, I can see that, it was my heart that gone bad, not my eyes! Where's the rest of him? I can actually see his legs!"

"Oh! Uh, well I took care of him while you were…well, *here*. So I did some training and exercised him. Put him through some of the K-9 program so he would be helpful when we get you home."

"Well, why'd you go do a thing like that? He's damn near skinny!" Moonshine climbed from her lap, up the pillows around her and began licking her face. "Well, I suppose you being able to walk does make it a tad easier since I won't be able to carry you in the sling for a spell. And you look a bit younger, so there's that. I suppose knowing a few words and being able to fend for yourself a bit may come in handy for now."

Blake let out a breath he didn't realize he was holding when Lou hugged her pet with her right arm and relaxed into him. His intentions had been good and not geared toward upsetting Lou. Now he could see that was just Lou being Lou, affections sometimes came out in a scolding manner, especially when she was the center of this kind of attention and there was a crowd.

After a good hour, and a plate of food together, the gang started to say their goodbyes when Lou started yawning more and more. She was still more tired and worn than she had let on, but they had expected that. Everly and Doc walked them out, helping with the left over meal, making promises to get together the next day for round two – leftovers.

Blake was the last to leave, leaning in to leave a kiss on her forehead, she held on to his arm and whispered, "Something's wrong, ain't it. I can't put my finger on it, but I have an awful feeling, like I know something and I just don't know what."

"You know I won't let anything happen, right? I don't want you to worry," he replied.

"I sure do. You're a good boy, Blake Cooper." She patted his cheek and gave him a weak smile.

"If you think of anything or something happens, you let me know, Lou."

She nodded her head and he offered a rare smile before turning to leave the room as Stone found his way in, followed by Everly and Doc. Blake paused where he stood, turned to Lou, taking in her relaxed expression, and left.

"Willy. The music in my head. That *was* you. I thought it was just a dream."

"Willy?" Everly asked.

"William Stone is my given name," Stone replied. "Stone Williams was a rodeo name...sounded tougher, marketable, they said."

"You'll always be Willy Stone to me, dear friend." Lou held out her right hand to him as a gesture to come closer and sit with her.

"I suppose I will, babycakes."

"Babycakes...it's been a long time since I heard that." She laughed at the nickname he had given her so many years ago, letting it wash over her and bring her a sense of something she couldn't quite define.

It quickly dawned on Lou that Everly was standing there and likely hadn't a clue what or who Stone was to her. But she watched the two of them, saw that they were anything but strangers, and the fondness they seemed to share matched their likeness to the eye. Everly knew and Lou didn't know how she felt about that.

"Oh, Evie…you must think something awful of me. I'm sorry child, I… When Willy left, and Hank and I married, everything just sort of fell into place, like it was meant to be or something. Willy had been gone for so long, I didn't think he was coming back. At that point, I didn't see no sense in bringing up things we couldn't change."

Stone let out a pained groan. "I did things the wrong way, Lou, but I was always around, watching from afar. As selfish as I wanted to be, I couldn't. You had a good life, a family, and I just couldn't bring myself to interrupt that, not when I was still on the road and had nothing to offer, and I'd already taken so much from you."

"It was me…I should have tried to find you first, given you a chance to…" Stone shook his head, cutting her off, with a silent exchange that only the two of them understood and ended with locked stares and sweet smiles.

"I'll admit, I was surprised, *still* surprised, but it doesn't change anything I knew growing up and I kind of like how quickly my family is growing now."

"The baby…" Not a question or guess, Gran knew. "When I woke up, it felt like a lot was different, like I had memories of things I didn't remember happening. Strangest thing. Willy and that harmonica, then you walkin' in a few pounds bigger in the middle. I think I knew before though. Something was in the air."

"You and I had a lot of long talks while you were…sleeping. I guess you *did* hear them all."

Lou's brow furrowed, and she nodded slowly while her eyes wandered, looking for answers to something still unclear, "I did. I heard a lot of things I suppose, some things I didn't want to hear, but I can't quite tell what they are…or who…"

"It's okay, Gran. Everything is fine. You're awake…let's just focus on that and you getting well enough to leave this place!"

"Yes!" Ready to bring the solemn mood back to a high, Doc took the conversation in a different direction. "We need to get you well enough to attend a wedding!"

"A wedding? Ohhh, I knew those two would come around. I saw them today, watching each other. Did Blake go all formal like, or did he piss her off first and go heat of the moment?"

"No." They all laughed, wondering if she knew something from those nights when Blake and Jessie were staying at the hospital with her. "Me and Ev. As soon as you're ready, it's happening."

"Yeah, and Stone offered to marry us, he's staying in town. Isn't that great?" Everly said, more anxious to see Gran's reaction to Stone staying in McKenzie than anything else.

Emotion overcame Lou, something that didn't happen often. She turned her attention to Moonshine, petting him slowly. "Well, isn't that a nice sentiment, thank you, Willy. You'll get to be a part of our girl's special day.

"We should probably let you get some sleep, Gran. You're looking a little tired. I can stay tonight."

Stone turned to Everly with a sharp look. "Nonsense, kid. You get home with your beau and start planning that weddin'. I'll stay the night, Lou and I have some catchin' up to do anyway. Just let me grab a coffee from somewhere around here and Nurse Carly told me about that extra pie."

Everly laughed, and linked arms with Stone. "C'mon, I'll

show you the way."

"I'll meet you out there, Ev. I'm just going to make a quick note in the chart for Doctors Sterling and Reynolds in case we miss them on rounds in the morning."

"Sounds good, meet you at the elevator then."

Doc logged into the computer that sat on the mobile cart in Lou's room, searching for her medical chart. He wanted to update it with his observations for the two specialists who were hired specifically for Lou as well as make concessions that typically weren't granted unless you knew someone. They knew a couple someones.

"There, all set. Moonshine gets to stay the night. If anyone asks, he's your therapy dog – I noted it in your chart too – those are allowed in the hospital. Technically, with all of the training Blake did, Moonshine qualifies as one, but no one has to know he isn't certified yet. It also helps that two of McKenzie General's biggest donors belong to you. No one will question McCain Charities or The Tayler Family Trust."

"I suppose not. Those boys, they really came through for me. Now…you get on out of here. I'll be fine until Willy gets back. Go have a wild night with my granddaughter."

Doc choked on the water he was sipping when Lou kicked him out and told him to go have sex. "Sorry?"

"You should be sorry, Mason Charles. Honestly, hurt the baby? You're a doctor for heaven's sake – guess I should be grateful Beck and Dawson saw fit to bring in a couple of doctors that knew better…*hurt the baby*. Most absurd thing I ever heard."

Heat began to rise, turning Doc's face a nice shade of rosy abashed pink. "I uh…*holy shit*…that's…no longer a *problem*."

"Well then…good. Seems that wasn't a dream either…or nightmare, rather."

19

EVERLY CRIED AGAINST THE WALL AS DOC PLUNGED INTO HER, faster and harder until she gripped him tighter, coming down around him, bringing him to his finish as well. Doc carried her to the bed, laying her down gently before collapsing beside her, both glistening in sweat, trying to catch their breaths.

"Wow, that was... That was..." Everly couldn't complete her thought with her words still trapped somewhere between ecstasy and calm.

"Something else...it was something else."

"I don't know what got into you, but I liked it. They say the man gets sympathy pains and gains sympathy weight... maybe you have sympathy hormones. If so, I hope they stick around."

He laughed at her wild assessment while standing in agreement that they were really good together in this way and he hoped it never stopped. "I'm just making up for lost time. I felt like I still owed you a few rounds...playing catch up."

"Is that what this is? Well, then, yes...you still have a ways to go Doc...might take a lifetime."

He rolled over to face her, his hand on her face taking the silliness to serious. "I'd love nothing more, Evie. I will spend my life *catching up* and doing whatever I can to keep you happy."

"I know you will. I love you Mason Charles. More today than even yesterday."

"Wow, it was that good? Note to self, my lady likes it against that wall over there."

She playfully swatted his ass earning her a deep seductive kiss that was blazing hot and stirring a tingle that would require another wall. The moment dampened like a cold shower when Everly's stomach rumbled with a long drawn out growl, causing them to laugh.

"So I guess we won't be finishing this up," Doc joked, moving down her body, resting his head on her belly. "Mommy's hungry kiddo, or is this you reminding us you're in the room?"

She laughed at his teasing, running her hands through his hair, enjoying the cute conversation he was having with the baby. He continued to talk, causing a different stir that made itself known in that moment. Doc's head shot up, eyes full of joy, when he felt the baby.

"He just kicked me! He kicked me in my face! Ev…that was him, right? He just…moved and stuff!"

"Yes…he or *she* just kicked you in your face." She laughed.

Doc rested his forehead on her belly again, and spoke to the baby. "I should ground you for that, but you get a pass because how were you supposed to know that was my face with mom in the way and stuff? And because it was really fucking cute."

"Language," Everly scolded through her giggles.

"I mean...stinking, really stinking cute. That was like a tiny little foot – he's strong!"

"Yes, he or *she* is very strong, just ask my bladder and right kidney."

"Ev, this is so surreal. I mean, we studied this stuff in school, we've both treated plenty of pregnant women and delivered babies, but this...it's like nothing I could have imagined."

"I know. I feel the same way. We made this little person that we get to love forever and I'm growing it...like right now...and it's moving and reacts to different things more and more like he or she has a personality already. Surreal."

Sliding up the length of her body, Doc left a hand on the round of her belly resting his head in the crook of her neck, peppering her with kisses. "I love you, Ev. So damn much it hurts. Thank you for this, for having our baby and for finally loving me back. This...this is everything."

Everly was overwhelmed by the emotions he stirred in her. There was so much to say, to share with him, but the words were more than she could speak. Sometimes the most profound words were those that were never spoken. Those are the words that filled your heart and rested in your soul, bringing you comfort on your best days as much as your worst days. Doc claimed her heart, flooded her soul and was her everything on her best as well as her worst days.

Another growl from her stomach crippled the sweet sentimental moment, ending it in laughter.

"I think the baby wants ice cream." She said.

"Ice cream? We don't have any ice cream."

"But the baby *really* wants ice cream...and the baby loves you a *lot."*

Amusement danced in his expression at her attempts to bribe him. "Fine, I'll go get you some."

"The baby…you're getting it for the baby."

"I stand corrected, I'll get some for the baby. You can return the favor later though." He crawled off the bed, pulling her up with him, holding her in a long kiss and smacked her ass before slipping into some sweats and a t-shirt and leaving for the store.

Walking out the door, he heard her holler from behind, "Hey, maybe some brownies too…and cookies! Yeah, cookies!"

"How about I just get cookie dough ice cream and cookies and cream ice cream…it's all mixed in already."

"No, it's not the same. Not the same at all, don't ever say that again. Oh…and marshmallows…we need those too…the little ones!"

Laughing, he asked, "Anything else…*for the baby?*"

"Nope…just coconut. Don't forget the coconut."

The door closing behind him could be heard from the bedroom and she missed him already. Lying in bed, she thought about their whirlwind romance that started as anything but – and how quickly they reached this point. Thinking back, she loved him all along but ignored it – it wasn't for her – until now. She couldn't wait until he returned home, she was hungry, the ice cream was just a bonus.

WITH TWO BAGS OF GROCERIES ON THE SEAT NEXT TO HIM, Doc laughed at the ridiculousness that was in the bags. He laughed at Everly, adding to her list as he made his way out the door, the grocery clerk laughed at him when he saw the spread on the counter for check out. Doc grabbed all of the sugary fixes his girl had asked for, adding beef sticks, green olives, and pickles for good measure because by the time he got home, ice cream cravings may have transitioned to something salty.

God he loved her, and he'd buy any number of ridiculous food combinations for her. There isn't much he wouldn't do for her. She challenged him, humored him, and loved him. That was everything he wanted and needed.

Pulling on to their street, he noticed the light on at Lou's next door. He parked in their driveway, but walked next door, nearly a whole city block between the homes, and tried the door. Everly must've gone next door for one reason or another, perhaps to check on the house, and decide what was needed for Lou's return.

When he tried the door, it was locked, not unusual since she was by herself, it was dusk and things had been a bit off in their world. He knocked, waiting for her to answer so he could help her with whatever she was doing and get her back home and in bed…ice cream optional.

When she didn't answer, an odd sense of foreboding overcame him and his knock became urgent and he yelled her name. She still didn't answer and he started with the doorbell too. Knocking and yelling, he was becoming desperate when he heard her call his name from her front porch.

"What's wrong, Mason? What are you doing over there?"

Relieved at the sight of her, he rushed across the adjoined lawn and pulled her into his arms, holding her tight.

"What's going on, Doc…why are you so wound up?"

"I saw the lights on when I pulled in, and when you didn't answer the door, I assumed something was wrong."

"I've been here the whole time. I took a quick shower and changed is all. Nobody has been next door for weeks – since Blake came for Moonshine."

"Then why are the lights on? Grab your key, the door's locked."

She quickly grabbed the keys from the entry table dish that sat right inside the door and started for Gran's.

"Oh, no...you stay here." Doc said, taking the keys from her hand.

"I'm not staying here, what if someone was in there, or *is* in there?"

"Exactly...what if someone is in there...you are staying here."

"Doc...why do you insist on learning things the hard way. I'm going with you, now let's go."

Picking his battles, he tucked her behind him and they walked back over to Lou's. Oddly, the lights were all off when they returned and that taste of dread returned, settling in his gut. The two looked at each other before he keyed the lock and slowly turned the knob.

"Wait here," he whispered, "let me check it out first."

She nodded as he wandered in, waiting impatiently for him to return.

"Ev, get the light switch," he said, and she flicked the switch on between the entry door and where she found Doc, Everly rushed to his side to see what the source of his vexing tone was. Nothing could have prepared her for what she was about to see and never be able to unsee. If there was ever a worry that something was awry or that someone was up to anything but good, that notion was now confirmed.

"Flowers," she said, scanning the space, "there's so many, it's like..."

"Like a shrine."

"Who would do this? Stone, maybe?" Everly questioned knowing Stone would be a stretch.

"No, he'd have no reason. Even if he did bring...all of these...why would he duck out? Someone was here, Ev. The lights were on. Call Blake, baby."

* * *

Blake thoroughly searched the house, more than once, taking in everything he could while Logan was on the outside looking for traces of pretty much anything that could lend them a clue. There was nothing…just flowers. They found themselves in the same position they were previously at the hospital…flowers aren't threatening.

"What do you think, Blake? Any ideas?" Doc asked.

"No. Nothing. It's just flowers. I bet half the town has a key to this place from over the years, that's just how McKenzie is. You go out of town and you have dozens of neighbors checking on the place."

"So you don't think it was someone breaking in? I mean, the lights were on, then off…there was clearly someone here, but they must've slipped out the back," Everly defended.

"I agree someone was here…flowers." Gesturing to the gobs of bouquets, Blake wasn't trying to be an ass, but was trying to deflect a bit so she and Doc wouldn't worry. "Look. Get the locks changed tomorrow. Logan has been doing drive-bys since the last incident, I'll just have him park here tonight."

A deep sigh of disappointment escaped Doc; he didn't feel any better now than before, even if Logan was now assigned to his driveway, but it was what it was and there wasn't a damn thing he could do about it but keep his girl close. He and Everly said their goodbyes and excused themselves back to their home to settle in for the night.

Blake did one last walk through, checking all of the doors and windows as he went. He stood in the doorway, ready to leave, taking one last glance over his shoulder before standing on the front step and scanning the area around them. Someone had definitely been there, many times.

There were light dusty dirt tracks, similar to those he saw at the hospital, and he suspected this had less and less to do with Lou, and more about a vantage point to watch someone else. Doc or Everly, he wondered. He couldn't ignore that smell…it was there as boldly as it had been at the hospital and at Everly's before.

Those oh so telling hairs at the back of his neck began to rise as they tended to do when there was menace in the air. He had a stalker in McKenzie Ridge and he would find out who it was, no matter the cost.

20

Days passed with little to no interruption from anyone or anything out of the norm, even the flowers had stopped. Everyone had gathered at Lou's house to prepare it for her homecoming. She was doing well, and even beginning to get around, but would need assistance for a while and used a walker to slowly move about, hence the ramp that was being built to get her up the steps and in the front door.

Obvious tension between Carigan and BJ left a curious, yet amused, vibe in the air as everyone watched Carigan go out of her way to get in BJ's way, just to ignore him. There were several displays of *assets* flashed when she did exaggerated bends or reaches in front of him. It was very much a *see what you're missing* display of teasing.

"What's going on with you and Baker? Hands in the wrong cookie jar already?" Tact wasn't Jessie's strong point, it was actually foreign to her, but she got right to business and the rest of the ladies in the kitchen appreciated her crass demeanor.

"What? No! I mean, not yet anyway." Her initial shock at

the question was quickly followed by discouragement. "He's leaving."

Sounds of sympathy trailed at the idea of Carigan being left, yet again, by the man she thought she was destined to be with.

"Leaving? But he just got here. What about the Bakery and taking over for his dad?" Everly asked.

"Don't know, he won't talk about it. All I know is Jed rejected all of the changes BJ wanted to implement and said the bakery stays the same or he'll find someone else to run it. Then I heard BJ on the phone with Veronica."

"Veronica? Who the hell is Veronica? Do we hate her?" Jessie asked.

"She is his business partner in San Francisco. I couldn't hear all of their conversation, but I heard him say, *I'll see you soon* and that was it. Then he told me he had business to tend to and didn't know when he'd be back."

"Oh, Cari…I agree those are pretty pointed things to say, but maybe there's a good reason for all of it," Everly defended.

"Of course there's a good reason. He didn't get what he wanted so he's going home…to his whore."

"So she's a whore? You met her?" Jessie laughed.

"No, but she's beautiful, smart, and loaded…she's a whore. I might have looked her up online."

Jessie tossed her head back in laughter before high fiving Carigan. "I have taught you well. We definitely hate her then. You should go over there and start flirting with Blake's new shadow…really teach Bart Baker a lesson."

"BJ, his name is BJ," Carigan defended, a sure sign that her anger hadn't muddled her protective nature where he was concerned and that she did still love him. "Besides, Logan is a few years younger than us, isn't he? He can't be more than early twenties?"

"Who cares. It's not like you're planning to bump uglies with him...or maybe you are and to that I say, have at it. Just make Bart second guess what he's leaving."

"No...I couldn't. It's just not...*me*. Besides, my brothers would have a fit, I'm sure they are in part responsible for him leaving anyway. I should have known better. I shouldn't have opened my heart back up to him. People leave on the drop of a dime...relationships, the forever kind, are rare. Guess my brothers are getting their way, he's leaving."

Carigan's words settled on Everly like a weighted blanket, consuming her every fear that she thought had been put behind her. Hearing how Carigan's fairy tale fling was so quickly coming to a halt was a sharp reminder that forever isn't promised. In most cases, it's a choice, and just like BJ was choosing a new tomorrow that didn't include Carigan or their plans, Doc could do the same.

Everly knew too well how quickly life could pull the rug out from under you and it was only a matter of time before it happened again. Too many good things had happened to her to cling to soppy dreams of forever. The only thing she was guaranteed was a baby...the daddy was only a bonus for as long as he wanted to be.

Searching the yard, she laid eyes on Doc as he interacted with the guys. She wondered what they were talking about. It seemed serious with a few supportive slaps to the shoulder and what looked like a stern talking to by Carigans brothers. Maybe Carigan was right, he was leaving and feeling the O'Reilly wrath before he went.

Doc seemed to be engrossed in deep thoughts of his own – was he rethinking his commitments in McKenzie too? Why not? He didn't have roots here, only a job and Everly while he was here. He didn't have to stay here to be a dad – he was more of a city boy anyway.

Everly's past and fears were haunting her to the nth degree and it was overwhelming her. Carigan's problems weren't her problems, yet she was owning them. Still not used to being happy and opening her heart, straying from the path and ready to bolt in the name of saving her heart.

She looked at the ladies, huddled around Carigan and said, "Forevers are a gamble, never a promise."

She walked inside Gran's house, alone…she needed to collect her thoughts and decide where she stood on the *forever*.

* * *

"What did you do to Squirt?" Wylie asked BJ with a puffed out chest and questioning eyes, referring to his kid sister.

"I didn't do anything! I don't know what's up with her. She just started acting…*weird*."

"Weird?"

"Yeah. She just started acting strange. She's snappy, and sarcastic, when she actually talks to me. She keeps saying *have fun in San Francisco* and *you must really miss Veronica, are you telling her what you did while you were here*? What the hell is all that about?"

Doc was watching Everly from afar, noting her body language as a heated Carigan ranted over what was probably the very thing BJ was discussing. "Who is Veronica and why would you miss her?"

"Roni is my business partner, we own the restaurant

together. I'm heading back to San Fran to finalize the paper-work…she's buying me out. Dad wouldn't let me implement the changes I wanted to at the bakery, so I'm opening up a spot next door. Best of both worlds, I can have my bistro while easily overseeing the bakery operations for dad while I'm at it."

Scratching his chin, Doc figured something had to have been lost in translation. "Does she know all of this? It sounds like she is missing a part of the story, man."

"She *is*! A really *big* part of it! I keep trying to tell her why I'm going to San Fran and that it's a quick trip so I can live here permanently, but she won't listen. She either walks away or just cuts me off. I swear I'm not doing anything wrong and she acts like I just cheated on her with a nun or something."

As silence fell over the men while they pondered BJ's situation, the brothers could hear Carigan make mention of their happiness over BJ's leaving and ultimately her heartbreak. Sure the guys had given them a hard time. They're her big brothers, it's their duty, but not one of them wanted it to end in heartbreak for their sister. Not because of them.

"BJ, you need to tell her…tell her everything," Luke offered.

"Yeah!" Liam chimed, "and say you're sorry."

"But I didn't do anything to be sorry for…"

Dace rolled his eyes at BJ's asinine remark. "So what? Apologize anyway, chicks like that shit. Besides, you're going to do something to piss her off for real someday so call it practice."

"But she won't listen, I've tried. And apologizing seems ridiculous, like I'm owning up to something I didn't do."

Liam rolled his eyes and pointed at BJ while addressing the other guys, "Is this guy for real? What isn't he under-

standing? Make her listen, man. Apologize, just apologize…
it's like taking one for the team or something. Women eat that
shit up…it works."

"Yeah, they're right," Dawson interrupted, getting nods
from the other two married men to his side. "Always apologize, and grovel a little. Let her think she has the upper hand.
Then she'll let you talk and when she realizes it's all a big
misunderstanding, you'll be out of the dog house and *she'll*
be apologizing for being so stubborn. Well…maybe. I'm kind
of making up that last part."

"Apologize. Grovel…make her listen," BJ repeated.

"Not to us, numb nuts, to her…go! Do it now, while all of
her friends are watching. That's worth bonus points!" Luke
awkwardly shoved BJ in the direction of the women then
stood back and watched to see if their bullshit pep talk would
actually work.

Everly walked back out to see BJ approaching the group
of women who had suddenly gone silent. Carigan stood with
halfcocked hips, crossed arms, and a fiery *I dare you to piss
me off* attitude.

"Uh, look, Carigan…"

"What? What do you have to say? Goodbye? Is that what
you…."

"Christ, will you shut up for just a minute?" Eyes wide,
he turned back to the guys, surprised by his own actions.
Nods of encouragement gave him a cocky sense of encouragement that almost got him in trouble.

Gasps from the women and squinted glares ripped that
confidence away as fast as it had come. They were intimidating on their own, damn scary as a group. A whisper from
behind him, *apologize,* had him talking again.

"Look. You're right, I'm leaving. I'm going back to San

Francisco." More gasps from the hotheaded hens in front of
him made his stomach flop. "And…I'm not sorry for it."

The more the ladies gasped and sighed, the more fire he
put into his words. Carigan's anger had plummeted to sadness
and it tore him up.

"I'm not sorry because I'll be back…soon. To stay for
good. I'm being bought out by Veronica and I need to sign the
papers."

"You're selling? But that's your dream…you can't." If
ever an example of why women were confusing to men were
needed, this would be the conversation that cemented it all.
Her anger over him leaving was now concern for him giving
up his dream to stay. She didn't want him to leave, begrudged
him for it even, but didn't want him to stay and let his
dream go?

He laughed at the twist of emotions she was firing at him.
"Yes, I can…and I am. I'm opening a new restaurant here,
right next door to the bakery."

"But shops on Main Street never come open, how…"

"The art gallery next door is closing, they're retiring. It's
mine if I want it."

Just as he was pulling her in for a make-up kiss, she put
her arms between them and pushed him away. "But I heard
you. I heard you tell *Veronica*," Veronica was said in a sing
song voice that was as annoying as the person herself, "you
couldn't wait to see her."

"That's because I can't. I can't wait to tell her *goodbye*.
I'm coming home, Cari. This…this is home, you're home."

"Oh, Christ, that's a good one, Baker. Give it up
O'Reilly. He fucking loves you, wants to marry you, have
little red headed babies with you…just go with him to San
Francisco if you're worried about it and take a side trip to
Reno to get hitched on your way back. Problem solved."

Leave it to Jessie to call it as she saw it and sum up a dragged out conversation that's dancing in circles to a quick conclusion.

"Come with me. Jessie's right, come with me."

"Of course, I'm right, captain obvious." Jessie rolled her eyes and tossed her hand in the air annoyed by his moment of ignorance.

"If you don't come with me, I'm just going to marry you as soon as I get back..."

"So what, I don't have a say in this?" Carigan mused.

"Say in what? You don't want to get married? Too bad... make a choice. Come with me or we do this in a few weeks."

"Of all the things to go all alpha macho on..." she teased. "When do we leave?"

"End of the week!" BJ picked Carigan up and spun her around while locked in a deep smoldering kiss. "Let's go home and...*pack.*"

Tossing her over his shoulder, BJ hauled Carigan to his truck, despite all of the protests from her brothers about waiting to get married, their parents being gone still, they were too young...and the list went on.

Blake stood at the edge of the lawn and watched them drive off while the rest of the gang began to pack things up for the day.

Jessie joined him. "What has you over here brooding alone? You look kind of creepy, staring off like that."

"Nothing. Just thinking. Creepy? Really?"

"Yeah, well, I know you better than you know you and something is wrong. You're worried."

"No, I never worry. I'm just...concerned."

"Same thing, genius. If it makes you feel any better, I feel it too. Like someone has been watching us all afternoon."

"See anyone? Anything out of sorts?"

"No, nothing at all. That's the sketchy part. Blake, what aren't you telling me?"

"I don't know. I honestly don't know."

They both looked up as the cold wet snowflakes began to fall...

"Storm is coming..." Jessie said.

"That it is..."

21

A STORM IT WAS INDEED. OVERNIGHT, ENOUGH SNOW HAD fallen to encourage tourists at the higher elevations to take chances in the fresh powder that locals knew better than to do. It was also a call sign of sorts to the city, to come and invade the mountains and make your snow angels. An accident resulted, in both cases, causing Doc to be called in to assist with multi-patient traumas.

An off-trail skier and a couple of vehicle related injuries kept him from joining Everly for her doctor's appointment in Arrow Springs, the next town over. Rather than cancel and wait for Doc, she went because this was the appointment where they confirmed the baby's gender. Working in a hospital, there would be plenty of opportunities for Doc to *take a peek* with an ultrasound machine at a later time. This also gave Everly a chance to put together a surprise baby reveal gift for Doc.

The snow was coming down, but locals were managing and she would be home before the big stuff really hit hard. And she was glad she went. Her appointment went really well, and she was overjoyed with the news her doctor had given her. With time to spare, before the weather turned for the worse in their area, she stopped and did a little shopping.

Sure, she could do that at home, in McKenzie. But small town gossip would get to Doc, before she could, and spoil her surprise. She spent time, picking out items that would tell Doc the story of her day, and that of their future. There were a few gender specific onesies, balloons in the right color, and a cute gender themed bassinet to put everything in to start with. A few other props were picked up to seal the deal and she was on her way back to McKenzie, a short straight shot up the highway.

Doc would be waiting for her at the hospital, they were to meet in Gran's room so they could share the news. Everly had other ideas though. She wanted to share this with Doc, privately, first.

They would never have this moment again, and as much as she loved her family of friends and Gran, this needed to be their moment first. Her plan was to stop at home and set up her surprise, then text Doc from the hospital parking lot to come down. They could go back up to the hospital later in the evening to share with Gran, and inevitably Stone, weather permitting.

Something had changed in her today. The old fears that had resurfaced and festered after Carigan's misguided fit had dissolved and no longer plagued her. Perhaps it was seeing the baby that made it all real for her and cemented the love that had been brewing for weeks.

She thought back to the night Doc told her he wanted a lot of babies with her and she giggled. Truth was, she wanted the same thing. If this man and this baby could stir the amount of love she had flowing through her, she knew there was room for more...a lifetime of more.

How they came about wasn't the ideal plan. Not so secret

relationship, surprise baby, and all that came with it was anything but a fairy tale leading in to a happily ever after, but it was their story and she wouldn't have it any other way. She was ready to be a mom and wife, two things she never imagined being a part of the checklist of life, but here she was, building a family.

Stirred from her thoughts by little kicks in her belly, she placed a hand over where the baby was kicking and began to speak to their little one.

"I know you're there." she giggled, "I can't wait to show daddy your first pictures and tell him your news. I think he will love our surprises we picked out for him. I bet he calls everyone tonight to tell them about you, he's going to be so excited. It's going to be a special night, little bug. You might want to cover your ears though, I don't want you scarred for life when daddy shows mommy how much he loves her. Scratch that, I can't believe I just said that to you…so inappropriate. Wow…so many changes are coming."

The snow was coming down harder, requiring her to slow her pace and keep her focus on the road. They may reach near white out conditions by the time she got home if the snow didn't let up. Pulling her head from her whimsy state, she made a mental note to save all of the warm fuzzies for when she got home. The snow was no joke and required all of her attention.

With each kick, her heart swelled as an emotional wave washed over her, looking down for a brief moment, she spoke directly to the baby one last time before shifting her concentration, "I already love you so, so much…"

When she looked up to watch the road, only a second later, she let out a blood curdling scream.

* * *

IT WAS GETTING LATE AND DOC BEGAN TO WORRY. EVEN WITH the heavy snow, she knew how to drive in it and she should have been back to McKenzie by now. She hadn't called, and wasn't answering her cellphone. Each call was going straight to voicemail now.

Since he was working, they planned to meet at the hospital because she was his ride. After calling everyone he could think of, and turning up nothing, Stone offered to give him a ride to their place to see if she was there and the phones were just out. The snow was just bad enough that it was possible she couldn't get any further into town and phones might be impacted.

Blake was the first person he called, then the last when he hadn't found Everly. Blake had checked all of the reports and there weren't any accidents or incidents that could have explained her disappearance. So he told Doc he would meet him at their house and they would figure out their next move from there. It wasn't like Everly to just fall off the grid without telling anyone, and with the weather they were having, and being pregnant, it was even less likely. Being home and unable to make calls, compliments of bad weather, was more likely. Or so they hoped.

When Stone and Doc pulled up, Blake was already there and they didn't find what they had hoped. It was obvious the minute the house came into view and her car was nowhere to be seen. Doc's stomach sank, fear found its way in, and it swarmed in a downward spiral that left him anxious and full of worry.

"Her car's not here, I'm guessing she isn't," Doc said, pointing out the obvious, but conversation kept his mind occupied and far from the doom and gloom it was leaning toward.

"I have Logan out checking the roads on every route to

and from everyone's houses that she may have stopped at. So far, he has cleared the area around Dawson and Sam's. He's searching the ridge by Morgan and Beck's, then he'll hit the other side out by the rest of the gang. With this weather, she may have pulled over and just can't call out. We'll find her."

Blake's cool and collected demeanor brought a sense of calm to Doc. If he wasn't worried yet, Doc would reserve worry for later, when and if Blake was. Confidence was an outward trait that Blake wore, and his instincts ran deep – it all went a long way with Doc right now. If anyone could resolve this and find Everly quickly and safe, it was Blake.

Doc let them in the house, Stone silently accompanying them from behind. He didn't say so, but Stone was worried. It was etched in his face as was the lifetime of regrets he was likely mulling over. Though short, the relationship between Everly and her grandfather was growing stronger each day and they were quite fond of one another – truly kindred spirits.

A waft of something Doc couldn't quite identify met them at the door, dancing on their senses. It was earthy with a hint of pine, and perhaps a bit of soft citrus and sandalwood. Nothing offensive, just a fresh, clean scent with a warm vanilla under note that was pleasant and oddly familiar.

"That smell. It's stronger now," Blake chimed, pushing past Doc in search of its source. And he found it.

Just inside the door, past the foyer, the living room came into view, knocking the wind from Doc as his emotions resurfaced. There were flowers on every surface throughout the space and into the adjacent dining room. With them were various candles in every shape and size. Some were fresh, some previously lit…the source of the smell.

"Evie loves those candles. I didn't know she had so many though. What is this? Why the flowers?"

"Maybe she was here. Did you guys have any big plans tonight? Is this...*romantic* or something?" Blake's question was well thought out, but didn't fit. Something was wrong, very wrong, and it didn't take his deep rooted intuition and experience to feel the menace in the air.

"Well, maybe she planned a surprise for me? She knows what the baby's gender is...maybe she was planning dinner or something? But where is she now?" Doc was at a loss and that heavy feeling in his stomach was lurching again. Everly wasn't the overly romantic type – sweet and endearing, yes, but flowers and candles galore? Not likely, it was too whimsy and frilly for her.

"Maybe she ran to town, needed to stop at the store? Could have stopped here to set this up before heading to the hospital to pick you up? One of us would have seen her on the roadside on our way here, you from the hospital and me from the House. I'll expand the search to include Main Street in case she went out that way for something in town."

"Those there are the wild flowers that kept showin' up in Lou's room. Why would Everly bring those in here when they marked something so questionable before? I don't know about this, boys..." Stone was right. Why would she? Those flowers marked several questionable moments that brought anything but joy, so why would she use them to celebrate a milestone?

"Fuck..." Between the familiar smell that he had been picking up everywhere, the flowers, and Everly missing in a snow storm, Blake knew he needed to react, and quickly. He felt something was coming, that there was a threat of some kind headed their way, but he hoped he would have more to go on and either intercept whatever it was or at least be better prepared for it. He had neither on his side.

Grabbing his cellphone from a clip on his belt, Blake

made a call. Doc and Stone were drawn to his dark edgy presence, their unfiltered anxieties feeding off of it. Clinging to every word, a living nightmare evolved when Blake's phone call laid out the cards for them.

"Dec...it's me. Get the boys together and meet me at Everly's...we have a problem."

22

It wasn't long before Declan arrived with all four brothers with equipment in tow and oddly dressed similar in dark fatigues like they were mission bound. Everyone knew Everly was unaccounted for, and had been on standby until they heard otherwise, so one quick call from Blake after hanging up with Declan, and the whole gang had arrived.

With everyone together, they went over what they knew once more. Nothing changed, nobody had heard from or seen Everly, and each had the same last conversation – she was excited to find out what the baby's gender was. Not a single clue outside of the fact that she was traveling one town over to Arrow Springs, a short twenty minute drive on a good day, perhaps longer given the weather. By this point, she was hours late, several hours.

"I just don't understand," Doc pleaded, worry evident, but disappointment somehow seeping in. "Everything was fine when she left this morning. She seemed fine. Do you think this is cold feet?"

"I suppose it's possible, but unlikely. Surely you would have noticed a change in her, something to clue you in," Dec offered, not entirely convinced this wasn't a voluntary disappearance yet.

Doc shook his head, rubbing his hand against the back of his neck as he paced back and forth, trying to come up with something, anything. "Nothing seemed off, but we also haven't found her or even her car. It's like she vanished."

"Before we got here, we did some quick preliminary investigating and know she made it to her appointment, left, and that her credit card was used at three different stores shortly after. That's when she falls off the grid. She had to have headed home after that...or somewhere anyway." Liam was the head of IT security in the brothers' company. He was a highly skilled tech pro, a hacker. "There aren't any cameras on the highway between McKenzie and Arrow Springs so that was a bust and we confirmed there were no accident reports or calls for a tow truck, assuming she broke down."

"Yeah, the weather is pretty rough, there isn't a lot of traffic on that old highway on a good day, today it would be next to nothing, I'm sure. Who knows when the last highway patrol passed through there."

"She left. She left me...us." Doc hung his head letting all of the unlikely negative ideas consume him and take over. "Did you guys see her when BJ and Carigan were having their...*issue*. Something spooked her. I saw it. She seemed fine after, but..."

"Son, that's a real reach, don't you think?" Stone scolded. "I know I'm new at this and still have a lot of learnin' to do, but I do know that girl doesn't waver. If she had it in her to leave, she'd 'ave done it right then and there. No games, no hesitation, and no façade. That girl has it real bad for you. Her life before you may poke and prod here and there, but I think she'd be hard for you to get rid of at this point."

"I suppose you're right. Lou will be home in a few days,

and we're celebrating the two engagements that day. She's too excited for both. I don't know...I just can't stand not knowing if she's okay and not being able to help her if she isn't."

Jessie put a rare comforting arm on Doc's shoulder and pulled him into her embrace, "She loves you, and that baby, Doc. You're everything to her and she's probably just as worried about you right now. We're going to find her."

All eyes were on Jessie in her moment of tenderness. They were either shocked expressions, or warm adoring ones, neither washed over her well. "What the hell are you all looking at, we have shit to do. What's next, Blake?"

And she was back.

Liam had excused himself outside, to grab something from the truck that he had left behind, and was now sitting in the middle of Everly's living room, setting up the device. It was something of a bulky laptop with a few extra attachments and an extra screen. He went to work, clearly in his element, fully immersed in whatever he was doing. He was definitely the computer nerd his brothers teased him of being.

"Okay, I am ready to go," he said, pecking away at the keys. "Searching signals now...should have her car gps and cellphone in a minute."

Blake chuckled in surprise. "Do you have, oh...say...a *warrant* for that O'Reilly? You know that's illegal and I'm obligated to intervene."

Jessie, of all people, put an arm around Blake and nudged him to follow her, even using his nickname. "Come look at the snow with me, Coop. I love this big window, such a beautiful view of the ridge."

"Jessie..." It was obvious what she was doing to help the cause, what he didn't know wouldn't hurt him and if he didn't see it, he wouldn't have to arrest anyone.

"Can you just stop being a damn GI Joe turbo Cop for a minute and look at the pretty fucking snow with me? Christ, you're a pain in the ass."

Subtle laughter could be heard over the ricochet sound of Liam's fingers padding over the keyboard in front of him at such a fast paced, the sound was only recognizable because they knew what he was doing. Liam enjoyed his work, the challenge was appealing and this task was no different. He was on a mission, one he intended to complete.

"Almost there." he announced, "Locking in…got her phone…and…boom! Got her car."

He pounded away at the keyboard before turning the larger computer screen around, facing the group, revealing information that looked foreign to most of them. He stood, leaning over the screen and pointed out what he found, giving an explanation.

"Okay, these are the coordinates for her car, past coordinates show that she did indeed go to Arrow Springs, looks like she made a few stops while there. It seems to be sitting on highway 91 now, doesn't appear to be moving. I have a cellphone ping on *Switch 59, Cell Tower 154, Sector Alpha*. That particular tower is off of highway 91, between McKenzie and Arrow Springs about a half mile from the coordinates that correspond with her car."

"Um, so, what does all of that mean?" Doc was hopeful this was good news and clinged to that notion until told otherwise.

"It means…I found her. Her car anyway and since her phone is obviously nearby, I have to assume she is still in the area too."

"What's near there, Liam?" Doc questioned, trying to visualize the area she was in and if there was any nearby help.

"Nothing, nothing at all. It's all road and trees through there."

"Good work Liam." Blake patted him on the back, a pleased look on his face and sense of hope in his voice. "Let's plug in the coordinates and get out there then. Sounds like she broke down."

"Let's bring the team…be prepared for anything…just in case. It's good *practice,*" Liam interrupted.

"You got it. Load up guys," Blake instructed.

As the rest of the group made their way outside, filing into the vehicles, Liam held Blake back for a quick conversation in private.

"Hey man, I traced her GPS and the tower hits like I said. I can see where she's been." The solemn vibrato to Liam's voice put Blake on alert.

"Right, you said that already. What's the problem?"

Liam hesitated for a moment, letting the breath he had been holding slowly leave him. "She hasn't moved. She's been sitting there – for a while. You can't tell me there hasn't been a single vehicle, emergency or otherwise, that's passed by her in that time. This isn't the city, someone would have stopped and helped somehow. I checked all of the towers, none of them are down, we would have heard from her by now. She's in trouble, man."

"Shit!" Blake stormed toward the door, Liam close behind. "Boys, get your gear, we're doing this for real."

An overwhelming sense of dread took over, leaving Doc dizzy with fear as he clung to the side of the truck. Something was wrong, really wrong. He couldn't let his mind wander too far because it lead to the shit nightmares were made of. He wouldn't let himself go there or worry until he had something to worry about, which was damn hard.

Stone placed a hand on Doc's shoulder. "We'll find her son, we'll find her."

Doc dropped his head and did something he didn't do nearly enough – he prayed, "Dear God let them be okay…"

* * *

IN A SMALL CARAVAN OF VEHICLES, THE GANG, NOW A potential rescue team, made their way down the snow covered highway, watching the ditches and old service roads for any sign of Everly so they wouldn't have to double back, should she not be where Liam's hacking had placed her. Morgan and Beck had called ahead to Sugar Spring Stables, asking for the horse trailer to be loaded so it was ready when they got there. If this was a real rescue, they would likely need the beasts to get into places made difficult by terrain and weather. Worst case scenario, it was good practice for a real emergency, like Liam and Blake had mentioned before.

Headlights on and wipers running intermittently, the snow came down harder as time went on, making it more difficult to see evidence that any vehicle had been out there in recent hours. They trudged on, creeping up on the location they hoped to find Everly and her car. When it finally came into view, its headlights still on and wipers going, that last half of a mile felt like the longest.

Not concerned with traffic or rules, they parked right alongside Everly's car in the middle of the road, barely coming to a stop when they rushed from the vehicles. Several ran directly to the vehicle, while some began searching the area around it because it was obvious on their approach that she wasn't in the car. It was empty.

Blake shouted from the vehicle, only his head inside so he wouldn't damage the crime scene, or evidence, should this be what they were dealing with. "I got her purse here, phone on the seat, keys in the ignition."

He reached through the steering wheel and turned the key, starting the vehicle, "It's running, almost a full tank of gas, and no emergency sensors lit up on the dash. Car seems to be fine. Inside is clean."

Sighs of relief surrounded the group when they heard what they had been waiting for. *Inside is clean* was code for *no blood* or signs of menace.

"I got four good tires, no body damage to the exterior," Wylie added, rounding the vehicle after checking underneath. "Also clean."

They were two for two, no evidence of foul play, *yet,* but where was Everly? Doc stood back and let the team do what they were trained to do, hard as that was. They might have felt better about the lack of evidence suggesting malice, but to him, it just meant they were that much further from finding her. He didn't want something sinister to be evident, but he'd do just about anything for a simple clue. Anything that could lead them to her.

"I got prints over here!" Luke yelled from just beyond the vehicle, off the road in what was typically a grassy area that lead to the forest beyond, now covered by snow. "Tracks are headed into the woods. These look too big to be Ev though."

"I have foot prints down here too…coming from the woods." Dace was squatting by the tracks he found, scratching his chin. "I agree, these are as big as my feet, looks like boots."

"Why would there be tracks headed into the woods and back out?" Doc questioned.

"Pregnant, maybe she had to squat behind a tree," Jessie reasoned. "You know…pee."

"No, I can't see her going all the way out to the woods for

that in the snow – just open the two side doors and use the side of the road. She's outdoorsy, she would have thought of something more resourceful then hiking into the woods. Besides, she would be back at the car." Blake had a good point, Everly was resourceful, did well in tough conditions. It's what made her good at Search and Rescue and why she was great on the Life Flight Chopper.

Declan observed the tracks from one brother down to the other and noticed something out of place. Something suggesting the foul play that was looming and they'd all hoped to avoid. He pulled off his black leather glove and placed his hand inside the first set of tracks that were just behind the vehicle, then did the same at the other set.

"The terrain between the two sets is consistent and though the snow has been coming down, it's still easy to see that one set is deeper than the other."

"So two people were out here?" Doc asked. "Someone helped her?"

Declan looked down with his hands on his hips, his timbre sharp and angry, "*Fuck*. No, no one helped her. The tracks match, same foot, same boots. It's the depth. The tracks going back into the woods are deeper than the other set, quite a bit deeper."

Jessie shook her head, trying to wrap it around what Declan was suggesting. "I don't get it, so there *is* two people? What does that mean? Why was one deeper and why is that significant. Try to remember we aren't all GI Joe special forces ninja types like you guys."

"It means," Blake took over, "that whoever walked out of those woods, walked back in quite a bit heavier. They were carrying something."

"Or someone…Everly," Doc deadpanned. "They were carrying Evie."

A slow nod came from Declan along with the words that would haunt this group for who knows how long, "It looks that way. I'm sorry man. Let's mobilize the team, and call it in. We have a full Search and Rescue on our hands and we don't know what kind of threat we are dealing with. We need to get into the woods and follow the clues. Let's get those horses ready, we're going to need them."

"We're down a helo," Blake added, referring to helicopter assistance overhead. "Too many accidents earlier."

Beck stepped forward, pulling on his gloves and pulling on a heavier waterproof jacket that matched his bottom half. "Blake, I can have a chopper here in minutes. It's out at my ranch in Arrow Springs. It's fast, and I might have had it equipped with…state of the art…stuff."

"What kind of *stuff*, McCain?"

"When I joined up on the Search Team, I added things… like things that could help if ever needed."

"Like?" Blake was getting frustrated with Beck's elusiveness due to embarrassment, but reality is, his helicopter hobby was likely going to help them find Everly.

"Like a hoist, net stretcher, various harnesses, ladders, all the first aid available for sale…and one of those infrared do-dads that can find people hiding or otherwise. It's the full deal."

"Get it here," Blake said, slapping Beck's shoulder, before walking off and hollering over his shoulder, "You did good, McCain, that *do-dad* might just come in handy."

Doc's world had just tipped upside down and spun out of control as the earth quaked beneath his feet and terror knocked the wind from his lungs. Everly was not just missing, she was abducted, and in danger to the point that infrared and helicopters were necessary. His whole life danced in limbo, flashing before his eyes as thoughts of where Everly could be, who could have her, and what they were doing to her, haunted him. He turned to her vehicle behind him where Wylie had been emptying its contents on the hood of the car, looking for hints of any kind.

Balloons were floating just above a series of items that were laying there, baby items. The closer he got, the more his heart sunk as each item registered. She *had* been planning to surprise him. There was a tiny onesie that said *My dad rocks* and one that looked like a batman suit – he had a band and geeked out over superheroes especially Batman. There was a little ball and blue mitt next to a plastic doctor kit – both things *he* loved in his life and would likely enjoy sharing with their child. Her gifts to him told the story.

It was undeniable…he had been right all along, "It's a boy – I'm having a son."

Tears welled up and contradicting emotions consumed him. How could he feel such a sense of pride and joy while being scared out of his mind.

"We're going to find her, Doc…" Blake's nearly whispered words were appreciated and gave him hope, but they did little to lift any weight or worry that took residence in his broken heart.

23

STANDING AT THE BACK OF EACH TRUCK, THE TEAM PREPARED for their search and ultimate rescue, putting on and preparing tactical gear such as bullet proof vests, helmets, and of course weapons. Not knowing what they were walking into, they had to be prepared for anything. It was a form of organized chaos that lead to a plan.

Moving out in the direction the tracks took them, the team disappeared into the woods. Some on foot to track the trail of evidence left, and some on horses to look ahead and get a better view of what they were facing, the team spread out in a line, briskly but carefully trudging through the snow covered brush and trees. The helicopter had arrived just before they moved out, taking Dawson and Carigan with it as well as Liam to run the search equipment. They hovered above, circling the team guiding them from the air as much as the team guided from the ground.

Quick progress lead them to an old forest service road, something quite common in those woods, but that's where the trail ended. No more tracks, a snow covered road, and the silence of snow falling in a spooked forest.

"What the hell?" Luke bellowed, "Where did they go?"

"Good question, the snow couldn't have covered their tracks or it would have covered all of them. It's as if they just vanished at this point." Wylie pointed out the obvious, but they were all thinking it.

"They didn't *vanish*," Declan reasoned, "they drove."

Looking between Declan and the blank canvas of a road before him, Doc was confused, "Uh, if foot prints can't disappear from snow, how do tire tracks...I don't see any evidence of a vehicle."

Blake rolled his head in frustration and anger, letting out a few expletives under his breath, "That's because they covered their fucking tracks. Shit!"

"Wait, how the hell does that work if they're *in* a vehicle, driving? Even a small vehicle, or snowmobile would leave traces at least as deep as those of their feet...I mean that's just obvious." Jessie had a good point, the obvious answer, however, wasn't what they were looking for. Not now, not with this piece of the puzzle. The answer was intended to be anything but simple or obvious.

"They had a vehicle waiting, probably right here." Blake waved his arm from left to right angled down at the ground in front of them. "Then, dragged the snow behind them as they left."

"If you look closely, you see an inconsistent pattern in the snow – it's too smooth through here," Declan took over, sharing his observations so the team would know what to look for, the subtleties, as they forged ahead. "And there are two narrow lines with quite a distance between them. We were looking for tire tracks, but those were covered by whatever they are dragging. It's probably the width of the vehicle and just heavy enough to camouflage the tire tracks without leaving too much of a trace, as we see here."

Jessie reiterated what Blake said, trying to wrap her mind around the absurdity as much as the reality it brought to the forefront. "Dragging something? To smooth the ground back out behind them? That means…"

A petrified steely look fell over Doc, his tone so even keeled and calm it was alarming, "It means this was planned. Someone staged this…the abduction, the waiting vehicle, a way to cover their tracks. Whoever has her…has been watching her. Why?"

"I don't know, man," Declan offered. "But we aren't stopping until we find out and have Evie *and* the *asshole* who did this…you got me?"

Doc's illusive nod indicated that he was still on board and understood the mission, but his blank stare suggested otherwise. He was overwhelmed – by everything – he didn't know where to go, what to think, or why this was happening.

McKenzie was a small town where everyone knew each other, there were no strangers. Even many of the tourists were repeat visitors and were known among the locals. How does a psychopath live in your midst and you not see the obvious signs that must have been there? How does this kind of crazy go under the radar?

He wracked his brain, trying to think of any possible suspects, but nothing hit him, not a single one. Everly had lived in McKenzie her entire life, had no family outside of Lou, and now Stone. Her only outside ties were to Portland, and those were limited.

This was too much effort and too much planning for a city friend, or foe, to put together and execute. This required vast knowledge of McKenzie, the surrounding area, and these woods. It also required knowing Everly's schedule and habits, but who would, or did, watch that closely?

He was at a loss, and felt defeated. He wasn't giving up,

but he wasn't feeling very optimistic either. Whoever this was, they were a step ahead and that was saying a lot, considering he was surrounded by a tactical team made up of some of the most highly trained men he'd ever met, with resources and experience beyond imagination. They had seen and dealt with the kind of stuff you only see in movies and then some. And they were stumped.

Sure they were catching the small clues most wouldn't, but they still didn't know where to go, or what to do next. They needed to think like a crazed lunatic and break his or her pattern and find Everly. That idea brought on an entirely new sense of purpose and intention for Doc.

He owned it, the dark, mystery of it all. He felt hollow without Everly, so it wasn't hard to go to such a diehard place that reeked of dark and ugly motives. In that very moment, Doc knew he was making good on his promise to Everly…he would do anything for her. He would even kill.

Stone was a new factor in Everly's life, and had been illusive himself in the beginning. It took them some time to catch up with the mystery man who he was known as and finally figure out who he was. But as Doc watched Stone, sitting on his larger than life brown steed, waiting for instructions, he saw his pain. Stone was out there for the same reason as the rest of them and it was all good intentioned.

Blake and Declan were huddled together, talking into their headsets to someone and motioning one direction to the other. They were revising the plan. It was in that very moment, where everything felt surreal and moved in slow motion, that he felt it. The pain that had been building in his heart that the distraction of fear could no longer cloak – his heart – it was breaking.

"Alright, listen up," Blake said. "Mission has changed.

Check your weapons, we don't know what we are hunting or about to come across. We're following the trail."

Colton, like Doc and Beck, was along to help, trained in Search and Rescue, but didn't think like the other guys did. Their experience ended with their escapades on the mountain rescues, this was far above their heads. "What trail? They covered it. Either direction, that little bit of a clue we had disappears. How do we know which way to go? How do we know we aren't burning up daylight and time on the wrong trail?"

"Just radioed the helo, they didn't see anything up ahead so they're heading west now. This road leads back to the highway making it the least likely direction our captor took or we most likely would have run into them on our way here. The chopper will zig zag back our way, scouring the area in case we missed anything." Blake was direct, this was in his blood. It was like it took him somewhere else, somewhere from his days in the military perhaps.

Declan picked up where Blake left off. The two worked in sync seamlessly, bouncing off one another well. They knew each other from past lives, crossing each other's paths often on various missions with their respective teams and outfits, which were never fully disclosed, handled together.

"We will head east, follow the road, flanking each side until we find our next clue. Given the starting point, and where we encountered the car, its apparent they picked this spot on purpose, and are using the woods to their advantage, so they can hide. So we follow, the deeper they go, the more protected they are so we need to make up time. The eyes in the sky will double back, after they clear the western section of the search area, and check our tracks. They have speed on their side so they'll make sure we didn't miss anything then work ahead."

"Okay, eyes wide, guys. Everything's a clue until it's not…"

Moving forward, the team spread out, just as Blake and Declan had instructed, and moved forward in a stealthy silence. With every billowing branch, every howl of the wind, they were on alert, hunting with clandestine like maneuvers. Doc followed suit, but a nagging inkling was digging at him and had the day's events running back through his mind as he tried to sort out what he had missed.

Everly never made it to the hospital. When they went to the house, they found candles and flowers that actually made more sense now, given the items they found in the car that suggested a surprise was brewing, yet she never made it to the house, so where did those come from? Had she done that before she went to Arrow Springs, but after she dropped him off at the hospital? That timeline or order of events didn't entirely make sense.

Then, finding her car the way they did, where they did, didn't support the flowers and candles being set up, unless she *had* done that before heading to Arrow Springs because she hadn't made it back to McKenzie Ridge in the first place? Or had she? Her car could have been stolen, but again, where was she, and why was her stuff still in the car?

His thoughts were spinning in circles, getting him nowhere except right back to the out of place flowers and candles that didn't make sense or fit the series of events. They were nagging him, distracting him, weighing on him… why? How did they play into Everly's disappearance?

Revisiting the what, when, and how, he considered the potential clue. The flowers were ongoing, they had been mysteriously showing up for weeks and a plan of this caliber had to have been planned for weeks as well. They had to be connected. As did that smell that only Blake noticed initially, but became more prevalent as time wore on. So many candles in one place had revealed the source of the odor, as the candles, Everly's favorite candles. That was the other half of the clue, had to be.

Someone had to have brought the flowers and candles to the house as a surprise, not for him, but for Everly, just like the single bouquet that had somehow made its way into their home a few weeks prior. Someone was in their home then, someone was in their home today. The same someone who had his girl. He felt it, the details were swarming around him, becoming more clear. He knew, he knew where she was…it was the candles, they held the answer.

When Doc stopped dead in his tracks, the team took notice and did the same. Staring off in the distance, his peripheral vision blurred leaving only the long snow covered road ahead in his view. The voices around him muffled to nothing more than static noise when the ground beneath his feet spun, dizzying him as reality struck him, and the answer crashed over him in a wave of confident optimism.

Finally hearing his name, his world straightened, and he turned his attention to the frazzled faces around him, an almost smile graced his face when he said, "Oh my God…I know who has her."

"Doc? You okay? What do you know? Who has Ev?" Blake's voice carried a skeptical overtone as he measured Doc's assertion – they didn't have time for games or false hopes.

"It's all coming together – it all makes sense. It's been right in front of us the whole time. *Fuck*, we've even talked to him, he's been around us. How did we miss it when it was so obvious?"

"You aren't making any sense, Doc. *Who?* Who has been right in front of us all along?" Patience was wearing thin with

Doc while he continued to think out loud and consider every detail that flooded in. Blake couldn't validate or disprove Doc's theories if he didn't know what they were.

"Think about it… Carly heard someone talking to Lou and thought it was me telling her how much I loved Evie and wanted to marry her. She thought she misheard someone in a different room but she didn't. But it wasn't me – it was *him*!"

Blake nodded, still skeptical, but he was listening. "I remember that conversation but…"

Doc put his hand out to stop Blake, eyes closed in annoyance while shaking his head. "Hang on, *damn it*, listen to me… The wild flowers, they grow out in the fields and woods. You can't get them at Meg's flower shop or the regular market in town. Someone is out here picking them, or what's left of them. There is one place you *can* buy them though…"

Doubting stares turned to those full of sympathy, assuming Doc was reaching for anything, Declan intervened, "Look, Doc, we'll all understand if you need to sit this out. You're too close to the situation."

"What the hell? The *situation*? Will you just hear me out? Christ!" The men nodded, and Doc proceeded, "The conversation in the hospital that didn't take place *did,* wild flowers that can only be picked out here or bought at the Farmers Market…the *Farmers Market*."

"Oh…" Jessie chimed, "June…June Burton. She sold the flowers at the weekend market along with her candles."

"Yes! Evie's *favorite* candles!" he replied, relieved that someone was finally understanding.

Eyes squinted, Blake tried to pick up Doc's theory, like Jessie was, but with no such luck. "Doc, we need more than June Burton, she's dead."

"Shit," Jessie said, "it makes sense. He was leaving her

gifts, everywhere. The flowers were never for Gran, they were for Ev because she rarely left the hospital. She finally did leave and the flowers were in her house. The candles and flowers today, he was planning something. Something interfered with his plan."

Declan gritted his teeth so hard a vein in his forehead began to protrude. The story still didn't make sense to the rest of the team. "Can you guys, oh, I don't know, fill the rest of us in on who *he* is?"

"To top it all off, when we did rounds, *he* grilled Carly about Ev and me...the pregnancy. He was always interested in Ev, fond of her, but this was odd. He seemed upset, distraught really."

"Can we just give *him* a name?!" Declan was done speaking in code, and Doc was so anxious it was all he could do.

"He's talking about Clyde Burton," Blake said. "The guy just lost his mom, June. She sold handmade goods at the Farmers Market – honey, potpourri, *flowers, candles*. Woods people, and he's all alone out there with his mom gone, his only real friend is moving on, and the flowers and candles… can't deny the connection."

"Exactly. He talked about Lou always being good to him. He's such an introvert it would makes sense that he went to visit, felt comfortable talking to her, but need to do it when no one was around, lacks social skills." Doc ran his hands through his hair, more memories falling into place, "God, he even *said* he was lonely, wanted to be around *people*."

"They live in the cabin at the top of that ridge." Blake pointed to a tall ridge in the distance, the highest in the area. "Access is on the far side. In this weather it'll take us a good hour or two to make it around that way and he already has a good head start, we don't have time to waste."

"Can we go up the side? Climb the face?" Wylie asked, looking for a solution.

"Let's use the helicopter," Beck offered.

Blake turned and looked behind him at the long road east that ended back at the highway. "We aren't any more than a mile in. Let's land the chopper on the highway and hitch a ride. It's about a fifteen minute run to meet them."

"Okay, I'll relay," Dec said, offering to give directions to the team in the air.

Their plan was in place. The helicopter met them at the highway to give them a ride and would drop them just outside of their target, the Burton cabin, they would hike in the last quarter mile or so. Even if Clyde were to see the helicopter, he wouldn't recognize it. They would have the element of surprise on their side, and hopefully make up most of the time they lost searching for Everly in the first place.

Before they left, the team divided once more, Stone was staying behind. "Look, son. I want to be there to help ya bring our girl home, but this old body and bad knee will probably cause you all more trouble than good. I'll stay here with the horses, you just call me if you need me to bring the horses around, or a truck…anything. I'll be there."

Doc patted his back, understanding how hard it must have been for him to make such a selfless decision. "I understand, so will Everly."

"I'll stay behind with Stone and help get the horses loaded. We'll be ready to move if we're wrong on this," Jessie added.

"That's right," Blake said, "you aren't going anywhere near that cabin, Jess."

Jessie straightened her shoulders, ready to fight back with Blake, but something about his protective nature and the look in his eyes, when he said he needed her to stay, left her off balance. All she could do was nod in agreement.

"I got your back out here, guys." Morgan was a good cop, but she knew her limits. She also had a secret that made danger less appealing than it once was. "If we need to move in a hurry, these guys will need me to help them get there with the lights and sirens."

"Alright, let's go." Declan climbed into the helicopter first and instantly started working on the rigging needed to rappel from the helicopter when they were finally in place.

With everyone in place, the helicopter took off...they had a mission to finish.

24

HOVERING JUST OUTSIDE THE AREA THAT LED TO THEIR target, the helicopter didn't even land. They rappelled down, two at a time, hidden under the cloak of a thick tree line. The helicopter left as quickly as it came, circling high in a wide birth around the area in question so they would be nearby if needed, but without giving away the team's position.

Like a stealthy elite team of operatives, they moved in quickly, using hand signals to silently direct each move and communicate with one another. They were like no other search and rescue group, with the unique expertise among them that had been passed on to the rest of their group, they were prepared for anything. It wasn't long before the tree line thinned and an open prairie came into view, an old dilapidated cabin sat front and center. A plume of smoke swirling out of the chimney, along with Clyde Burtons old truck parked in front, told them there was someone home.

Adrenaline coursed through them as anxieties ran high, they had found their mark and it was go time. Clandestinely moving around the cabin, each taking a different position or point of entry, they were ready to execute the detailed plan they put together on the chopper ride in. Shit was about to get real.

Doc and Beck watched from the tree line through the intense maneuvers about to take place. Blake and Declan flanked the front door, ready to kick it in as soon as Wylie broke the front window, that hadn't been boarded up yet for winter, and tossed in a stun grenade also known as a flash-bang. The space was so small that the exploding *bang* created such a force, it tossed the front door open, making it easier for the team to access the inside.

Each stretched a wide band from their neck over their faces to filter the smoke from the grenade, making it easier to breathe as they charged through the cabin, clearing the small space in only seconds. Doc and Beck rejoined the gang when Dace gave them the all clear, only to find that the cabin was empty. An obvious struggle had taken place, blood spattered on multiple surfaces, but no sign of Clyde, or Everly.

They combed the space, looking for evidence, finding only a locket in the corner of one of the bedrooms. It belonged to Everly. It had been placed there on purpose, neatly laid out so it would be obvious to anyone looking closely like they were. She left them a clue.

Doc smiled weakly. "She got away…"

RUNNING AS FAST AS SHE COULD, EVERLY STUMBLED WHEN the overwhelming grogginess she felt kept trying to reclaim her. A tickle on her forehead prompted her to raise her hand and brush at whatever was there. Startled by the dampness she felt, she quickly pulled her hand away and it was covered in blood – her head was bleeding somewhere in her hairline.

She tried to remember what happened, how she ended up

in the Burton cabin, but her last clear memory was of driving down highway 91, toward McKenzie, before slamming on her brakes. She had looked down for less than a second and when she looked up, there was someone in the road. Swerving to miss him, she hit a small snow berm on the side of the road and that's where the memory ends. Maybe she hit her head on the steering wheel?

Head wounds bled worse than any other, she knew that, and it didn't help that she was running. She stopped for only a moment to rip the bottom hem of her already torn shirt and tied it around her head, covering the area of the wound. As much as she wanted to slow the bleeding, she was more concerned about leaving a blood trail.

Back to an even paced run, she continued forward in the direction opposite of the cabin. More and more of what happened came back to her, and she was beginning to wish it hadn't. Chills crept up her body and they weren't entirely from the snow but from the chilling ordeal that was unfolding in her mind as she continued to regain her senses.

The man in the road had come to her door as she was getting out to see if he was okay. In hind sight, probably not her smartest move, but given her profession and choice of pastimes, it was in her nature to protect, heal, and fix. What happened next wasn't anything she ever could have imagined, even in her wildest of dreams, or rather...*nightmares*. The conversation that took place was straight out of a made for TV movie or a novelist's thriller.

"Are you okay?" she had asked.

He gave her a broken toothed grin. "I've been waiting for you. I was afraid something happened."

"I'm sorry, what? Waiting for me? Here?" Everly had looked around, trying to make sense of what he was saying, or better yet, why?

"I had a nice evening planned for you. For us. Your favorite flowers, those candles you love so much. It was going to be perfect. I was going to make you mine."

"You were...wh-what?" She slowly backed away from the man until she was backed up against the car door that was still open.

"I heard that bastard on your answering machine. Doc said he was finished up and waiting for you. Couldn't risk him showing up and ruining everything. He already tried to ruin what we were meant to have. So I came to you."

"Y-you were in my...*house?*" The fear was all consuming, the pieces were falling into place.

"I've been in your house, Lou's house, I even watched you sleep at the hospital. So sweetly sleeping, next to Lou like that – it took all I had to keep my distance then, but not now. I thought our plan was ruined when that prick called until I saw your appointment reminder on the refrigerator. Then I knew...I was to meet you here. Brilliant really – nobody would know."

Sheer fright washed over her and weakened her knees, almost collapsing her. She drummed up the adrenaline and strength to push through and quickly spun on the door, trying to make it inside the car to get away from him.

She wasn't fast enough. She hadn't hit her head on the steering wheel at all...she had been struck with something hard and sharp.

Everly lost time after that because her next memory was waking in a cold damp place, God knows where, huddled in a corner. It was dark, windows were boarded from the outside, and it smelled of spoil, old dirt and mildew. Someone was coming, but she was too disoriented and weak still to react.

It was him, again. He had a wicked grin full of menace,

his eyes roaming over her with a type of desire that made her feel ill.

"Please...don't hurt my baby."

Whatever he was thinking or feeling just a moment before was quickly replaced with disgust and anger. "Doctor Charles used you, ruined you. He's filthy, undeserving, but don't worry. I will take care of you...and *our* baby. He didn't even have the decency to marry you first, just took what he wanted and left you in this condition."

His villainous words matched his unkempt appearance. He was dirty, unshaven, and brought an odor with him that couldn't be described. Everly wasn't only stricken by his troubling words and appearance but also how different he seemed. She had always known him to be quiet and harmless. This version of him was anything but.

"Are you ready, Everly?"

"For *what*?"

"Tonight. Our...wedding night." He stood in the broken down doorway, watching her as he began to stroke himself.

She recoiled, trying to bury herself deeper into the corner as if it provided protection from what he threatened.

"Aww, don't be afraid. I know you're nervous – you didn't think I knew, did you?" he asked, his wicked smile of rotten teeth making her cringe.

"Knew what?" she asked, trying to gauge her fate, and how hard she would have to fight.

"That you love me too. I see it. When everyone else hides from me, or looks at me in disgust with their nose in the air – there you are, the only one approaching me, asking me how I am, if I need anything. And when you finally walk away, that sexy sway in your hips – I know it's for me when you look over your shoulder and flash that smile that says it all."

The bile in her stomach began to rise, making her feel ill. "You'll never get away with this."

"I already have. They can't find you, there's no trail."

A crashing sound came from behind him, knocking him to the ground, causing Everly to huddle under her arms, shielding herself from whatever had just happened. Grunts and moans accompanied the sound of flesh upon flesh in a scuffle that she didn't have time to decipher. That was her chance, she ran and hadn't looked back. She wouldn't stop until she got to the ridge.

NOTHING MORE THAN A SHACK WITH A FEW BROKEN DOWN buildings – the men had scoured the grounds looking for anything. The only sign of Everly being there was the locket – the obvious sign of a scuffle their only other clue. She had put up a fight, they thought. Chairs were overturned along with the lone table. There were shattered glass lamps and the smell of spilled kerosene everywhere. And the blood...a *lot* of blood.

Moving outside, the team picked up what looked like two sets of tracks, trailed by blood. They hoped it was Ev, it was all they had to go on, but the second set of tracks meant she was being chased. Following the tracks in a wide line so they wouldn't miss anything along the way, they came to a dead end at the creek. Another vanishing act where their clues disappeared.

"This has to be Ev. She's smart, especially out here. She knew to cover her tracks - I bet she jumped in the creek and started running. No trail for whoever was chasing her," Blake assumed.

"Agreed. But which way did she go? Upstream? Downstream?" Doc asked, looking left to right, running his hands through his hair. "She has to be freezing and who knows if she's injured. If the baby…"

"If she's running, they're both still okay. Let's not borrow trouble and assume both are still okay," Beck offered as moral support, hoping their efforts were leading to a happy outcome.

Blake took a long look left, to the east, then west. "She knows this area. She's been out here hiking, climbing, even training for SAR. She'd head west, toward the ridge, and try to get to the highway from there."

"Highway? She doesn't have gear…how would she get down the face of the ridge?" Wylie asked.

Doc stared to the west, nodding confidently, believing in Blake's theory. "She's a skilled climber – resourceful – smart. She'd find a way."

The helicopter flew in from the west, heading up stream, Declan signaling them as they did. "Helo's headed upstream, just in case we're wrong. They'll catch up with us down stream once they clear the east side."

"Alright, let's move, cover both sides of the creek," Blake ordered.

"Hold up. They flew over a wrecked truck off the access road – no tango," Declan said, no tango meaning they didn't have eyes on Everly or anyone else. "Not much snow accumulated on it…it hasn't been there long. They dispatched a team to investigate…has something hanging off the back bumper."

"Back bumper…to drag the snow and hide tracks," Doc assumed.

Blake's jaw tightened. "Another vehicle? Shit, we might have more than one suspect?"

25

EVERLY PICKED UP THE CREEK, RUNNING THROUGH ITS FRIGID water, trying to hide her tracks and lose her captor. She knew he was behind her, she felt it like he was breathing down the back of her neck. The fear motivating her to keep going, despite growing tired and sore in the freezing temperatures.

The creek ran along the tree line for a great distance, helping to camouflage her, but when that tree line thinned and the creek veered away from the forest's protection, she was no longer on a safe route – she needed a new plan. Continuing through the path of the creek would take her to wide open space, leaving her a sitting duck and obvious moving target. She had a head start, but she didn't think she could outrun him much longer. She needed to play smarter now, not faster.

Just ahead laid an old fallen tree that had become nothing more than a stripped bare log over time and was falling apart. Using it as a bridge to the forest would still leave tracks. Even if she kicked over them as she went...there would be evidence she had run across there, and it would lead her chaser in her direction. This is where smarter was more important than faster.

She laid parallel to the log, on her left side, and pulled herself along the log. It was slow, and hard, but didn't leave an obvious trail, just a slight dip in the snow that was level from one side to the other. That close to the log and with the snow still falling, no one would be the wiser.

Catching her breath at the other end, several yards into the thick veil of the forest, she finally got to her feet and pressed on. She was leaving tracks now, but they only gave her away if he figured out that she was in there to begin with. Her hope, and prayer, was that he was going to run right by that log and follow the creek, which would take him further and further away. She would have time to get to the ridge and escape down the side where he wouldn't think to look for an injured pregnant woman. Smarter.

Her breath caught when she heard him call her name. Either she had lost a lot of time, or he was just that fast, but she could tell he wasn't far behind and was counting on him being on the creek side of the tree's still. His voice came again. It went from frantic to angry with each call – one of worry – one of hate. A distinct difference in each call, she wondered, were there two voices?

The voices got closer, and came more often so she ran harder and faster, despite not being able to feel her legs or feet any longer. She pushed on, fighting it for her baby… fighting for Doc. The tears threatened, but she wouldn't let them come. There would be plenty of time for that when she was safe.

* * *

Blake and the team stopped when they heard the shouting for Everly, just up ahead. Oddly it brought relief because it meant she got away and he hadn't found her yet. It also brought an entirely new level of fear because they knew he must be closer to her, closer than they were, and that voice was full of anger and rage.

"I got something over here," Luke called out. "She was here, I'm sure of it."

Standing by the old log that Everly had used to throw off her captor, he bent down, grabbing a handful of snow, then dumping it out. He looked up, following the length of the log before standing with a smile on his face.

"She *is* smart. She's in the woods. That way," Luke said, pointing south into the trees, before turning west and pointing downstream. "Our guy is that way. If he were in the woods, we wouldn't hear him so well…we're right on his ass."

Though he should feel lighter from such news, Doc couldn't shed the sense of trepidation that was haunting him. "Are you sure? We can't be wrong on this."

"Look here, the snow is shallower along the log and the snow is packed. It's fresh powder everywhere else." He stepped closer and grabbed another handful of snow, walking it back to the guys with an open hand. "Blood. Gotta be her."

Blake chuckled and swatted Luke's back, "She dragged herself along the log to hide her movement. That's some heavy tactical shit right there. She *is* smart."

Standing still and silent when another round of yelling came, they were able to hear a difference in the shouting. There were two distinct voices, two different intentions in their tone, and two different locations.

"Son of a bitch," Declan said. "We *do* have two. One in the woods, and a hot one on this side not far behind him. Who the fuck is the other guy?"

"The muffled one in the woods doesn't want her as bad as the one up ahead. We need to split up."

Just then the helicopter flew over, quickly disappearing around the bend of trees.

"We got eyes! We got eyes! Just around that bend. They got him! They got him!" Luke bolted in a dead run after word came over the radio. He followed the path of the helicopter, with half the team at his side.

The rest of the team ran along the log, disappearing into the trees where they quickly picked up Everly's trail. It wasn't long before Everly's tracks were matched with a second set; someone picked up on her and was on her tail. Moving faster than the snow probably should have let them, they were determined to get to her first.

"She could be hiding," Luke said, breathlessly. "She needs to know we're here."

The team in the woods began yelling her name, hoping she would recognize it was them, despite how much the thick forest muffled their sound and carried it in odd directions. The Creekside team was silent, marking everyone's position with each yell. Emotion was coursing through Doc's voice with every word he yelled for her.

He wasn't just calling her name, he was telling her he loved her, that they are there, that she's safe – he wouldn't let anything happen to her. Those words were as much for him as they were her, they were also a threat for the asshole on her tail. He hoped like hell both Everly and their suspect heard him loud and clear.

"Helo lost visual!" Luke yelled. "He's in the trees, he's in the trees. Eye's wide boys, he's in our space. Team two is on him, make your mark before you shoot – our guys are in here."

The intensity overflowed, boosting their drive. Blake was

on a hunting mission and he always got his trophy. This guy wasn't getting away and he'd be lucky to be alive when all was said and done. His team finally had visual – he was in their sights. They spread out, forming a large circle around him where they would slowly move in and trap him with nowhere to go. He was still running after Everly, or where he thought she was, but they were faster, and closing in quickly.

Everly made it to the ridge and shot out of the woods with little time to spare. The voices behind her were close, she needed to disappear quickly. Laying at the edge of the ridge, she slowly swung her legs over, feeling for a place to plant them and started her careful descent. She knew this rock, climbed it many times; she just needed to think through every step and she would be fine. One wrong step on the snowy cliff and she was done.

Shoulders above the edge, she looked up as two voices caught her attention, both men coming out of the trees at the same time. Clyde Burton? Where had he come from and why was *he* there? He was there to help her.

Right behind him was Doc, followed by three O'Reilly brothers. The sight of Doc lifted the weight that she had been carrying on her shoulders since waking in that God forsaken place. Her relief was short lived when Doc aimed a weapon at Clyde, the brothers doing the same, matching his target. He had it wrong, they all had to have had it wrong.

"Stop or I'll shoot, Burton! Don't fucking try me!" Doc's anger seethed through clenched teeth hoping Clyde would give him a reason to pull the trigger.

Panic and a narrow ledge made for a dangerous state. Clyde was roughed up, bloodied and his clothes torn and she knew why. He had been the one to rush the cabin and give her the chance to escape. He *was* there to help her.

"No! Doc! Don't shoot! It's not him!" she yelled.

She saw Doc's stance soften and his head tilted to one side in confusion. The helicopter blew over, startling her rigid state, and everything converted to a state of slow motion for both Doc, and Everly.

The slight shift from her startled movement was enough for her to lose her grip and begin to fall. She heard her name being called out by several of the others, but none of them could get to her fast enough. She hadn't even realized she was falling until she landed on a narrow ledge, flat on her back, in a bluff of snow.

Suddenly aware of just how cold she was, - daylight escaped her – everything blurred into darkness. The last thing she heard was a blast from a gun.

* * *

"YOU KILLED HER!" A MAN STOOD AT THE EDGE OF THE TREE line, gun aimed in Doc's direction after firing a shot and missing.

Tobias Smith was an off the grid recluse who was rarely seen anywhere near civilization. He traded wares with others out in the woods, and only came to town to sell his wood carvings at the Farmers Market. He didn't like anyone, Everly must have been the exception. He was the man who took her.

Clyde stepped in front of Doc and yelled back at Tobias. "You! You did! *You* hurt her! You *took* her and now she's…"

With Clyde so close, Doc picked up that all too familiar smell – the pine, sandalwood, and citrus.

"You were there," Doc said to Clyde. "The candles, that smell, it's your mother's candles."

Clyde nodded, "I watched over her. I watched *him* watch her. I didn't want him to hurt her. She's my friend – I didn't want him to hurt my friend."

Tobias wandered closer, away from the tree line. "I sure did. I was in her house, I even got into the old woman's house. Lou knows she's mine. We talked, and she knows. You violated her Doctor Charles. I'm doing you a favor by righting your wrong and marrying her."

"She's not yours," Doc whispered back with a tight glare and gritted teeth.

"Oh, that's where you're wrong. The feel of her skin against my hand while she slept next to that hospital bed made her moan. *I* made her moan. I took her to save her. I held her body in my arms, felt her against me. I will take care of her in ways you wouldn't. You're nothing more than an animal." He paused to adjust himself. "You ruined our night, our *wedding* night."

Fury ran through Doc, disgusted by Tobias's words, but more so by the arousal he gave himself simply by talking about Everly the way he was. Doc lunged at Tobias, ready to finish him, but he was met by the end of a gun, squared between his now wide eyes. The air was knocked from his lungs at the sound of gunshots.

Opening his eyes, he realized he was still standing but Tobias was flat on the ground, bleeding out, struggling to breathe. Standing at the edge of the tree line were Blake and Declan, weapons drawn and still on their mark. Slowly moving in, they finally dropped their weapons to their side's when Tobias's weapon was kicked out of the reach and no longer a threat to any of them because Tobias was *dead*.

Doc bolted to the edge of the ridge, where the helicopter was hovering, and watched Everly from above. Luke was already there, rigging the gear, so they could get down to her. He rappelled down the face of the ridge to her, Luke staying close to his side. Doc wasn't used to this kind of activity and most definitely not used to treating someone he loved so much that Luke brought balance, by offering to help with the rescue.

She was semi-conscious, her face and head bloodied. Her arm laid at an unnatural angle and appeared to be broken – all things that would heal – he prayed what he saw was the extent of her injuries. As the basket stretcher lowered from the helicopter, he prepared her for transport and discovered the one injury that may never heal. There was blood between her legs, staining the snow beneath her.

"No…oh, God no." Doc broke down, the day's events becoming too much.

Luke took over, giving his friend a minute to get through that moment and collect himself, by asking questions that required Doc to focus. There was time to lose their shit later.

Everly was the first to go up where Dawson anxiously waited for her – Doc was quick to follow. Once seated at her side while Dawson went to work, stabilizing her for the short flight, she opened her eyes and said something that would break what was left of Doc's heart, and haunt him forever.

"Our baby."

With the helicopter disappearing into the distance, the rest of the team began to rappel down the ridge to waiting vehicles now staged below. Clyde stood there with tears in his eyes before finally walking away, back in the direction of his cabin.

"What about that guy?" Dace asked, gesturing to Tobias's lifeless body.

"He isn't going anywhere," Blake replied. "Recovery team is twenty five minutes out – he'll be fine out here…he likes being alone."

26

BEING AFFILIATED WITH THE HOSPITAL AS THEY WERE, AND well connected with the money that funded it, came with privileges. The gang kept each other company, and sane, in Gran's hospital room, waiting for news, while Doc and Everly were admitted to the room next door after clearing the emergency room.

"I'm never letting you out of my sight again." Doc whispered to a sleeping Everly, resting his head on his hand that held hers. "You're my world, my life…my everything. I can't do this life thing without you – I love you too much. I need you, baby. God I need you."

Her soft hand brushed his face, earning his attention. Her raspy voice finally came. "I love you."

"Ev!" Quick to his feet, Doc looked around, unsure what to do or who to call despite being a doctor himself.

Her face was swollen, already bruising, her head taking the bulk of the trauma with stitches to correct it. She smiled the best she could through the pain. "Sit."

Tapping the nurse's call button over and over again, he

took a seat. "Thank God you're awake. I was so worried, I was afraid…"

With her hand to his mouth, she shushed him, not wanting either of them to relive the hell they had escaped. He kissed her hand, then did it again for good measure – that would never get old.

"Doc, you were in the room when they gave me something to sleep. I'm fine. Hurt like hell, but fine."

Awareness struck and her drowsy eyes were now anything but – she stiffened as fear crept in. "The baby!"

Doc gently placed his hand on her belly. "Shhh, shhhh. He's fine, baby. He's just fine."

"You know…"

"I do. I've already thought of a few names. I was thinking Bon Jovi – sounds French. Or maybe Slash – no one will screw with a kid named Slash. Great band name too. Then I was thinking maybe he won't be into music as much as super heroes so maybe Bruce Wayne or Clark Kent?"

"Not a chance, Doc. Not a chance."

"Well, since I was right about him being a boy, I feel like I should get an extra vote."

She laughed at his silliness and appreciated the attempt to lighten the mood, but despite his efforts, her mood shifted to serious again. "Clyde?"

"He's fine too, baby. He had an eye on you all along."

"He saved me. Saved the baby. If it weren't for him, I would never have made it out of there when I did."

Carly came in, responding to the call button Doc had pushed so many times. She began to check Everly over and chart her findings when the rest of the gang slowly pushed through the door, front and center was Granny Lou in a wheelchair pushed by Stone.

Affections were quickly exchanged then Everly asked for

someone to fill in the blanks. She had the gist of what had happened but some things still didn't make sense to her.

"When I woke, I had no idea where I was. It wasn't until I ran that I realized it was the Burton place. How did Tobias end up there?"

Blake explained that Tobias had knocked her out on the highway when she ran for the car and carried her to the truck he had waiting on the Forest Service road. Clyde was already in the truck, under a tarp in the back. It was Clyde who caused the truck to wreck in the ditch where it was found, he broke out the back window. Then he hit Tobias over the head with a shovel, knocking him out.

"Clyde took you to his cabin to hide you while he went for help. He was afraid to move you anymore than he had. When he got back to where the wrecked truck was, Tobias was nowhere to be found, so he turned around and went back for you."

"He broke back in and charged Tobias – I do remember that now. He looked at me and nodded, that's when I ran. I heard the fighting, but just kept running. That's probably what saved my life."

"Tobias can't hurt you or anyone else – not anymore." Blake's monotone deliverance left a chill in the air that oddly left them all relieved. That man was out of their lives, and the threat was no more.

The long silence that followed was finally broken when BJ walked in with gluten free, organic donuts that were frosted blue, each one said *boy* – those ingredients were just as organic as the rest he used in the sweet dessert he had prepared. Passing around the tasty treat, they all began to toss around potential baby names, *Hippy* and *Granola* among them.

Everly looked around the room taking in the amount of

joy and love she was surrounded by. Family wasn't always made up of blood, but those you chose to complete you. She had that here, in McKenzie, with the people surrounding her. Her life had so drastically changed in a relatively short time. Her life that had been full of limits was now limitless and she finally felt free to *love* and man did she love hard.

Doc whispered in her ear, laying a hand on her shoulder. "You okay, baby?"

Placing one hand over his and laying her head on him, she rested her free hand on her round stomach just as her little boy kicked, reminding her he was there. "I'm perfect…just… *perfect.*"

EPILOGUE

Lou finally came home, five days later when Everly did. Her prognosis was good, she was getting stronger each day and was expected to regain most of her strength and mobility with physical therapy. Her physical therapist was a young hunky guy, new to McKenzie Ridge, and about to be broken in quickly by Lou and her dirty old lady friends.

As for Everly, she was put on bed rest for six weeks while the injuries she sustained during her fall healed. Unfortunately bed rest included no sex, which Doc was okay with, Everly…not so much. They made due, though, grateful for the second chance they were given.

The couple decided they would get married right there in McKenzie Ridge, just as soon as the bed rest had expired. Once the doctor gave his blessing, they would wed. More importantly, with raging pregnancy hormones, they could celebrate their wedding night properly with hot steamy sex. Everyone had their priorities and Everly's were of the naked and wild variety.

Megan went to work on preparing a dream shotgun wedding that would be magazine worthy if she had her way.

She would be planning a baby shower for Doc and Evie's little boy too. He was to be named Rocco Jagger Charles, RJ for short. Doc promised endless sex to get his way on the name. If she was being honest, Everly liked it so it was a win win for her.

Party planning was in season because Meg had two other baby showers to plan. Sam and Dawson were expecting their third baby, a little girl due a short few months after Rocco. McKenzie was booming with babies – the other baby shower was for Morgan and Beck.

Morgan had opted out of Everly's rescue because she knew it would be too much for her and the pregnancy. She was newly pregnant and twins were on the schedule. The three ladies gave Megan baby fever and she hoped that she and Colton would be next.

"You guys are like a bunch of fricken bunnies. This town is only so big, you're all going to have to move."

"Bets on Jessie being next? Any takers?" Doc teased.

"Screw you, Doc. I hope your baby is bald."

"Most babies *are* bald." He retorted.

"Then I hope he hates Batman, and music."

"Those are fighting words, Jess."

"Yeah, well so is jinxing me with a kid."

Blake watched from the corner, wondering just how serious Jessie was about that statement. He wasn't into having kids, but practicing how to make them was something he could handle. When she caught him watching her, he shot her a wicked wink to which she flipped him off.

The engagement party that two of the group's couples were supposed to be having had become more of a homecoming because one of the couples was missing. Carigan and BJ had left for San Francisco so BJ could sign the necessary papers to sell his half of his restaurant to his business partner.

They made it a day before heading straight to Reno where they were married.

Something about tragedies and near death situations prompted expedited forever's. Life was beginning to feel like it was on fast forward and everyone wanted to grab their piece of happiness. BJ and Carigan planned to take their time getting back to McKenzie, enjoying their honeymoon all over the Pacific Northwest.

They stopped in Portland to welcome her parents' home from Ireland, only four of her brothers were there, finally home from McKenzie. Their last stop was in the San Juan Islands off the Puget Sound – Beck had set them up at his lavish home that sat on a ridge, of course, in Deception Pass.

Stone had moved into the small guest house that sat in the back corner of Lou's property where Everly once lived. The sale of his large Texas ranch was underway, as was the purchase of Sugar Pine Stables where he was already moving his best riding bulls, including Ol'Twister, for breeding and show horses that he couldn't say goodbye to. Retirement looked good on him, and he was happy to be back in McKenzie, he was *home*. There might even be a second chance at love for him there too.

The happily ever after's were falling into place, for all but one. Lydia. The party had finally died down and everyone went home when both Everly and Lou needed to rest. Lydia had put her son, Jax, to bed for the night and as tired as she was, couldn't go to sleep herself. She was really good at putting on a happy face during the day when she was around other people – she felt safe in McKenzie – most of the time.

After the ordeal she went through with her now deceased husband, living on the run, and in fear for her life and the life of her son…she struggled with feeling safe at night, when it was dark, and she was alone. When it was dark, and quiet, she was left with her haunting thoughts. Every sound, every shadow, it all spooked her. Her routine now was to stay up late, until she couldn't fight sleep and she would finally succumb to dreams over nightmares out of sheer exhaustion, albeit with the lights and TV still on.

She was nearing that time of night, ready to head to her room when there was a knock at her door. It was well after midnight, and she wasn't expecting anyone. None of her friends would ever think to come by so late with a little one in the house. It just wasn't like them in general.

Paranoia rolled in, and adrenaline had taken over. Going to the hall closet, she reached for the gun she had hidden on the highest shelf, out of Jax's reach. Turning off the safety, she slowly went to the door, jumping when another knock came, harder and louder.

She stood there a good minute, recalling what she had been taught about handling and firing a weapon. She was taught how to shoot by the very man who protected her on the run, and then ran from her when their journey came to an end. Declan O'Reilly was easy on the eyes, delicious in bed, but bad for the heart.

With her hand on the door knob, she waited for a third knock before throwing the door open, startling the person on the other side of the door, banking on the element of surprise.

A sharp gasp escaped her when she saw who was standing at the other end of a bullet. Declan O'Reilly. He was back and standing on her front step with his hands up in surrender.

"We have a problem…"

* * *

I hope you loved reading Fearless as much as I loved writing it! I can't wait for you to read the **EPIC** *conclusion to McKenzie Ridge,* **REDEMPTION!**

We've all been waiting for Blake and Jessie - Redemption tells us everything we need to know about these two series favorites...watch out for that **PLOT TWIST***!*

Get your copy of REDEMPTION, now! Available on all major retailers!

ABOUT STEPHANIE ST. KLAIRE

USA Today Best-Selling Author & Screenwriter, Stephanie St. Klaire is a multifaceted romance writer who has found her calling making readers bite their nails in suspense and hang on the edge of their seats with bated breath, as they wait for the next startling mystery to be unveiled.

Whether she's off the grid hunting her diabolical killer's next victim or plotting gritty crime thrillers that will leave you questioning her sanity, she always brings the chaos and the heat. (Watch yourself or you just might end up a character in one of her stories!)

Equal parts Hallmark and Criminal Minds, SSK balances her dark side by writing rom-com as her alter ego Stephie Klaire.

The Pacific Northwest native currently resides in Portland, Oregon with her husband, five children, and two ferocious lap dogs— where every day is Taco Tuesday and Christmas isn't just a season... it's a state of mind.

*Get a **FREE** ebook when you sign up for SSK's non-spammy newsletter...*
www.stephaniestklaire.com/newsletter

Join Stephanie's private Facebook Group & Other Places to Find SSK:
www.stephaniestklaire.com/findssk

WHAT TO READ NEXT BY SSK

Lethal Jeopardy

Dangerous Chaos

Corrupt Justice

Stand Alone

Chameleon Effect

FREE BOOKS & SALES

Stephanie always has FREE books and sales running and
they're constantly changing…
For current Freebies and Deals, go to:
www.stephaniestklaire.com/freeandsales

REDEMPTION CHAPTER 1 - FREE SAMPLE

"I need you..." Jessie whispered into the phone, catching Blake by surprise. "*Please* help me, Blake."

He knew this day would come. He just hadn't thought it would come so soon. With her past threatening to resurface and take her out, Blake saw red when he heard the terror in Jessie's voice. Blake switched his cell phone over to speaker and set it on the nearby coffee table while he quickly slipped into his boots, not even bothering to fully lace them up. In quick motion, he tossed his holster over his shoulders and tucked a loaded weapon in on each side before loading one into his ankle holster.

There was no telling what he was being called to do, and he wanted to be prepared for anything. History has a tendency to repeat itself, and Jessie's history was one that made a best-selling thriller novel look like roses. It sent a shiver down his spine.

In a final measure of preparedness, he clipped his knife to his belt, tossed on his black leather jacket and grabbed his phone before flying out the door.

"Where are you?" he asked, in a low monotone voice.

Quick heavy breathing came through the line, letting him know she was still there. She finally answered, giving him relief, "I…I'm in the closet. Hiding."

"Where are the kids?" he asked, referring to Dawson and Sam's children, who Jessie had been watching. If he remembered correctly, Colton and Meg Sparks' daughter, Olivia, was there, too. He made a mental note of who should be there, and what or who to watch for, so there wasn't an element of surprise that could put any of them in danger.

"I-I don't know. I d-don't hear them right now. Are you almost here? Tell me you're almost here, Blake. Sam and Dawson aren't due for a while. I didn't know who else to call." Her tattered whisper revealed a level of fear he hadn't witnessed coming from her.

Jessie was a combat boot wearing badass who didn't take shit from anyone, and she certainly didn't get *scared*. Grown men have cried in her presence and been brought to their knees as a consequence of her wrath. Jessie was a force of nature, who wasn't easily backed into a closet – especially by choice. A chill coursed through him at the sound of her whisper and what she was finally forced to face.

"I tried to subdue them, but I lost control of the situation. And the smell – it's overwhelming – I don't even know what's causing it, and I'm afraid to look." She took a pause, her breathing still erratic.

"It's okay. I'm on my way. I promise you're going to be okay." And God did he hope he would make good on that promise. If anything happened to her, especially on his watch, he wouldn't be able to live with the outcome.

"I think I can hear them. Oh, my God, I think they're going through everything."

"They're tossing the house? Do you know if they're looking for something specific? Or what they're after?" he asked as the sound of a creaking door came through the phone.

He sent a quick text to Logan Traynor while keeping Jessie on the line. Logan was his new partner since Morgan Jameson had gone on maternity leave, and an extra combat-ready back up might be the difference between life and death. Logan also happened to be Blake's deceased best friend's son – someone he gladly took under his wing when Logan transitioned from enlisted soldier to civilian life – he trusted Logan with everything.

This kid was loyal and highly trained as a special operative for various government services, having followed in his father's footsteps, which also mirrored Blake's. Logan looked up to Blake, would do anything for him, and didn't require an explanation to drop everything and jump into action. He didn't know Jessie's story like Blake did or the trouble it was brewing – nobody did – except Blake, and if Jessie knew how he came about it, she'd skin him alive, right after she kicked his balls all over the place. There was no telling what Blake was about to walk in on, and whoever was with Jessie wouldn't expect Blake or Logan. He really was the only person Blake could trust with a mission as dangerous and delicate as this.

"There's shit everywhere. Blake hurry. Hold on…" The line went quiet for what felt like an eternity before she finally returned. "I heard one of them – they're looking for *me*."

"Keep calm…and quiet. I'm almost there, Jess."

So close yet so far away – how cliché, he thought. The woman who pushed his every button, who he fought with most and infuriated him more than anyone could, was now the woman he was fighting for. From cliché to irony, fate had an odd sense of humor…and terrible timing. Truth be told, despite their angsty banter, he cared about her and didn't wish her any harm, which was why he needed to get there and fast.

Time seemed to slow, allowing a sense of panic to seep in, something Blake wasn't accustomed to. He was ex-military – worked for branches of government that were *off record* and had seen things the average civilian couldn't imagine. Calm, cool, and collected – it's how he handled everything, until now. Until this. Until *her*. Though she aggravated the shit out of him, he needed her to be okay.

McKenzie Ridge was small and didn't carry a lot of traffic this time of night, despite it being high season for tourists. Despite its size and lack of obstacles, he couldn't seem to get from point A to point B quickly enough. He knew what was coming for her, even if she hadn't told him, and he feared he would be too late.

"I think they have weapons, Blake. Where did they get those? What the…"

"Jessie, what's going on. What do you see or hear?" he asked, trying to keep tabs on the situation so he could defuse it quickly once he arrived.

Once more, the sound of the creaking door came through the phone - only this time, it was much faster, as if the door had been yanked open.

"They found me. They know I'm in the…" The sound of a quick scuffle and muffled voices cut her off before the line finally went dead.

With his police lights on, he sped through town, killing the siren when he finally reached the dark isolated road that Dawson and Sam lived on. There were very few homes on that road, and they were spread out with acres between them, so he parked up the street, deciding to use the wooded surroundings to covertly find his way in, so as not to alert the intruders of his presence. The element of surprise would give him the upper hand and allow him to neutralize the threat promptly. As long as he wasn't too late – he wouldn't let his mind go there.

Blake didn't like trouble in his town, especially when it involved his people. This was the kind of trouble that really got under his skin – murderers and rapists. This brand of *trouble* had recently been released from prison, for *good behavior*, after spending the better part of a decade behind bars. Jessie had been the one to put him there, hence his return to make good on his promise to *get even*. Her assailant wasn't the kind of guy to let a grudge go either, especially after what he did to Jessie that landed him in prison to begin with. He had unfinished business, said so himself before he was cuffed in the courtroom and hauled off to the state penitentiary.

With the high-level security clearance Blake still held, he had access to anything and everything. It wasn't hard to find anything out about anyone with his reach. It may not be entirely appropriate to use his authority to keep tabs on those he cared about, but it was the only way he could really protect them. When he read Jessie's case, it made sense of everything – why she dressed the way she did, why she kept people at arm's length with her abrasive attitude, why she was…the way she was. Even more reason to get to her in a hurry – she was in real danger.

Worry stretched to anger as he wondered how this guy made it into his town, unseen, when Blake had eyes everywhere, watching for him. Something had been missed; there was obviously a flaw in the plan to keep Jessie – and McKenzie Ridge – safe. At a near run down the rural street, he was weaving in and out of the tree line, relying on the dark night sky and shadows it created to keep his cover. Blake was frustrated – time felt like it was working against him.

When there had been trouble in town the previous fall, he had assigned himself to Jessie, to watch over her and keep her safe until they eliminated the threat that had been brewing for years. The threat against her then had been minimal compared to what she faced now, which drove him harder. But, when all was said and done, and life had returned to normal, there wasn't a reason to shadow her, and she was quick to point that out.

The only way to get her to agree to his protection would be to tell her he knew everything, and that wasn't an option. So, to keep her safe, he watched her from a distance, except for tonight when she caught him following her and made him leave. Another failed plan on his part.

There wasn't time to evaluate where he went wrong in his attempt to keep trouble away or why Blake even let Jessie get to him in such a way that he left her so vulnerable. He'd reflect on that later. Right now, he had a job to do, and it was to get into that house and take out the threat so Jessie wouldn't have to worry any longer. So he wouldn't have to worry any longer.

As he rounded the corner, coming up on the long driveway that led to the house, he was surprised to find it wasn't guarded. Was this asshole that brazen? That he would just come in and do his dirty work alone in an unfamiliar house in an unfamiliar town? Prepared for anything, Blake made his way to the house, still vacant of any guards. *Odd*, he thought.

The lights were on inside, easily seen from the front of the house, and he saw shadows moving through the curtains. A front door entrance would come without surprise – they'd see and hear him coming. So, he went around back, moving quickly and without a sound. Up the back steps and in through the unlocked back door Blake Cooper went, silently cursing Jessie for making it so easy for anyone to get in. Even more reason to kick his own ass for giving in to her stubbornness and leaving her alone. Surely, she knew there was a threat headed her way and that *he* was out of prison – they send letters to the victims, alerting them of such. Why would she be so reckless, especially with kids in the house?

With his weapon drawn, he maneuvered through the dark halls of the house, following the sound of muted voices. Oddly, they were somewhat inaudible, a dialect that he wasn't familiar with as it just sounded like gibberish. There was more than one voice; he could at least tell that, despite not understanding the conversation – it sounded like there were at least three. *No problem*, he thought. He was trained to handle more with just hand-to-hand combat; this would be over before *they* knew it.

One familiar voice finally came into earshot – Jessie. She was negotiating, probably for her life, so their attention would be on her. Perfect.

"I-I won't tell…I promise," he heard her say anxiously - he could almost see her big doe eyes wide with fear as she shifted from foot to foot, awaiting his rescue. "Just let me go, and we'll forget this ever happened."

With his back to the wall, he slowly and silently slid toward the room and gave a quick look around the corner when he reached the end. Confusion set in. What the hell? He peered around the corner once more and couldn't believe what he saw.

REDEMPTION CHAPTER 2 - FREE SAMPLE

Making his presence known, Blake stepped into view. The scene was anything but what he expected to walk in on – it was chaos...it was troubling...it was pure pandemonium. He'd never seen such a mess in his life.

Holstering his weapon, he traipsed further into the room, trying not to trip over the debris he encountered.

"Jesus, it took you long enough!" Jessie said from the toddler rocking chair she was sitting in.

All attention was quickly averted from Jessie to Blake at his mention. "Uncle Blake!"

Taking a knee, he crouched to the level of the 4 feet and under club, accepting their welcome.

"What the hell is going on here?" he asked.

"I can't wait to say bad words like you when I grow up, Uncle Blake!" Ellie said. Ellie was the precocious daughter of Sam and Dawson, a real handful but in a good way.

"Bad words aren't for pretty girls – I shouldn't say them either," he replied, fully aware that she would rat him out to her parents later.

"But, Aunt Jessie says them all the time. Isn't she a pretty girl?" Ellie asked, to which Jessie raised her brow, awaiting his response.

"Pretty difficult – I'll give you that," Blake chided while taking to his feet.

"Suck it, you diiii-arn nice guy!" Jessie was scolded often enough for foul language around the kids that it seemed she was finally starting to get it. She also wasn't fond of using *nice* words; saying them pained her, hence the death glare she tossed Blake's way was evidence of that.

"Suck what?" Ellie asked, looking around. "Oooh, did you bring suckers?"

"Not this time, kid. *Aunt Jessie* didn't tell me she needed anything to...*suck.*" Two could play at this game, he thought.

"That's because I knew *Uncle Blake* needed one more than I did. He likes to suck...*really, really hard.*" Jessie was determined to get the last word, especially with Blake because that's just what they did.

"These guys? This is what you called me over for – who you were hiding from?"

"Ooh! Hide and seek!" Ellie shouted, clapping her hands while jumping up and down in sugar induced excitement.

"No, El. We're done with that game after losing your brother," Jessie said under her breath.

Blake's jaw dropped in disbelief, certain he had to have heard her wrong because *Gavin* was Dawson and Sam's toddler son. "*Lost*? You *lost* Gavin? How the he-hecky does that even happen"

Clearly enjoying how aggravated she was making him, she crossed her arms and tossed on her famous smartass smirk. "Hecky? Really?"

Ellie Lou leaned in and whispered, "I think he meant the bad word but didn't wanna get in trouble."

"Can we get back on topic? How did you lose a thirty

something pound...*human*?" With his weapon holstered, he crossed his arms, waiting for her response – there really wasn't an answer that would justify losing a toddler while playing hide and seek, but he couldn't wait to hear her try.

"He's smart! He hid in the drier! I didn't think to look there because...well, he's *thirty pounds*!

"The *drier*? Are you kidding me?" Blake ran his hands through his raven black hair, looking around the space, taking in the scattered toys, pillows, and multiple blanket forts surrounding him – troubling, chaos, pandemonium.

"Did they do this?" he questioned, to which she nodded, scanning the space herself with raised brows and an over-whelmed expression. "I don't get it. They're normally really good kids. Like *really* good."

"Me, neither. They're a bunch of hooligans. That cute and sweet crap is just a façade," she said, eyeing the blue eyed and pigtails ring leader, Ellie.

Right on cue, Gavin stood in front of her and tossed her some of that cute and sweet she had mentioned. With his hands on her face, he planted a sloppy kiss on her cheek and said, "I love you, Yessi."

"See what I mean?" Jessie sent a *see what I mean* look to Blake, catching him in a rare smile before turning her attention back to Gavin. "Yeah, well, I love you, too...especially when your parents are here, rug rat."

"I see what you mean...*hooligans*."

An exaggerated eye roll later with a matching discon-certing sigh, she replied, "Don't be fooled by all that slobbery cuteness – they're like mini assassins in the making. And I think you're involved in that somehow with all your...*G.I. Joe* crap that you do."

Because karma was real, and Jessie had it coming, the kids went crazy in that very moment, Jessie their target.

When one of the little ones put a lampshade on her head, they began to run circles around her as she still sat in that damn toddler sized rocking chair. She didn't budge, not even a little. Funny as it was, Blake – being Blake – had to pull together a semblance of order because he knew it wouldn't be long before their friends returned home, and this mess wouldn't make them happy. That's when he noticed it.

"Uh, why are you just sitting there, and what's with the lamp?" he questioned.

"I took it apart, trying to get...free."

"Free?"

Jessie shook her wrist, generating a clanging sound that alerted Blake to exactly *what* she had been trying to free herself from. A tall chrome floor lamp that she was currently handcuffed to.

"You're kidding me."

"Do I look like I'm kidding?! I'm sitting in a pink kid chair, hugging a fuuu-dging lamp." It didn't matter that she caught herself before dropping an F-bomb because the kids had heard it enough to know what she really meant, and it wasn't *fudging*.

"Aunt Jessie wants to say a bad word! Cover your ears!" Ellie shouted, to which the other littles complied.

Safe from little ears, she got it out of her system, "A *fucking* lamp, Blake. I'm hugging a fucking lamp that has this odd thing around it, so the cuffs only go so high. I have to sit low to the ground or put this big ass lamp on the couch so as not to break my delicate little wrist."

"Hate to break it to you, but there isn't anything delicate about you."

Jessie's head spun so fast, he wasn't sure how she managed it without injury. "Cover your eyes, kids."

Destructive hooligans, maybe, but they listened when it

mattered, and right at that moment it really mattered. As soon as their little eyes were closed and covered, Jessie tossed Blake a gesture to let him know just how *delicate* she *wasn't*.

Though completely amused, seeing Jessie cuffed led to all sorts of thoughts he'd rather not have at the moment – especially in front of the children. Quick to change the subject, he addressed other lingering questions, of which he was equally quick to answer himself. "Where did they get handcuffs, anyway? Sam and Dawson are in the medical field... Ohhh."

"Yeah, you catching up there, big guy?" she laughed, enjoying his embarrassment.

"Wait, is that cheetah print?" he questioned, not even sure why he asked because he really didn't want to know about their friends' bedroom habits.

A little voice interrupted yet another awkward moment for Blake, but it was only the beginning, "Bang, Bang!"

"Hey, what's the rule, buddy? Don't aim your gun at someone, even playing. It's not.... Oh, my God." Blake's eyes went wide with surprise, and he was rendered speechless when he realized just what he was being *shot at* with.

Much to Jessie's amusement, she couldn't help but laugh – hysterically. Especially when Gavin took his weapon to Blake's leg, slapping him with it repeatedly in some odd form of toddler hand-to-hand combat move.

"Oh, my God! No, no, no, no buddy. That's...that's a... *not* a gun!"

Trying to regain her own composure, Jessie added insult to injury by saying, "Actually, I think he's using it as a *sword*...a little more fitting, considering. Don't you think?"

Blake was frantically looking around, with his hands in the air, as if trying to keep from touching anything Gavin was. Handcuffs were one thing, but *this*...he just couldn't go there bare handed. While Jessie tried to catch her breath between bouts of laughter, Blake used a handful of nearby baby wipes to handle the vibrator he was wrestling away from Gavin.

"*Don't* touch anything, Gav. Not a thing. That's a disgusting...*no, no*. Stand right there, bud. Don't move," Blake scolded, holding the pink rabbit vibrator straight out in front of him.

With tears staining her now red face and hugging her stomach with her free arm, Jessie struggled to get the words out, "It's...it's...a *vibrator*! He just *slapped* you wi-with a *vibrator*! That rabbit...the rabbit isn't a trigger it's a..."

"*Stop*! I know what the *rabbit* is. How the hell did they get you handcuffed and find their parents'...*toy box*?" Embarrassed, something that didn't happen often, he whispered the last part, not sure what else to call it.

"Uncle Blake said a bad word. Don't forget to fill the swear jar," Ellie hollered from across the room where she had poured out an entire tub of building blocks.

"I'll fill the whole *damn* jar...no problem!" he said under his breath, waiting for Jessie's reply.

He pulled out his own handcuff key, hoping it was just as *universal* on the cuffs from the sexy shop as they were for his standard issue cuffs he used on criminals. Before he tried to unlock Jessie, he took to one knee and carefully laid Gavin's weapon on a heap of baby wipes. O*ne thing at a time*, he thought.

"Don't judge me. I put these guys to bed like I was told to. I came back out here to clean up and must've dozed off. I woke up with Gav's *gun* to my head, cuffed to the lamp," Jessie said with a shrug as if it wasn't odd at all.

"Your forehead." He scanned the room, shaking his head, taking in the chaos still in progress while he went to work on the cuffed lamp. "It doesn't make sense – I've never seen this. Not even on their worst day. What did they eat for dinner?"

"Oh, we had a picnic and watched movies. They were totally fine then."

"Picnic?" he questioned while getting back on his feet.

"Yeah. With sundaes, cookies, and I brought cupcakes…" Finally free, she rubbed her wrists and let out a sigh of relief.

"But *what* for *dinner*?" he repeated.

Tossing him a dirty look that said *what don't you understand*, she spoke slowly and repeated herself, "Sundaes, cookies, cupcakes…I think there were juice pouches, too."

"That's *not* dinner; that's a sugar high. Probably more sugar than they've ever had their whole lives…*combined*," Blake judged.

Taking to her feet, her hands went to her hips, offended by the scolding she was receiving, "That's not my fault. That's bad parenting if they can't handle their sugar!"

"They aren't alcoholics learning to hold their liquor – they're kids – they need real food."

"Well, I'm *cool* Aunt Jessie. Cool Aunt Jessie brings cookies, not carrots."

Her reasoning had him shaking his head in disbelief. "Maybe *cool* Aunt Jessie can just spring for pizza next time."

She shrugged her shoulders, no longer interested in his two-cents. "That sounds like something *boring* Uncle Blake would do."

Gavin had been patiently waiting for Blake, standing at his side with both little hands up, fingers spread, not touching a thing, just as he was told. Blake reached down and carefully picked up the R-rated gadget with baby wipes in one hand while scooping Gavin up under his other arm.

Because life was just unfair sometimes, Logan appeared from around the same corner Blake had, gun drawn.

REDEMPTION CHAPTER 3 - FREE SAMPLE

Confusion consumed Logan's expression as he looked around, holstering his weapon.

"Uh, this isn't what I thought I was being called for. I don't do…diapers, man," Logan said, scanning the messy room with a hint of fear in his eyes.

"False alarm – I forgot to call you off. Sorry about that, but thanks for coming in such a hurry. Hope it isn't too late to get back to whatever *we*," he grumbled, tossing an annoyed look at Jessie, "interrupted."

Logan smiled. "Carly said she would wait for me."

Carly Lewis was new to McKenzie Ridge, having moved to town only a year prior for a nursing job at McKenzie General Hospital. It didn't take long for her to make friends with the McKenzie gang since their professional paths crossed often. Both Carly and Logan had moved to town around the same time and were enjoying not only their new surroundings and friends but also each other's company. They had quickly become inseparable, only parting ways when each was working.

Logan's love-struck look quickly merged to one of shock

when he zeroed in on what Blake was holding – it wasn't the toddler he was pointing at when he asked, "Is that a..."

Before he could get out another word, Blake cut him off, irritation evident in his tone, "It's exactly what you think it is – have a good night, Logan."

Jessie broke out into laughter once again, enjoying the discomfort the evening's antics brought to Blake. Batting her eye lashes a little more than usual, in a sugary flirtatious tone she knew would get Blake's attention, she said, "Later, Traynor. It was *really* good to see you."

She knew she succeeded in pissing him off with a little jealousy when he turned a scowl to her and said, "You get those two in bed, and I'll toss this one in the bath real quick. After playing with a...*gun*, hand washing doesn't seem... sufficient."

"You mean *sword*?" she snickered.

When the kids protested the idea of bedtime, Blake started negotiations. "If you behave and go to bed, I'll take you for a ride in the horse buggy out at Morgan's ranch this weekend."

A master negotiator, it seemed – the kids quickly complied. Jessie was impressed – why did this come so easy to him? Apparently, there wasn't anything Blake wasn't good at.

Blake quickly bathed Gavin and put him to bed before heading outside to bring his car up to the house and get his dog. Baby, his pint-sized companion, went everywhere with Blake because she suffered from severe separation anxiety. After caring for Lou Shaw's dachshund while she was battling a major health scare the previous fall, Blake had a hard time parting with it. He had bonded with the dog.

Colton Sparks was known for his brood of special needs pets and always seemed to have a quirky rescue needing a home. He thought Baby and Blake would make a nice team. Baby needed discipline, and Blake needed a companion. What Blake ended up with was a neurotic pooch that lost its shit and destroyed everything around it if Blake was out of earshot or sight.

Fortunately, he found his vehicle intact. The thirty or more minutes Baby had been left unattended didn't cost him a torn-up truck. This time.

With his handful of dog under his arm, he entered the house and was pleasantly surprised to see that Jessie had already done a great deal of cleanup. He was also surprised to find her snuggling a rosy cheeked toddler, Olivia. What surprised him more – how quickly she brought the room to some form of order or that she was being sweet and nurturing – he wasn't sure. Either way, this was a good look on her.

"This one won't sleep and feels a little warm. I think she's about to gnaw that finger off."

When Olivia turned to see who Jessie was talking to, she sat up and reached for Blake with her chubby little hands.

"Traitor – now I have to clean." She peppered a handful of soft kisses on the tot's head before handing her over to Blake.

Jessie was good with the kids, usually because she acted like them, but affection wasn't her thing where anyone else was concerned. It took Blake by surprise, once again, when she showed affection and hinted that she may have a soft side.

With his mouth to her forehead, he confirmed her suspicion, "She has a fever. I'm guessing molars – she's teething."

He plopped on the couch with a *Baby* in each arm, settling in for the evening.

"Why do you take that dog everywhere. Isn't it embarrassing?" she asked, caught in a stare down with the dog.

"You know why. She needs me."

"Want to borrow a purse?" she asked.

Confused, he asked, "A purse?"

"For your dog…isn't that what all the ladies are doing?"

"You're an asshole…"

She smiled as she walked away. "Uh oh, Uncle Blake owes more money to the swear jar."

"You're really good at that. I don't get why the kids like you so much," she said, nodding her head at the toddler snuggled into his neck.

"It's because they know I won't let them climb in a drier."

"How was I supposed…forget it. You play *manny,* and I'll clean-up."

Jessie did her best to ignore Blake while she went to work, cleaning up after the fun the kids had earlier. Every time she walked by, however, she couldn't help but swoon, even just a little, over the sight of Blake snuggling a tiny tot and pup. It made her a little more than crazy that he could stir butterfly like flutters, low in her belly with just a look.

He was the epitome of an alpha man's man, who screamed testosterone driven machismo with his every move and every word. Built was an understatement – his muscles had muscles that were clearly defined through his standard black t-shirt and ass hugging jeans. Though nobody really knew his entire story, they *did* know that he had an extensive military background full of covert ops, undercover, badass, American hero activity.

She would be lying if she denied his dark secret past wasn't a turn on. He was hands down hot – he was also a pain in the ass. Sure, Jessie was known to give him shit – a *lot* of shit – but that didn't mean she didn't appreciate his chiseled features and crave-worthy physique. Add a baby and tiny dog to the mix, and you have a whole lot of sexy. She'd never tell him, though; she'd take that to the grave.

It was late in the evening when Jessie finally finished straightening things up and restoring order in the house. Blake and Olivia had dozed off…Baby, too. She felt Olivia's head, happy to discover her fever had gone down, and her rosy cheeks were no more. Before sitting down next to her little clan, she pulled a blanket over them and put her feet up, then she, too, gave in to sleep.

* * *

Waking up in unfamiliar surroundings was one thing, but waking to the flash of a cell phone camera or two, accompanied by snickers, could only mean one thing. Blackmail. Having realized she fell asleep wasn't as big of a deal as realizing that it wasn't a pillow, she was resting her head on, but Blake's shoulder. Add to that the fact that his arm was around her shoulders, and her arm stretched across his abdomen in a comfy embrace with the toddler and dog still snuggled in, and they provided a nice little show. A picture worthy show, apparently.

Jessie and Blake were known for their love-hate relationship – they *loved* to *hate* each other. Their angsty banter, and attempt at mutual loathing, wasn't something that anyone who knew them – with the exception of the two of them – bought. Their family of friends knew that they were quite fond of each other, just living in denial, even *meant* for each other.

"Well, didn't expect to see you here, Blake," Sam Tayler

teased with camera aimed and one hand resting on her very pregnant belly.

"I had to rescue Jessie; she was *handcuffed* to your lamp over there," he replied with a raised eyebrow, waiting for the punchline to settle in.

"I was wondering how Jessie would fair, having all three at once," Megan Sparks chimed in, rubbing her equally swollen pregnant belly. "Wait, did you say, hand…cuffs?"

"Well, Lamaze went great. Thanks for watching the kids. Have a good night," Sam said, wide-eyed as crimson red crept up her cheeks.

Two could play at the blackmail game, Jessie thought. "Yep…cheetah handcuffs. They're over there on the counter. The kids *found them*."

"Oh…f-found…th-them?" Sam stuttered, obviously worried *them* implied that the children had found more than handcuffs, and Jessie was happy to address the *concern*. Because she was an asshole.

In true Jessie fashion, she smiled and winked before eliminating any memory they had of walking in on her sleep-snuggling with Blake. "Yep! The pink vibrator too. The one with the little tickler thing on the…"

"Yeah, yeah, yeah. I know what you're, uh, talking about." Sam looked at the handcuffs once more, appearing to search for said pink object, too.

"It's in the trash," Blake deadpanned.

Sam gasped, "The trash? Why is it in the trash?"

"Because your son was shooting people with it." As much as Jessie didn't like to side with Blake, this was too good to let him have on his own – Sam's kids put Jessie to the test – it was well deserved, if you asked Jessie.

"And hitting them with it," Blake added. "Feel free to dig it out of there."

"If I were you, I'd be more inclined to make your man put out; that thing's what broken marriages are made of," Jessie teased.

Colton reached for his sleeping daughter while Meg's belly bounced in fits of laughter.

"Jessie, please. I know you have one too. We were together when we bought them," Sam admitted, suddenly defensive. "Besides, Dawson works a lot and...I'm pregnant...and, and...hormones...and..."

"Holy shit, are you going to cry? Dawson, go get her toy out of the trash, will ya?" Jessie asked, suddenly feeling bad.

Dawson put his arm around his wife's shoulders. "Nah, she does this a lot. It'll pass. It's the pregnancy hormone thing."

"Yeah," Sam choked, twirling her finger in a crazy motion near her temple. "Hormones...crazy..."

Blake turned to Colton. "I think she's teething, fever broke, but her finger is a little swollen from chewing on it. I got her to sleep, though."

"Awe, you certainly have a way with the little ones. They'll do anything for you," Meg said, sweeping wispy hairs off her daughter's forehead, confirming her fever had passed.

"Just like the rest of the women in this town," Jessie added, grabbing her things.

Blake turned to her with a *go to hell* look. "What is that supposed to mean?"

"It means you do your *I'm stone cold Blake Cooper with no personality but have good hair-look at my big boy muscles* bit, and women faint everywhere," Jessie accused.

"Big boy muscles? I suppose I do have great hair."

Jessie rolled her eyes, letting out an audible guffaw, and said, "I'm out of here. The kids were good until they weren't.

I'm busy the next three times you need a sitter, okay? Then, I'll think about it."

She kissed Olivia's head once again and headed for the door. "Don't forget your dog."

"Wouldn't think of it," he said, scooping up his dog, following her to the door. "I'll follow you home – make sure you get there."

"I don't need a babysitter. If you haven't had your fill – kids are that way," she said, tossing her thumb over her shoulder, inside the house. More snickers could be heard from inside as the door closed behind them.

"I'm not babysitting – it's just good manners."

"Nothing happens here – it's McKenzie," she said. "Besides, how do you know I'm not headed to the Pump House for some drinks?"

"Actually, we had trouble here, twice, back to back, not six months ago. Trouble can happen anywhere. And you work tomorrow; I know you aren't drinking tonight."

"I don't need you watching over me anymore. It's getting a little creepy."

The previous fall he had watched over her when a threat had come to town for someone else, but since she was connected, it warranted a body guard of sorts. Or, at least, that's how Blake sold it.

"You called me for help tonight, remember? Was there a *reason* for that?" he asked, knowing full well there was a reason that she didn't know *he* knew.

"That…that was different. Everyone else was at Lamaze – you were all that was left."

He smiled; she was deflecting as expected. "Lou…Lou was at Lamaze? That's got to be some sort of record. She's gotta be at least seventy years old now. I'll have to remember to send flowers tomorrow."

"Point taken," she said, climbing into her car. "Don't follow me, Blake."

She slammed her car door and sped off.

Blake was quick to catch up and follow her home. He couldn't help but fume over her stubbornness. What did it hurt if he wanted to see her home – most people would be grateful. Not Jessie. She was frustrating – went out of her way to inconvenience people and be a royal pain in the ass.

He suspected that she was just antagonizing him, trying to act tougher than she felt, but getting her to admit it would never happen. She carried the weight of the world on her shoulders with a terrifying past, and that past just got a whole lot heavier. Sure, he said it was just *good manners*, seeing that she got home okay, but he needed to be certain it really was safe. It was only a matter of time before it wouldn't be.

REDEMPTION CHAPTER 4 - FREE SAMPLE

When Jessie saw headlights in her rearview mirror, quickly approaching, she held her breath until she saw it was Blake. She told him not to follow her, but she was pleased to see it was him and not *someone* else. Even if he was an uptight, Dudley Do-right, pest.

If he wanted to tail her home, she'd make him work for it. She punched the gas pedal and took off, speeding through town. Not the safest way to go about pissing him off, but at this hour of night, there wouldn't be any traffic.

When he caught up, riding her ass, she could see his angry expression in the mirror. If he was anything, it was relentless. He kept up and trailed her all the way home, even pulled up behind her when she parked in her driveway.

Without even a glance his way, she got out of her car and went to the door. Before stepping in, she turned his direction and flipped him off in thanks. Flipping people off was pretty much Jessie's way of communicating everything. Though she couldn't see his face past the bright lights shining her way, she knew he saw her…she could feel his eyes on her.

Closing the door behind her, she leaned against it and let

out a laugh. One of her greatest pleasures was getting under his skin. Her mood quickly changed when she pushed herself off the door, ready to head to bed, and something had her attention.

She stood still; there was something in the air, not a smell or sound, just something. Something was off, like someone had been there though she hadn't a single idea how she sensed that. Intuition maybe?

Jessie remained calm, listening for movement or some sign that she wasn't alone. But, it didn't come – all she could hear was the sound of her own breath. There was nothing noticeably out of place, she discovered, as she slowly made her way through the house.

Her cat, Flea Bag, should have greeted her by now and hadn't. Another indication that something was terribly wrong. *Where is Flea Bag*, she thought. *Just come out, and prove me wrong...please.*

From the living room, she moved to the kitchen at the back of the house, following a faint odor that was all too familiar in her line of work but didn't make sense...smoke. It wasn't just any smoke; it was that which was emitted from burning wood. Living in the tree filled mountains where forest fires were almost an annual occurrence, that smell was unmistakable. Where was it coming from?

An odd glow, which she hadn't noticed until now, drew her deeper into the kitchen and to the adjacent dining room window, grabbing her attention. A sense of anxiety rose like a warning bell. She didn't know what she was about to discover, but her instincts told her she wasn't going to like it – at all. It became brighter, bolder, unmistakable as its shadows danced across her dining room walls. Fire.

Confused, she stood staring, wondering just how and why there was a fire roaring in her backyard fire pit. She hadn't started it before she left, nor would she have left it unattended. She was a firefighter and knew better. The trees surrounding her property were perfect fire fuel – especially this time of year as they were heading into fire season.

There wasn't any movement outside along the tree line, but she suddenly felt vulnerable, like someone was watching her. Or could be, anyway. She backed into the shadows of her house, watching the fire grow, wondering who started it and why. Deep down, she knew. The fire, symbolic of a campfire, gave it away. She was almost certain of it.

She had been counting down the days until he would be a threat again – he found her faster than she thought he would. Hitting speed dial, she slowly lifted her phone to her ear, waiting for him to answer. Surely, he would; he had to. When he did, all she could whisper was, *help.*

* * *

"She's such a pain in the ass. Why do I always drop everything for her?" Blake asked the only one listening – his dog. "She's rude, no *crude*, not an ounce of feminine charm...*at all.*"

Baby whined, tilting her head, clearly confused by the conversation they were having on the drive home.

"I always have to...*protect* her. Why can't I just leave her alone like she *wants* me to, Baby?"

Baby laid down, resting her head, keeping her eyes on Blake. Another little whine escaped her, getting his attention.

"I know what you're thinking, and you're wrong. I don't like her – especially like *that.* Oh, what do you know; you're still too new here...and you're a...girl."

Blake knew exactly why he continued to look after her, to protect her. Jessie infuriated him with her foul mouth and rude behavior, but deep down, he understood why she was the way she was. Somehow, that knowledge earned her an ungodly amount of grace and a free pass to be an asshole. Anyone who had been through what she had – and survived it – deserved a lot of patience.

She loved as hard as her exterior façade appeared to be tough – she simply didn't want anyone to know just how much she cared because that left a person as vulnerable as a sheep in a pack of wolves. The last time she outwardly cared – it nearly killed her and left her with scars that ran so deep he was sure she would have rather died. He understood that depth of pain – the vulnerability – the fear of *love,* better than anyone.

It was the source of his own façade – why the world was always at arm's length – why he loved from a distance. It was also why he kept tabs on *his people* and protected them so fiercely. He didn't want them to know the kind of pain he knew – so did what he could to keep them safe from pretty much everything. He failed before, and he'd carry that burden and sadness for the rest of his life – he wouldn't fail those he loved again.

His phone rang, pulling him from his thoughts. He rolled his eyes when he saw the name scroll across the screen – Jessie probably wasn't done flipping him the bird and wanted to deliver the verbal version of such. His thumb hovered over the red button on the screen that would send her away, but that odd tingle that made the hair on the back of his neck stand up was nagging at him to answer.

"What now?" he chided.

Her voice stalled. He could only hear her breathing until she finally whispered, "Help."

Déjà vu, almost, it was exactly what she had said earlier in the evening to summons him to diaper duty. Yet, something about the wavering in her voice and sense of fear kept him on the line.

"You said that earlier, and I was assaulted by a toddler with a…"

"Blake…" There was that fear again. "I'm serious. Someone…someone has…been here."

"If I get there, and it's just to clean Flea Bag's litter box…"

"Flea Bag is missing – there's a fire – please…hurry." Her voice cracked on her last words.

She wasn't kidding this time; he could hear it in her voice and feel it in his gut. Making a quick U-turn, he floored it, headed back to her house. One key word tipped him off – there was a fire. He knew what that meant as well as she did. The fact that Flea Bag wasn't in the house was another clue as he was strictly an indoor pet. She mothered the shit out of that cat and barely let him out on a leash due to all the wildlife in the area.

"I'm on my way. Stay on the phone," he said. When she didn't answer, he went faster. "Jessie? Answer me."

"I…I'm here. I don't understand – why the fire. Why did he start the fire? What does it mean?" she rambled.

"Who, Jessie? Why did who start the fire?" he questioned, giving her a chance to tell him what he already knew. It would be so much easier that way than carrying around this secret.

"No…no one. Just whoever d-did it."

"Jess, if you know something…"

Her heavy panicked breathing came through the phone before her words. "I don't, okay? Why aren't you here yet?"

He forgave her sharp harsh tone, expected it, really. As much as she needed him in that moment, she was pushing him away from her truth. She was scared.

"I'm almost there. Where are you in the house?" he asked, trying to keep her focused.

"Din...dining room corner. There...there might be someone...in the woods."

"Do you see someone?"

"No, uh, I just feel it," she replied.

"Okay. It's okay. Just stay right where you are. I'm out front. You're going to hear me come in the front door. Okay?"

"Okay," she agreed.

"I'll clear the house first, then I'll come for you. Don't. Move."

"O-k-kay."

His heart pinched at the fear drenched sound in her voice. "Jessie?"

"Yeah?"

"I'm not going to let anything happen to you. Okay? You're safe."

She heard the door open but could barely hear him move through the house. If she didn't know he was there, she probably wouldn't have heard him at all. He was being Blake – covert ops – undercover military – Blake, doing what he did best. He was protecting her.

The house was clear, no sign of forced entry or evidence that anyone had even been there. He went to her – the sight of her huddled into the dark corner, trembling in fear, crushed him. Jessie was strong and fierce; this experience had left her anything but. After holstering his weapon, he pulled her into his arms, both of them letting out a sigh of relief. As quickly as he had her in his arms, he then had her at arm's length, looking her over, making sure she was all in one piece.

"Are you okay?" he asked, looking over his shoulder at the roaring fire through the window.

"Yeah, just…" she choked a little on her words, choosing not to finish.

"I know," he said, and he *did* know. He knew exactly what had riled her because it was exactly what had him watching her, even from a distance, night and day.

"You didn't start that fire?" he asked, turning his attention in the fire's direction.

"Of course not – do you think I'm stupid enough to leave a fire unattended? Besides, it just started when I got here – it was just taking off."

"I'll go look around out there – you stay here and lock the door behind me." He drew his weapon again and went out back.

Despite his specific instructions to stay put, inside, and lock the door, she followed him outside.

"I said stay inside," he scolded in a low voice.

"Yeah, well, I'm going where the gun goes."

He walked in front of her and tucked her behind him. "Fair enough. Stay behind me."

Weapon aimed with a bright flashlight right below, he scanned the perimeter of the property, watching for any sign of menace.

Slowly moving forward, they reached the fire when a meow startled them – Flea Bag. He was sitting in one of the outdoor chairs surrounding the fire. She hadn't seen him because the back of the chair faced the house, blocking her furry companion.

"Were you enjoying the fire, boy?" she scooped up her cat and snuggled him close, taking the seat he had been sitting in.

"I said, stay behind me…"

"I'm checking Flea over. I need to make sure he is okay," she defended.

"Fine. *Stay there*! I mean it…" he replied before walking

the perimeter of the property, looking for anything or anyone out of place.

When he returned, he slid his flashlight in his back pocket and holstered his weapon though he kept his hand resting on it. "There's no evidence suggesting there was anyone in the house, and I don't see anything unusual out here, but it's dark. I'll look again in the morning."

"But the fire…" she added.

"Maybe a prank? You're not exactly nice to everyone; kids are out on summer break…could be…*anything*." He knew better than to think it was a prank, but he didn't want her to worry all night because he sure as hell wasn't relieving her of any worry by telling her he already planned on sleeping in his car up the street tonight. Watching her house.

"And you're McKenzie Ridge's finest?" she questioned, not sold on his assessment as she held up a box of wood stick matches.

"Okay. It's a box of matches. So, whoever started the fire left their matches. That doesn't prove anyone was inside or that this is more than a prank. It's obviously kids if they left evidence." He was failing miserably at explaining this incident away as anything other than what it was – a targeted message – a warning – a *threat*.

"Really? Well, Flea bag can't unlock doors, much less open them. Oh, or lock them from the outside. He's an indoor cat, hates it out here." She pointed out the obvious, then dropped the bomb. "And it's not like him to start a fire and wait for a tray of s'mores."

"He could have slipped out when you left," Blake reasoned, knowing full well she was *right*.

"Okay then. Explain this…" She held up the box of matches again. "These are from my kitchen drawer."

REDEMPTION CHAPTER 5 - FREE SAMPLE

A long pause stood between them before Blake finally gave in and gave up on trying to control her reaction to what he knew was more than a prank.

"I'm staying the night," he insisted, heading for the house.

With her cat under her arm, she was quick to follow, and protest. "Uh, no, you're not."

When he ignored her, she tried again. "Blake, I'm serious…you aren't staying the night. Not an option."

Blake went straight through the living room and through the front door, pulling it closed behind him. Scratching her cat's head, she leaned against the door and let out a sigh of relief. It was bad enough she had to call him for help – having him sleeping over was worse.

Not only was he bossy and demanding, he was hot as hell, and all three qualities bugged the shit out of her. He made it hard to hate him with all his pushy, macho, *let me protect you*, bullshit that made him so desirable and charming. She didn't want to find him desirable…or charming…but he was making it hard. She was a strong, independent woman, who fought her demons alone for years. She didn't need a man to fight them for her, even if *this* man reeked of hot sweaty sin of the all night sexy variety.

She shook her head, clearing her thoughts, erasing the part where Blake and sexy combined. He was an *asshole*, she told herself. A dictator, even – he was practically a terrorist with his cocky, *do it my way, the world is mine to protect* crap that he was constantly acting on.

Suddenly, she was thrust from the door when it opened behind her with a little more force than just opening it would require. She face planted into the wall, flinging her cat across the entry when she lost her balance. *What the…*

"Were you trying to hold the door closed so I couldn't come in?" Blake asked, confused by the force the door required and Jessie's wall hug.

"No, jerk. Don't you know how to knock? I was leaning against it until you *shoved* me into the wall."

"Why were you leaning against it if not to keep me out? Why not just use the lock?"

"Touché. Why *didn't* I use the lock? It's normal for people to just…let themselves into my house in the middle of the night."

"I told you that I was staying over."

"And, I said you weren't, and then you left."

He grinned, happy to rile her up, and held up his dog. "Had to get Baby. She can't sleep outside all night in my truck."

"Your dog? Nooooo. She can't stay here either. Flea doesn't like dogs…or other animals…or *people* who aren't me."

"Well, I wonder where he learned that? They'll be fine. If you don't make a big deal about it, the dog and cat won't."

He sat on the couch and put Baby on the ground while he unlaced his boots.

"What are you doing? Tie those back up; you aren't..." she paused when he removed his belt and slid out of his shoulder holster. "Blake, you're not staying! Put all of that back...on. I swear if you take off your shirt, I'll shoot you with your own gun!"

With his head tilted to one side, his raised eyebrow matched the curl in his lip. "You know, ladies don't usually tell me to put my clothes back on."

Then, he continued to ignore her and fluffed a couple of throw pillows before grabbing the blanket off the end of the couch, tossing it out the length of the couch, unfolding it over his long legs.

"Are you serious?" she asked with a high-pitched squeak.

"About the ladies?" He knew exactly what she was referring to, but getting her riled brought him an odd sense of joy.

"About..." Her jaw dropped when he tossed his arms behind his head and crossed his ankles – this guy really was staying.

"Oh, forget it!" she ranted. "You're impossible. A big... *bully*! Let's go, Flea."

"Bully? That's the best you got? *Bully*? You're Jessie Clarke...you invented ninety percent of the vulgar words of the world, and the best you could come up with was *bully*?"

When her cat followed the dog, half his size, to the couch and snuggled in with Blake, she tossed her hands up in the air.

"You're an *ass*!" she said, pointing to Blake before shifting her attention to the animals, "And you two suck!"

His ornery smirk had her in fits. "Are you going to say anything?"

"Are you done?" When she nodded, he sat up, and proceeded. "You called me for a *reason*, correct? Why?"

"Yes, you're…the police."

"I am…one of many officers. Yet, *you* called *me*. Not the backline to dispatch, not even 911. Me."

"So?" With her arms crossed, she shot him a sharp glare, daring him to go on.

"*Soooo*, you called me for a reason, Jess. You don't have to tell me, but I *am* staying. In the morning – with daylight – I'll get a better look outside."

"Then, come back in the morning."

"Jessica…" He saw a slight shimmy when he used her full name. "Do you know who it was? Who was in your house? Who started a fire in your backyard?"

"And let my cat outside…" she added.

He rolled his eyes. "And let your cat outside? If you know or suspect – if there's something I should know, tell me. Please."

Blake didn't really need her to answer any of those questions; he already had the answers. He needed her to tell him though. He needed her to share her story so he didn't have to pretend that he was in the dark anymore. She was afraid for a reason, and he was there to protect her from it – so he gave her a chance to trust him and be honest with him.

She called him because she was afraid, and he didn't blame her, given the terror she had lived through so many years ago. A terror that was coming for her. Jessie's façade that she had spent nearly ten years building was in play. She was in self-preservation mode – it was either that or crumble – he could see it.

When vulnerability swept across her face, and her eyes wandered as if searching for answers, he thought she just might tell him. He could see her considering both sides, at battle with herself, trying to decide if she could trust him with something so delicate. Then, she stiffened, gave a subtle shake of her head like she was pushing everything on the surface back down. She wasn't going to tell him.

Blake was a patient man. He wouldn't push her. Her brave front was back, despite being petrified as she should be. Jessie would tell him when and if she was ready. If he pushed too hard, she might figure out that he already knew, and how he found out would crush her. He had violated her privacy and, in a way, was lying by omission, at the very least.

It didn't matter how good his intentions were. The way he went about looking into the pasts of those he cared so deeply about was wrong. But, it was also the only way he could truly protect any of them, whether they wanted him to or not. If he was honest with himself, it was more for him than them because loss and pain haunted him daily, and he would protect himself from it, as much as them, at any cost.

"No, nothing. I know…nothing," she said, fearful of what he might think of her if she shared her truth. If he knew her secret. The steely, tough girl front was back in place as she straightened.

But, she almost made a mistake when she said, "If I… *knew*, I'd take care of him myself.

"Him?" Another opportunity to get her to share, but she recovered quickly.

"Whoever…him…her…whatever. Goodnight, Blake."

Jessie disappeared down the hallway and slammed her door for good measure.

* * *

She wasn't ready. *She may never be ready*, Blake thought. Jessie had called him for help, so it wasn't that she didn't trust him. It was that sharing her secret was like reliving it, and her past was a heavy burden she didn't wish on anyone. Blake could relate to that more than anyone. It's why he kept his own secrets.

Blake would carry that burden for her – as long as she needed him to. In the meantime, he would watch for anything out of the ordinary, any potential threat, and guard her from it. Even if she thought he hadn't a clue what or who he was protecting her from. Like tonight when someone had let himself in her house, lit a fire to taunt her, a silent but real threat. It was just in his nature to take care of those around him – he wouldn't fail this time. He would redeem himself one way or another and, hopefully, overcome the guilt he carried and never let down those he cared about most.

He wouldn't let Jessie down. Blake made a silent vow not to rest until the bastard who'd hurt her, wanted to hurt her, was back in jail. Or...*dead.*

GET YOUR COPY OF REDEMPTION, TODAY!
AVAILABLE ON ALL MAJOR RETAILERS!

Made in United States
Troutdale, OR
07/01/2024

20927202R00166